Nest in the Bones

Stories by Antonio Di Benedetto

Translated from the Spanish by Martina Broner

archipelago books

Cuentos completos by Antonio Di Benedetto first published
by Adriana Hidalgo editora S.A., 2006

Archipelago Books
232 Third Street, #A111
Brooklyn, NY 11215

www.archipelagobooks.org

Library of Congress Cataloging-in-Publication Data
Title: Nest in the bones : stories / by Antonio Di Benedetto ;
translated from the Spanish by Martina Broner and Adrian West.
LCCN 2017001393 | ISBN 9780914671725 (paperback)
LCC PQ7797.B4343 A2 2017 | DDC 863/.64--dc23
LC record available at https://lccn.loc.gov/2017001393

Cover art: Xul Solar

Distributed by Penguin Random House
www.penguinrandomhouse.com

Archipelago Books gratefully acknowledges the generous support from the
Lannan Foundation, the SUR program, the National Endowment for the Arts,
the New York City Department of Cultural Affairs,
and the New York State Council on the Arts, a state agency.

Archipelago Books would also like to thank Adrian West for his generous
involvement with the book.

Nest in the Bones

Stories by Antonio Di Benedetto

·

from *Animal World* (1953)

Nest in the Bones

I'm not the monkey. My ideas are different, even if we did end up in the same position, at least at first.

My father brought him here, same as the palm tree. He's got too much land, too much money. He planted that little palm tree, and he liked it too, as long as it stayed young and dainty. But when it started growing and growing, he got tired of it, because it was ungainly and bristly, it wasn't adapting, he says. He quit paying it attention, I suppose because he's not the type to look up into the sky, at least not over there, where the palm tree stood. Instead he looks toward the mouth of the river, where storms gather, since for better or for worse, the harvest depends on the rains.

He didn't realize the monkey would never adapt, not just on account of the climate, but also because there was no way it would take to the family; and that's what he wanted, for it to be like a member of the family. He wasn't all wrong, maybe, since the monkey did take advantage of odd moments of consideration – when my father would show a bit of insight – to try and earn the place he'd been promised. But in the end, his place was the palm tree. My father wasn't much for festivity, nourishment, or petting: in general, he barely fed the thing, and didn't take much care to train it right. The monkey ran off, taking refuge in the palm tree, like a son returning to his mother. He only came down to scrounge or eat whatever food some kindly soul laid out at the foot of his dwelling. He lived alone, alone the way the withered treetop looked up there in the heights. He turned reclusive, meditative, no good for anything save the procurement of sustenance. Maybe because of his ill humor – because the greenhouse he'd envisioned never wound up getting built – my father cleared all the vegetation from the zone where the palm tree stretched slowly upward, like a heartsick sigh. The tree fell, the monkey fell, and the monkey took cover among the crates and trunks until, riled up by the blood from a decapitated chicken walking around in its death throes, the dogs leapt at him, and no one stopped them.

~

I'm not the monkey, but in my childhood days, my father also ordered me kept away from the table for one minor infraction or another. I don't have a palm tree, but I made one out of my house; or not my house exactly, but the rooms, the parcels of land, a walk, a book, a friend. My palm tree had many branches, and maybe that's why I came to think I wasn't like the monkey. Maybe it all depended, like with the monkey and the palm tree, on my birthplace and the inadequate destiny that followed. I don't know. Maybe I should have been born in another country, or maybe that's not it. Perhaps I shouldn't have been born in this era. I don't mean to say I ought to have been born into the Middle Ages or in the same year as Dostoyevsky. No. Maybe I should have been born in the twentieth or twenty-first century. Not because I think life will be easier then, though it's possible that it will be. But since I can't be born a century from now, I've tried to make it easier, as much as possible, by finding some use for myself.

When I figured out the monkey had been useless, I was able to get a grasp of what I considered a useful destiny, if only for the sake of others. His hollow head gave me ideas about what I could do with my own. I wanted – and it was easy to do so – to turn it into a bird's nest. Willing and exultant, my head filled to bursting with birds, for my sake and for theirs as well. I reveled in it, in the happiness of that sturdy, secure, and sheltering nest I was able to give them, and I reveled in other ways too. Like that time at my mother's tea benefit, when I stepped into the half-light, interrupting what was not quite revelry, my scheme both calculated and anxious, and she asked me, defiant and dismayed, how I could do such a thing, whistling in the middle of a gathering of ladies. And I said, my lips pried from my mouth by a smile of suffering at her ignorance, that it wasn't I who was whistling, and I provoked in her the innocent astonishment of a person witnessing the transit of a musical, tangible, and perishing god.

⌐

It wasn't always like that; a few years, maybe only a few months. With the change, I've come to doubt as to whether making a bird happy will make all the families in the coming centuries happy, too. If we all put our heads to the service of general happiness, maybe it could work. But our heads, not just our feelings.

I did it with mine, and it held blissful sparrows, canaries, and partridges. Now the vultures have nested in it, too. But I can't do it anymore. They're unaccountably voracious and have sharpened their beaks to devour the last bit of my brain. They go on pecking past the bare bone, I wouldn't say with rage, but as if at the behest of an obligation. And even if their pecks were affectionate and playful, they could never be tender. They hurt dreadfully, they hurt down to the bone, and make of my pain and torture a constant flow of grief, rent and hysterical. I can't do anything about them, nor can anyone, because no one can see them, just as nobody saw the birds that chirped before. And here I am, my nest bursting with opportunistic, insidious, and ever-present vultures, and with every peck of every one of their thousand beaks, they crunch every bone of every part of my entire skeleton. Here I am, hidden among the trunks, waiting for one of those people who formerly fed the monkey to take pity on this captive and free the hounds.

But please, may no one who hears my story let the horror overwhelm them; may they rise to the occasion and not give in, if my words should embolden them to the good purpose of populating their head with birds.

Reduced

From the moment he showed up in my dreams he was already, in a certain way, my dog. Since I don't have a dog in the daytime, but I do have numerous adversities, it's a good thing to recover with a nocturnal puppy, the kind that doesn't even make you leave the bed. All you have to do is fall asleep with the longing, which it would be pointless to explain, for those hours of diversion – frivolous and childish, I admit – and then he appears, ready to play or even, with his superior canine comprehension, just to tamely keep me company.

If you asked me, I wouldn't know how to tell you what he's like. But in dreams I could pick him out unfailingly from a pack of identical siblings. Even if, from the beginning, he was evidently and indisputably a dog, when I think of him, something gives me the sense that he's different, because his arrival was slow, as though he only gradually came into being. That's why his name, Reduced, feels contradictory to me, though it does make sense with relation to his physical dimensions. It's not that he's shrunk, even less that he is dwindling as we speak. But I also wouldn't say – and this too is important – that he is growing, even a bit, no matter how much I watch him, despite how we say, if with slight exaggeration, that young dogs evolve almost by the day. And so he has a touch of the immutable that doesn't exactly put me at ease. If Reduced, my Reduced, this little pup, so blissful, so good, such a dear friend, in other words, is unchanging, it is because he has the fixity of dreams, of dreams and nothing but. Hence my Reduced is like a stubborn nightmare that always recurs, ever the same, ever torturous; and though he cannot in the least be considered a nightmare, and if he were, he would be a nice one, still, he makes my heart quiver the way nightmares do, not when he vanishes, but during the day, in light of the not-at-all remote probability that at night he will not return.

It is for this reason, admitting he is a dream, that I need him to move into my waking life. If he is one, then I will have a dream in this miserable life of mine, sunless even as the sun shines over it. If he is one, I won't have to fear that one of these nights he will disappear forever, for even if he's done nothing to justify this conclusion, still, he might grow fickle and pass over, with his shadow-steps, into the dreams of one of my neighbors. If he lives, on the earth, it is indisputable that he could die. But I will think of his death the way I think of my own: as something that doesn't come, even if you long for it, so long as you don't go looking for it.

I've talked this over with Reduced. Outright, I confessed my misgivings, which he might have had some sense of before, because he's very perceptive, very alert. I asked him to give up the night and to come. He asked me not to demand an answer until last night. His reply didn't correspond precisely to my request. He said he liked being my dog, and we could spend more time together; but he proposed something in turn that obliges me to delay my response until I have thought it over well.

I should answer him tonight. There aren't many hours left, and I have to come to a resolution, hard as it is to decide on Reduced's request. Because Reduced has asked for me to accompany him, to accompany him in dreams.

We Fly

As if standing before a tranquil, inoffensive mystery, which it may well be, and yearning, unlike me, to talk, she tells me about her cat.

He is one. Of course he is, but... To start with, he's an orphan, taken in out of compassion, no one knows his ancestry. He's a cat, and he likes water. What he likes about ditches isn't the muck, but the cloudy current. He huffs as he hurls himself in, he lands hard, splashes; he sinks in his maw and makes like he's drinking, but he isn't drinking, it is a pure act of gluttony. You could think he was a dog and not a cat. Then there's the matter of his indifference to other cats. But won't look at dogs, either, except from a distance, and not even a street fight will rile him up. When he opens his mouth, his voice is hoarse and horribly off-key, so you can't tell whether he's mewing or barking.

I pretend I'm surprised. But I don't open my mouth, because if I asked a question or made a comment, she'd ask me why I think that and I'd have to explain and then I'd get trapped in a conversation. Anyway, she's not talking to me any longer: she's talking to herself. She repeats what she already knows, and she tries to learn more from it.

He's a cat and he likes water. That's not enough to conclude that he's a dog. The question's not even whether he's a cat or a dog, because neither of the two fly, and this little creature flies, he started flying a few days back.

I expect her to ask me if I think it's some kind of witchcraft. But no; to all appearances, she doesn't believe in witchcraft. I don't, either, though it did cross my mind. Or, rather, I thought it would cross her mind. But no.

"Aren't you amazed?"

"Yeah, sure. I'm amazed. Of course. I'm amazed."

I could be amazed, of course. But I'm not. I could be amazed because a cat-dog is flying. But I don't just talk. I think. I think she imagines I must be amazed because what she believed was a cat might be a dog or what might be a cat or dog could be a bird or some other flying animal. I should be amazed because the thing isn't what it's thought to be. But I can't be. Am I amazed that you aren't what your husband thinks you are? Am I amazed that I'm not what my wife thinks I am? Your little animal is a cynic, that's all. A seasoned cynic.

Purity Saved

Anyway, I should have stopped reading long ago. I should control myself, to keep from wasting too much light; I should control myself and sleep the right number of hours and not be a despicable sleepyhead when I go to work tomorrow.

The feverish cats, beings whose love is bellicose and essentially nocturnal, have taken the book from my hand. Beneath the moon, I believe, love can be more idyllic and more beastly. Maybe, in a relationship, it is the candor of the sun that nurtures those disclosures that lead to tedium and disenchantment.

My own little cat, my Fuci, must dwell among those cats; whether idyllic or beastly I do not know, but certainly unrecognizable. Unrecognizable for me as well, though I watch over his development and even see him in my dreams, when I dream that he is a leopard. I see him as a leopard, like an ordinary father whose son has surpassed his aspirations and taken on the proportions of a giant. A normal father, unable to stifle an inner voice that calls him, simply, son.

Thus I call my Fuci-leopard Fuci, nothing more. Fuci, I say to him, as a greeting and show of affection, when I visit him in the field in the park where he reenacts an old custom of his from his days as a cat. Back then, curled up and drowsing, he would sidle up next to any saucepan that smelled good. Now that he's a leopard, he drowses in the field where three hens are pecking, waiting, I suppose, for their death, so he can eat them without lapsing into flagrant criminality. While he waits, needs have arisen which, though they don't make him forget his longing, relegate it to the condition of a possibly ruined hope, and have imposed another life on him and another situation. His present state is that of a head of household. He lives, with his cubs and his chosen one – who puts me in mind of a hyena, and may even be one – in an abandoned oven, where the field's verdure goes dead, unable to make inroads into the salt earth. My Fuci-leopard lets no one approach him, save for me, though the presence of his wife, who doesn't care for me at all, disrupts our communication a bit. At those times, I limit myself to standing at a distance from the oven and looking, just looking; and while I look, I utter the name Fuci, as in a one-sided conversation, for all that intimate and caring. Because now I see in Fuci's visage, sad and tenuously severe, the burden of obligations, and I think, no matter how much a leopard he is, deep down he's just a cat, and they can't weigh a cat down with so much responsibility. I know this well, from my personal experience, as a man.

If he returns now, from the roofs and his allotment of love, he will find in me, beyond the customary protectiveness shown by man to cat, the solidarity of those whose problems have gotten the best of them.

It must be him, and tonight he must be a leopard, judging by his strength and ungainliness as he opens my door.

No.

It's not him. It's a man, a man whose presence is perplexing. I have a second to see he doesn't need a knife or gun to kill me, and neither is in view; and a second to see that, if he weren't there, the sky could be beautiful, revealed through the open door.

Fortunately, I'm a boy and still have many years left.

But how will I free my Fuci from that lawbreaker?

from *Clear Stories* (1957)

Huddled

In the house, now bereft of the mother, the boy moves softly from room to room. He looks through them slowly, as if discovering their contents or the height of the walls anew.

His aunt doesn't interest him for those few hours she stays there, taking care of the kitchen and the washing. Silence reigns between them like oblivion.

He only trusts his father, he takes refuge in him, during his midday break from work and at night, which he always hopes will be long.

Unusually, his father stays home one weekday afternoon. The boy is happy. But some men come, and they take the furnishings from the dining room and leave them on the curb. His father is giving them orders. The boy goes to the kitchen, and the father observes him, without speaking, from what may be a natural diffidence, accentuated by events. Then the men walk into the kitchen, saying "Now it's time for the kitchen," because they need to take away the cupboard and the table. The boy can tell, and he slips off to the lonely courtyard, where there's nothing but a few crates of rubbish, and he hides behind the crates. His father watches him, comparing him glumly to a frightened little mouse.

The debts, from his wife's long, incurable illness, and the rent, which is exorbitant, given his new financial situation, compel him to take a room in the pension. But deep down, he's glad, because his home is broken, and his sister-in-law's presence won't make it better. It's not getting better; it's turning ugly. And he feels he should give her the chance to annul a pact and responsibility that no longer have the favor of affection.

He's alone now, with his little boy. Maybe forever, he says to himself.

He sends off the suitcases full of clothes in a pickup, along with the boy's little bed, and the chair, which his body has grown used to.

He shuts the tailgate and crosses the street to catch the trolley. While he waits, he stares at the drawn windows, without curtains. He remembers those curtains his wife hung up. Who could have taken them?

The trolley comes down the other block. It's time to say goodbye. To say goodbye to the house. In the foregoing days, when he imagined this moment, he thought it would be solemn. And yet… he sighs. He feels the boy's little hand in the shelter in his own. He digs through his jacket pocket, takes out a couple of coins, and stretches out his arm to wave to the conductor.

He turns in the key to the owner of the house, catches a different trolley, and gets off two blocks from the pension.

He walks, the solitary man, with a little mute figure grasping his hand, and like the boy, he doesn't say a word. Who would you talk to, who would you explain this nothing to?

When they arrive, before going in, he decides he needs to tell him:

"Bertito, this is where we're going to live."

The boy looks at him. He looks at the building. He looks back at his father. This last look is a question.

The father can't answer it. He wants to bring the situation to an end. "Let's go in," he says, takes the child in his arms, steps up, and rings the buzzer.

He's taken Saturday afternoon to finish the move. He can put the clothing away and arrange it without rushing, he even has time to spare, and he ends up ruminating on how little he has left. The boy watches him work. He's sitting on the bed, where his father put him down an hour before.

"Papa, I'm tired."

His father is surprised:

"What do you mean, boy? It's six in the afternoon…"

He looks at him, trying to see shades of the weariness the child claims to feel. They aren't visible. But he's taken aback when he finds a glimmer of turmoil in his eyes. They're looking away off somewhere, those little eyes. As though wishing something wasn't where it was. He observes him closely. A voice filters in, a woman's voice. A woman is singing. He reckons she's pacing outside the bathroom door, waiting her turn for the water.

He tries to understand the boy. He assumes the voice intimidates him, so free, such a jarring contrast to the silence of his recently abandoned home. The boy senses a strange presence in that place where they have to live, and he doesn't care for it, but he knows he has no right to complain.

"It's OK, Bertito. You can sleep. I'll get your bed ready right now."

The boy makes a face to show he agrees. With just his face, nothing else, he says: *That's fine. That's what I need.*

The night was calm. His father greets the day with the confusion that arises from change of bed and surroundings. Once awake, he feels invigorated and composed.

He rouses the boy:

"Bertito, get up. They're going to clean the room."

He takes him to the bathroom. He gives him coffee and milk to drink. The boy obeys, leery and passive. But he doesn't speak, he doesn't show joy, satisfaction, or even curiosity.

His father thinks: *It's the change. He'll get over it soon.*

He thinks it will be good for the boy, and for him as well, to go to the movies, to the matinee. But they can't, not so soon, not after what's happened.

He opts for the park. The child lets himself be taken along.

They return after nightfall. The cool air enticed them to slow down, but then it was hard to find a bus. The father is in a hurry. He doesn't know what time dinner is served on Sundays.

It seems like a different building. From the sidewalk, through the open storm door, they see the courtyard blighted with dancers and music.

The father feels something in his throat. Something hard to swallow. Not for him – why should he care? – but for the boy. Down there, by his side, he feels a trembling, from bewilderment, perhaps from fright. He doesn't dare look at the boy. Before facing him, he looks for a solution. He suspects he was wrong to stop. He should have gone in without hesitation. He looks at the boy. The boy is peering inward, as if shriveled, as if his soul has withdrawn. His father wants to believe it will all be fine. Luckily, his room is the first one on the left, and has a door that opens into the foyer. There won't be any need to cross the courtyard.

Then he decides. First he tries to cheer the boy up:

"Look, Bertito. A party. That's nice, right?"

The boy shakes his head.

"What, you don't like the party?

The boy swings his head back and forth obstinately.

His father decides its time to act with fortitude.

"All right, let's go."

He hadn't counted on the boy's determination. He tugs at the little hand, and the tiny body resists. If he tries, he can drag him off. But...

He picks him up. The boy flails with his arms and legs, in open rebellion.

"Let's go for a hot chocolate."

The boy tries to break free, to hurl himself to the ground.

"Churros and chocolate, and cookies. Whatever you want."

He clarifies:

"Not here, somewhere else."

The boy calms down and gives in.

They have their chocolate in a bar with pool tables, a place only men go. Awe-struck, the boy watches the nearby game. When he finishes his cup, he rests his head on the table, and his father knows he'll put up no more resistance.

The dance isn't over. It's eleven.

He puts Roberto to bed.

He'd like to go down the hallway, to the bathroom, but he holds back; he'd have to mingle with the dancers or sidestep them, without knowing how. They are so unfamiliar to him...

He reads headlines, looks at photographs in the evening paper he bought at the bar. He yawns. He undresses. Before he turns off the light, he goes over to see how the boy is sleeping. He lifts up the sheet. The boy's eyes are open in desperation.

His father wants to tell him, *Sleep, boy, go to sleep.* He wants to say it in the most tender and protective voice, but nothing emerges from his throat.

Labor Union, retirees' section. An office worker rushing through his work, though he won't be able to escape his desk until twelve o' clock sharp.

And yet, by twelve fifteen he's made it to the pension. He's delivering a complaint on his child's behalf. As he walks down the hall, he sees the door to his room remains closed. He is surprised, but it doesn't stop him.

"First of all, Miss, good day to you. Now: I thought this was a family home."

"Mr. Ortega, you know perfectly well this is a boarding house. There's a sign out on the street."

"Yes, I know. A family pension is what I meant to say."

"And so it is. Does anyone say otherwise?"

"The facts do, Miss. The facts."

"What facts?"

"The dance last night."

"What's the harm in that? You think this is a nightclub? You think people are dancing here every night?"

At first the owner wasn't willing to give ground to a guest as new and as frazzled as he. But she sees she can reach a compromise: the motive of his irritation is circumstantial and insignificant.

"Look, Mr. Ortega, let me explain."

She explains: this happens only rarely. The dance was for boarders only. No outsiders. The truck drivers showed up from Córdoba, and since there are tourist girls staying in the pension…

Ortega listens and makes his assumptions: *Tourists and truck drivers. Thrifty tourists. Truckers flush with cash…* He sees he's let his anger be assuaged. The owner's defense is unobjectionable. So much so that she feels in her rights to bring up a much more delicate matter that has displeased her.

"Now then, Mr. Ortega, can you tell me what's going on with your boy? Will he be this way every day?"

The boy. The closed door. Just then, the father feels that the slightest touch could make him lose it.

He wants to run. He needs to see. But first, he needs information to back him up.

He left the boy there. When the girl tried to go in to do the cleaning, the boy started shouting. The girl was stunned and refused to go in if the boss didn't come and mediate. When the boy saw the owner, he got even more upset. And it was clear there was nothing wrong with him, he wasn't shouting because he was sick, he just didn't want anyone in there, that was all. So the women shut the door and there was no more noise. The room was a mess, and the father would have to deal with it.

"Is that all?"

"Is that not enough?"

The repetition of this episode the following day obliges him to come up with a system. The maid comes in at seven. Before sweeping the sidewalk, after dragging out the trashcans, she does Ortega's room, while he can keep a handle on the boy, in other words. Ten minutes are set aside for the trip to the bathroom.

But what about the rest of the day?

"Bertito, I can't stay here. If you wanted, you could leave the room while I'm not here… In the courtyard in the back, there are chicklets."

A flicker of interest lights up the boy's eyes. It dies out. The father struggles to reignite it:

"Little yellow chicks. Teeny tiny. Like this. They fit in your hands. Like this, make a little hollow with your hand."

The boy allows his father to bend his hand.

"You want to see them? I'll take you."

The boy closes his hand. His father sees it has become a fist, and it hurts him that already, the boy's hand foresees the hardships life will bring.

Quarter past eight at night. The father arrives. He doesn't waste a minute on friends, on window shopping, on bulletin boards. He can't deprive his child of respite from a confinement that has already lasted nearly a week until he hits on a solution or the boy stops stubbornly shutting himself up. The father trusts the way out of this will come on its own, through the dictates of nature alone.

The father arrives. The room is dark. He can tell from looking at the transom window outside. He enters, stretching his hand toward the light switch and uttering his wounded reproach:

"Always the same, son, and in the darkness, no less. Why? Why?"

The light appears, obedient to the flick of the switch, revealing the room in its completeness, but for him, all it discloses is the presence of the boy, sitting still, holding a certain part of his body in his hand.

"Papa, pee."

The boy doesn't answer his father's reproaches. He offers no reply to his questioning. He demands:

"Papa, pee."

"I'll take you right now. Let me put this away and…"

But the boy interrupts him, prodding:

"Papa, pee."

It's a plea.

The father understands. He throws the folders on the table, tugs the boy by the hand, and takes him down the hall.

When they get there, the child has wet his pants.

Afterward, while they wait for dinner, the father sits on the edge of the bed, observing this face, which seems to reflect neither guilt nor shame, but betrays the expectation of a punishment that cannot yet be written off.

The father is beyond confused:

"Can it really be, boy…? Not even when you're dying to go…?"

Ortega asks for permission. Half an hour to go to the store.

He returns to the office. The paper wrapping doesn't hide its contents. Someone figures it out. A suggestive smile. Ortega can tell. He hadn't thought of this. Nor had it occurred to him to leave the package in the coatroom. He can't put it on his desk now. He stashes it in the wastebasket. A coworker laughs heartily. All his colleagues giggle for a moment. But no one makes a wisecrack to keep it going. Ortega relaxes.

At twelve, he removes the package from the wire basket.

The boss, who hadn't participated in the merriment, says:

"Taking it with you? I thought you were going to use it here."

The others latch onto the joke.

Ortega isn't offended. He smiles. He bears it. All of a sudden, he suspects there is a secret culprit at play, and leaves, thinking he should look for a solution with the least possible delay.

He unwraps the package. The object is familiar to the boy. It's not so long since he stopped using it.

He unbuttons his pants.

His father cups the boy's face in his right hand. To keep from smacking him, he thinks, once he knows that his hand is occupied.

He interrupts him:

"But son, if I'm here, I can take you to the bathroom."

It's too late. In light of the reproach, the boy has tried to contain himself, but things are already running their course, and in consequence, the floor gets wet.

The father smiles in resignation.

"Well, we had to try it out sometime. Might as well be now."

His return to the room, after eight at night, shows that the device has served its purpose perfectly. They will have to eat right away, then and there. He'll have to take the thing off. He'll have to take the boy, too. He's dirty, he's soiled his clothes. But the thing comes first.

He picks it up. He goes to leave. The door opens. The door that reveals that woman.

He turns back. He leaves it inside. He covers it with a newspaper.

He takes the boy off to the bathroom, with clean underwear to change him.

When the girl comes to set the table, he asks her to take out the chamber pot. She hesitates, unsure whether, at that hour, such a chore falls within the scope of her obligations. Hereditary resignation leads her to answer:

"Sure. Right away."

The girl sets out the bread baskets from the kitchen, one for each room. Ortega's is the last one in the building, since she works from inside out, and when she gives him his, her hands are free. She picks up the implement and goes to the courtyard.

The father hears loud complaining. It's a man. He's yelling. The girl says something to him.

The father jolts. He doesn't understand the words' meaning, but he suspects they have something to do with him.

The girl comes back with the bowls of soup. She's upset. Ortega asks her what's happened.

"The gentleman from Room 9. He says he won't stand for me touching those things when I'm serving dinner. I said you told me to do it, I'm not doing it because I want to. The Señora got mad at me, too. I had to wash my hands before I could go back to serving."

The father can't defend himself, he can't discuss the matter with anyone. He looks at the child bitterly. The boy is aware of his glance. He had picked up his spoon. He leaves it there now, next to the plate, and lowers his forehead.

It's decided, they will change pensions. Roberto refuses to live in this one, he rejects it, maybe because it is their first lodgings in foreign territory. Roberto feels surrounded by enemies, and his declared hostility to his father no longer adopts merely illusory forms.

It takes a few days to find what he's looking for, not because he's choosy, but because he needs a room close to the bathroom. Experience demands it, and it's not a hard thing to find. Besides that, he needs – or wants – it to be at street level, with its own exit, or at least with a door that opens into the foyer, like the other. This came to him all of a sudden, as a consequence of a certain idea, one he didn't want to admit and that presumably has already faded away, though not without obliging him to find a room with that location instead of a different one.

For the boy, the move means nothing. He heeds to his calling as a shut-in, and at most, assents to going to the bathroom without the company of his father.

"Hang-ups! Hang-ups!" the father wails the day he concedes failure.

"What if he's ill…?" the new owner suggests, less discreet but also less selfish than the former one, trying to include herself in the problem that is dividing father from child.

"He eats, doesn't he?" the father replies violently.

"Yes, that he does."

"He does everything he has to do, right?"

"Yeah… Everything, you could say that… He does some things. But he doesn't do what other boys do."

"Not what other people do, little or big. It's his character, Miss. His character. That's not something a doctor can fix."

The woman has no more answers. She falls silent, focused. Then she hazards an opinion:

"Character… it could be. Or maybe it's grief."

Grief.

The word grabs hold of the father's heart. Grief.

He remembers that he has forgotten grief. He has.

When the conversation with the owner has reached its end, he tries to justify himself inwardly. He makes a list: one, two moves, predicaments with the boy, debts, the cruelty of creditors.

And yet, regardless of anything that might absolve him, there it is... grief, so distant, so muffled in so few weeks.

But not in the boy, in the boy it can't have gone away. And he never talks to him about his mother... to keep from making him suffer, or so he thought up to now. Because his own heart, like the house they left behind, has expelled her.

In the morning, he buys a picture frame, the size of a postcard. He waits for night, a time more suited to airing sentiments. More fitting, as well, for a father to utter those few words an older man can say to his little son and hear his heartbeat.

"Papa is going to show you something that you and I love very much. But don't cry, my boy."

The boy is surprised at this declaration and the accompanying demand.

The father unwraps the picture frame and places it on the table, which is already wiped clean of the crumbs from dinner. He opens the leather billfold where he keeps letters, receipts, and personal documents.

He takes out a photo. A portrait, a portrait of his wife.

That's how she was, he says to himself.

That's how she was a few months before she fell ill.

Contemplating the photograph unnerves him in a way he hadn't imagined. The heat of emotion, the desperation of absence overtake him. It was a mistake, he sees, to keep the photo hidden. Maybe if it had been there among his things, it would have comforted him through those grim and adverse circumstances.

That's how she was...

The father realizes the boy has been watching him the whole time. Unsure it was right to put his feelings on display, he hesitates before showing him the photograph. But he's decided – and if it has to happen – he will cry with his boy, together, for the first time, for what they both have lost.

He puts the portrait on the table, in front of his son.

The boy looks at it.

His father will ask him if he recognizes her, because the boy hasn't opened his lips, hasn't gestured, hasn't tried to pick up the photo. But there's no need to ask. The boy says:

"Mama."

Nothing more.

He looks up at his father, as though asking him if there is anything else to see.

His father is mortified. He begins to suspect the boy might be an imbecile. What he's done at the pensions… his lack of reaction to his mother's portrait…

He leaves the photo in the frame. It's still there in the morning and at midday. At night it's gone. The boy has taken scissors to it, and with his clumsiness, he's decapitated her.

"What have you done?"

His tone is so harsh, the question alone is a punishment, and the boy starts to cry. But amid sobs, he makes his wishes heard:

"I want more, I want another one to play with."

His father becomes enraged, and strikes him.

When he has him in his hands, like one defeated, he carries him to bed. Not to the boy's bed, but to his own, the one that came with the room, a big, old bed made for two. He curls up beside the boy. While he listens attentively as the sobbing dies down, as if its abeyance might diminish the harm he'd done the child, he gets a hunch, and the desire to see if it's right or not stirs him.

The opportunity to see comes later, after he's convinced the boy to get out of bed and eat his soup.

Anxious for an answer, he asks:

"Berto, Bertito, son, what happened to Mama?"

A trickle of water flows from the boy's eyes. The father is afraid of hurting him, and of hurting himself, by digging deeper into the boy's thoughts. In a wary voice, ready to retreat if he wounds him, he ventures:

"Berto, Bertito, where is Mama?"

The boy raises a hand, with a gesture of befuddlement, dejection, and utter incomprehension, and says:

"I don't know, I don't know, Papa. She left me alone. She abandoned me, Papa."

It is clear that a wail is welling deep inside him, making his chest quake repeatedly before emerging though his mouth and his eyes.

And his father can't console him because his head has dropped down onto the tablecloth and he is crying, too.

Now his father has had two meaningful experiences.

First, he has learned that, if he forgot his own grief, that didn't mean it was lost, and that very present grief is why he is now so volatile, so sensitive, that he has covered his face with tears.

Second, he believes he has reconciled with his son. He no longer blames him for his mishaps, and even conceals, as much as possible, the repulsion he feels at the boy's stubborn retreat into the room.

"When you're older, you'll have to go to school, Bertito. How long are you going to keep going like this?"

He's tried to get him to make friends with the girl next door. As always, Berto agreed to step out with his father; but playing, speaking with that creature the same size as him, no, not that, no.

His aunt can't take him in and his father prefers it that way.

A visit from her, the third or fourth since they've lived in the pensions, came to an unpleasant end. The boy got angry, there were shouts, a broken cup. On her way out, the aunt denounces him in the presence of the landlady:

"He's an animal."

The owner tries to help, despite forming part of that multitude of beings the child will not allow near him.

Then she pulls the father to her side with a bit of advice:

"What you need is a woman, and what the boy needs is a mother."

A woman.

Another word that was stolen from Ortega. Another word taken from him, and hidden.

The owner has no way of knowing what is going on. It's not a woman he needs. Indeed, one cause of his upsets is his disorderly behavior with those unknown women of the night, when he slips out into the street, leaving his boy in the care of sleep, his one unfailing guardian. With the better part of his time spent at the office, and the foam of his spare minutes skimmed off for his son, how could he maintain a regular relationship with a woman? How might he find a respectable woman who would put up with his situation, his boy, his inexhaustible debts? No, it isn't a woman he needs. And anyway, what woman? The owner is talking about a different kind, that much he understands, but he's a man, he's impatient, and that keeps him from being able to choose.

It's the hour when Sunday starts to fade. Ortega is sitting with his boy next to the lake. The boy is licking an ice cream.

Lots of women pass by, and the man observes them; he likes to watch them, that's all, he doesn't get carried away or let his feelings run wild.

But that one coming over, the one with a dress that both reveals and veils her restive body, invades him like a premonition. She comes over as if looking to meet someone. That much is obvious, because she's walking alone, but she doesn't seem to feel alone. The man has no choice but to look her in the eyes, and she has no choice but to look at him. In the eyes.

It's enough. He is pierced, wounded by desire. He has to follow her, to catch her. He tells the boy to walk. He orders him to walk. Off she goes, with her rapid step. Him behind her. He stays back, because the boy can only take short little steps, and gets lost amid the legs of the people walking slow, out for a stroll. His father grabs him by the hand and tugs. He lifts him up. He makes him drop his ice cream. He is saved from tears of protest because the child is accustomed to mute resignation.

The woman is no longer where Ortega can see her. He puts the child on the ground. He recovers his outward composure. Still, he is stricken with longing. Why? He doesn't know. He thinks for a moment. It's that when he saw her, she saw him as well. She's not a woman from the street, and for some time now, he's been unused to the suggestiveness of a woman's gaze as she crosses eyes with a man.

He has to find her.

Clearly she was on her way to meet someone. Who? Who? Here was the answer: she was off to meet a group of friends. They're together now, arm in arm, festive, like girls, though none of them is one. Now he'll have to walk past her. Past them. He'll have to content himself with seeing her as he passes by. How do you address a woman who's arm in arm with others?

The man is hoping to catch another of those intimate glances. Instead, he meets eyes with three, four other women. He doesn't want to see them, not anymore, because their stares harbor duplicity and malice and, to make their thoughts plainer, withering laughter frames their expressions.

Suddenly, the man is aware of what it is the women are seeing: a man engaged in a romantic conquest, following a woman where the lovers go to stroll, with a boy on his arm he can't tear loose from, who follows him in consternation, forced to witness the secret affairs of grown-ups.

A thought arises in the father's mind: he's lost respect for his son. A strange idea, he tells himself. But there it is.

On Monday, the father brings home a magazine so the boy can cut out the pictures. He always does that now, but this time, he's chosen one with alluring photos of women. At the kiosk, it struck him that the size, contrasting volumes, and blank backgrounds, which highlighted the women's silhouettes, would make them easier for the boy to cut out with his scissors. While he waits for lunch, he opens it up. He looks at a few of the pictures, and the magazine changes recipients.

When he arrives, the boy asks him, "Is it for me?," and the man nods.

But before he leaves again, he puts it in a drawer the boy can't reach. Sad, the boy ponders the ruination of his game.

"You can't cut this one up. I'll bring you another tonight, with little colored cats and ducks."

And he does, at night. But it was the afternoon hours that the boy wanted to fill: the cushion that goes on the chair so he can reach the table is made of raw linen stamped with flowers; the scissors found their way to it, setting the printed flowers free, and releasing the shabby filling of straw and dirty wool.

His father hopes to hide the remains of the ravaged cushion, which doesn't belong to them, but forms part of the pension's scant accessories. He'll put a pillow on the chair. Tomorrow he'll buy another cushion. But the girl comes in without knocking and sees the man on the ground, cleaning up the straw.

The Señora finds out from the girl. She comes as though summoned.

She stops at the threshold. The boy retreats behind the man, who has stood up. He doesn't flee because his father's there.

"It was so pretty, that cushion… I shouldn't have given it to you. These are things boarders should bring with them."

"I'll pay for it, Miss. It's not worth so much."

"No, it's not about what it's worth, in the end. It's… You know, what's the point in saying it. It pains me. But his aunt was right. The boy's an animal."

"Miss! How can you say such a thing! And with the boy there, listening to everything. Do you have no compassion? If it wasn't for…"

The woman understands she's gone too far. She regrets it, it wasn't what she had in mind. She just said all that to cover up her annoyance at losing the cushion.

"It's fine. You're right. I apologize. Goodnight."

With all those words, she hopes to put out the fire. She wants to run away from the flames.

But the father is still burning, hours later, and he needs to get away to somewhere with fresh air.

When the boy's asleep, he goes.

It's midnight.

He picks up a woman on the street.

Rage clouds his reasoning. He hits on the notion of avenging himself for what the owner did to him: he'll stick it to her in her own house. There must have been a reason, he recollects, why he looked for a room close to the street, though he'd never thought he would take advantage of the location. What if they found him out? Well, that would be the reward. He would change residence, but for the owner, the insult would remain. And the boy? He's asleep, he's asleep. He'll surely stay that way. Besides, with all he has to put up with from the boy, he can't be blamed for giving a little back. And even if the boy does see, if he hears, he won't understand.

He takes the woman home. The boy is resting. When she notices his body in the bed, the woman rebels. The man puts his foot down, and she gives in.

Afterwards, he follows her out to the corner.

When he returns, the boy's no longer in bed.

Where is he? Where?

The man looks in the bathroom, in the courtyard, without turning on the lights, calling for him softly, his words suffused with anguish. He peeps out at the sidewalk. He returns to the room to look in the corners.

The boy is under the big bed, right where the two walls meet.

His father sighs, relieved, before asking what he's doing there, inviting him to come out.

When he speaks to him, he doesn't get an answer. He can see the boy huddled there, eyes round and luminous like a cat's. How those eyes look at him…!

He presses him. He offers reasons: he needs to sleep, he can't stay there, nearly naked… And anyhow, did something happen?

He tries changing methods, first with this tone:

"Are you playing…? Playing what? Maybe you could come out and tell me."

Then a second tone:

"Berto, Berto, the boogeyman is coming."

He puts on a frightening voice, throws his shirttail over his head, and starts crawling under the bed.

The child screams.

He can't be allowed to scream at this hour.

The man opts for a more primitive plan: moving the bed. He starts dragging it, careful not to raise any hackles with the noise, and watching out so the boy doesn't get snagged on one of the legs. The boy comes along, grasping the metal railings next to the mattress. He can't resist his father's strength, but his father isn't looking to fight with him.

Livid, he says, "You'll stay there till…," shuts off the light, undresses, and lies down.

For a while he holds his breath, listens for noises, tries to spy on any possible movement his son might make. Nothing reaches him.

He falls into a deep sleep, like after a night of love.

He wakes up feeling threatened, as if some menace had caught him unawares. Someone's pounding on the door. He looks at the child's bed: it's still empty. He shouts: "Hold on."

He throws on a bit of clothing.

He cracks the door. It's the girl.

"No cleaning. No cleaning today. There's no need for you to come in and clean right now. I'll tell you later when it's all right for you to come."

He realizes he's contradicted himself, and he tries to smooth it over:

"The best thing would be for you hurry and bring my breakfast. I'm in a rush."

Until she returns, he pretends he's forgotten the boy, that he isn't worried about him.

He takes the tray at the door and places it on the table.

He calls:

"Berto."

He calls again:

"Bertito."

He tempts him:

"Milk, Bertito, with croissants and jelly."

He bends over to look and see if the child is asleep. He's not asleep, and those eyes, looking like they will never close…!

When he leaves, he says out loud, self-assured, like someone who knows best:

"You'll come out in your own time."

He hands over the tray in the kitchen. There's no need to tell the women not to go in while he's away.

At twelve-ten, he returns, with the intense hope that the boy has reacted as he wishes. That he's dropped the attitude, that there's no need for reprimands, threats, punishment, or pleading. That there's no need to explain anything or bring back up what's happened.

In the room, everything is so far from his wishes that he does what his own father did when he was a boy, what he swore he would never do when he became a father himself: he unclasps the buckle from the leather and pulls on the strap. Now he's armed.

"Are you going to come out, or…?"

He stays standing there. He grasps the buckle, letting the belt hang, so the boy will see that long strip of leather scraping the ground.

"Are you coming out…?"

The boy's sole response is silence.

For the third time:

"I said, are you coming out?"

And he kneels, as though preparing for a sacrifice, and whips the belt blindly into the corner. One, two, three blows get lost in the softness of the air, then he knows he's hit the target, because he can feel it in his hand and hear it in the cracking of the belt.

He pulls back. The belt goes limp, lies there under the bed. The man has let it go. Both hands closed, he is leaning on the floor, because his head, filled with blood, is weighing him down brutally. He's afraid he hit the boy in the face, he's afraid he made him faint: he hasn't let slip a single complaint, an ow, a show of fear.

The man looks, terrified, afraid he's ruined everything.

There he is: alive, stern, panting, a horrified cat, a tiger cub tucked away in his final refuge, scared of being torn apart by dogs.

Getting lunch is more complicated than getting breakfast. The girl makes so many trips… But still, he manages to keep her out, and later from asking why he wants to keep a plate of food in his room.

Before he leaves, he bows to humiliation. He's worked up the words all through lunch, all through siesta, which he didn't take advantage of.

"Berto, Bertito. I'm sorry I hurt you. I'm sorry I hit you. Berto, Bertito, will you come out and tell Papa you forgive him? Will you come out? Will you come out, Berto?"

He waits.

But he has to keep going:

"Fine, it doesn't matter. I forgive you. I'm not mad. I'm not getting mad anymore."

He pauses again. Another pause that begs for a response. He doesn't get it.

"OK, Bertito, bye then. See you tonight. You must be hungry. I've left some food for you on the table. It's probably cold, but that doesn't matter, you'll like it all the same. You can eat while I'm gone."

He takes all the steps between himself and the door. They are few, but they hurt, because he doesn't want to take them.

He opens the door, still not resolved to go, to leave him there like that.

He says, very softly:

"See you tonight. See you tonight, son."

He sighs and shuts the door.

He walks out to the street. The radiant clarity waylays him: *How can there be so much sun, today?*

At eight-ten, he stretches out his arm, barely past the doorframe, and turns on the lamp.

He doesn't talk anymore, he doesn't ask with words. He looks. The bed is undone, with the same disorder as the night before; the plate that held the food is now empty; the disused device has emerged from the nightstand and will have to be covered up with a magazine.

The father understands things will be harder from now on.

No

Dreams, more punctual than memories, came to tell me for the third time that the sky of her years of absence was closing.

I began to feel the day like a melancholy, painful burden.

I had to wait for night for the solitary commemoration and simple ritual of my worship of love.

In the morning, they ordered me to go to a public office which has a yard out front and a fence of slender bars. While I waited for the paperwork to find its destination inside, I passed the time walking along the gravel path.

A nun appeared, accompanied by a little girl with the awestruck look of a recently orphaned child cast into the world, and as she walked toward the building, her gaze settled on my eyes. We were close to each other, and I could make out her very fine peach fuzz and a small mole, light brown, also over her lip. She was young, and I don't know if what her look stirred up was sorrow or nostalgia for affection, which was the same as not having it, because it was born at the wrong time.

When the nun walked away, which happened just afterward, I watched her intensely. She responded to me with a clear stare, pure and distant. She stepped onto the sidewalk, paced alongside the fence, I walked past the street, and she left without turning her head.

At night, I walked to the railway station. It might seem like a strange place for my offering. Ah, I am capable of building up my feelings in silence, and in solitude as well. But something is necessary to bring a memory into being, and what I had of her were those hands, which held onto mine as the train pulled away.

On the night of the third anniversary, in the midst of the turbulent platforms, I couldn't mutter that tender phrase that I have in mind for her now. Because to say it, in a fleeting – perhaps miraculous – state of purity, I'd have to concentrate and isolate all the strength of my emotion and my thought.

I started up on the elevated bridge where the people pass over the trains from one platform to the other. The night was cool, and like a black box, the bridge seemed uninhabited. I scaled the three sets of stairs, and up top I found a woman posed as though waiting. Though I could have reached solitude on the other side of the bridge, it bothered me to come upon her, for it gave rise to that creeping intimation of desire in relation to women. And this wasn't the moment to give in to everyday urges.

I descended the three sets of stairs on the other side. I followed the second platform to where the rails cut it off.

I went back. The woman had stayed in the same place. Despairing of finding the proper moment for my recollections, I closed my eyes and said her name very softly, "Amanda…," and uttered the spiritual words I had chiseled in my mind for her. But even without watching what was going on around me, I got distracted, and failed to achieve the illusory communion I had enjoyed other times before.

I started walking back. A man appeared, and a woman joined him. They came down before me and mingled with the other people in the world.

Had it happened, had the mystery of evocation been lost?

Oh, yes, it was diminishing inside me as I walked, returning myself to the city's heart. Because after a few blocks, outside voices began to prevail. First came those of three women who had finished their shift in a restaurant kitchen, as they said. Two were talking and the third sang softly, for herself and herself alone. And I thought how the third, the one who was singing, was enjoying like no one else the good fortune of having finished a day's labor.

Then a friend recognized me. And spoke to me. And I spoke back.

"How are you?"

"Doing well."

"Glad to hear it."

"And you?"

"Good."

That was all, because he took off running to catch the bus. But again, I was communicating with the others. Even in myself, I was going back to being like all the other men.

At a kiosk, I bought caramels. They were for my sister's children, though when I reached the house, I knew they'd be asleep. She was working, and the noise of the sewing machine was the only voice in the house that hadn't died down. I laid them next to her hand.

She stopped her sewing to greet me, and turned around to look at me with humility and gratitude. It hurt me that she thanked me for everything, even if only with her eyes. For two years now, we've been so alone, she and I, and the kids, that I could only define us as a small community brought together by need, and naturally inclined to each other by sentiment.

"Are you tired?" she asked. I said, "Yeah," and she repeated, "Yeah. You're tired." She said it with such a wounding tone, one that struck me as so wounded, that I felt her sheltering wing close over me.

Then I knew I could talk with her about Amanda that night, because soon the nostalgia came back to me. And the nostalgia struggled with a measure of pride, the pride of being able to confess a love so muted and so destitute of a future. But I didn't speak.

Four days later, when I'd come back home for lunch, by the sewing machine, still at that hour, a letter with my name on it was waiting for me in the place I'd left the caramels.

It was from Amanda, the first letter from Amanda that had made it into my hands in the entire time I had existed. It was from Amanda. There was no need to open it to know. Among my papers, I had a sheet of notebook paper with a school exercise she had lent me, and I never gave it back, because I was distracted, because I forgot it, because I don't know why, because in my grammar school days it never occurred to me I'd end up loving her, and so much.

"Dear friend…" Such a common opening, yet for me it wasn't, because I was bursting with longings and ressentiments. She told me she had flunked out in the second-to-last year of her program. She had given up her studies to get married the autumn before.

I knew it. I knew it all when it happened, and I didn't find out from her.

A friend came. He told me about our common friend, how she was seeing someone, and I listened as if her existence were the furthest thing from my interests. But I withdrew, as if home from a battle I had lost. That battle never happened, except inside me.

For a time, amid the fog of the proximity of loss, I gave myself over to scheming. I cooked up plans to obstruct their matrimony. Never the simplest thing: telling her what was happening to me. This was a time when I still feared deep responsibilities.

Back then, I was slave to the conviction that their marriage had something both terrible and inevitable about it.

When I found out it had occurred, I consoled myself with the belief that the image of her as a girl, as a fiancée who hadn't been mine, would go on belonging to me, forever.

I dedicated to that credo the secret part of my heart, while paradoxically, in the home of my widowed sister, life turned me into a minor sort of godfather to the family.

Nothing in the letter gave me the right to think it, but still, I thought: "Why *couldn't she help* writing me?"

I dug into my suspicions, in my letters I goaded her to confess, but she revealed nothing in words. Still, she never mentioned her husband, as if he didn't exist, and if I sent off two letters per week, I got two from her in return, and if they were three, then the postman would bring me three, and her answer was so swift, so clearly written with my own words fresh in her mind, that what we had was now a living, breathing dialogue.

And one exalted night I plucked an amorous truth from the place where my most guarded feelings lay tucked away. Written on paper, it seemed to belong to me no more, as if it were Amanda's now. I put the paper in an envelope. I took it, that very night, to the main post office. I couldn't give myself the chance to regret it.

I waited three days, four, the normal period. I had to suffer all those instants that make up another day. The letter arrived, and I knew my declaration had provoked neither acceptance nor reproach.

Then I begged. I begged her to tell me something, to give me a word, even one of condemnation or forgetting, to offer some solidity for my position on this earth, which depended so heavily on her.

Three days later, an envelope arrived at my house with a small portrait: the figure that provoked in me a hidden, bloody battle with the enchantment of a costly ideal.

Was that her answer? I refused to let hope disappear.

Our dialogue lapsed, through my willfulness and silence, until I was sure I would be able to travel: permission from work, the necessary funds, the ticket bought, and the certainty of a date carved in stone.

I asked her for nothing, I could require nothing of her. Just to wait for me, and not when I got off the train, where passengers cut such a lamentable figure; not in her home, and not somewhere secret; just for her to tell me, before my departure, in two lines, a time and a place.

She waited for me in her city, on a path trimmed with trees tall as the poplar rows in my province, but thicker. When I arrived and set eyes on it, I was happy, feeling that for our vital occasion, the setting showed touches of grandeur.

She was there on a still-empty terrace, with twenty or thirty café tables from the pastry shop where we were due to meet.

With nothing between us, save a few empty tables that were easy to ignore, her presence became clear to me, sweet and grave. She greeted me without extravagance, as saints greet children on prayer cards, with the benevolence and peace of the sinless.

How should I speak?, I asked myself as I felt my body move forward. How should I speak to that face, that stare? How should I choose my words, how should I think in words?

She remained in her chair, and above the table I saw the sharp outlines of the serene torso and noble face of her welcome. Gently, a new feeling took hold of me, which forbid me from coming too close to her side, and made me collapse into the chair in front of her, with the table separating us. Twice I said her fated name: "Amanda... Amanda...," and I took her hand, which was at rest atop the white marble.

Oh, my God! How it moved her to see me so. In her eyes, a tear was born, so discreet, it clung to her eyelid. And I repeated her name, as though putting a name to my love. And she had to say my name, because it welled inside her, I know, because it crumbled in her mouth with a sob. And she said to me, oh, she said to me!, "My love," and she sobbed.

I leapt up from the chair, and when I reached her, she fell into my arms and said it, said it: "My love, my love..."

But hers was the voice of one uttering the name a dearly beloved lost, and as I embraced her I wanted to ask, in desperation, why, until I felt her lower body twist away, marking an irreparable distance between us.

Afterwards, we gave each other the most beautiful and saddest hour of my life. But without tears. When we said goodbye, I placed my hand over hers, while it lay on the marble of the table; I squeezed it tight, very tight, and we smiled, one to the other, with bitterness and bravery.

from *Decline and Angel* (1958)

Abandonment and Passivity

A burst of light speckled the drawer of men's clothes, but was immediately snuffed out. The light then shifted to the ladies' clothes, which changed continents: from the dresser drawer to the suitcase, deprived of the silky tidiness they had known when they were freshly ironed. A luster, overlooked, withered and shrank on the bed. The one-piece swimsuit was stripped of the two-piece bikini's company.

When the door shut noisily, to announce the suitcase's departure, the glass of water, still intact, pressed down the handwritten note, echoing, on the table's esplanade, the vertical presence of a vase of excessively red artificial flowers, streaked with a tender pink that clashed with the furious hue surrounding it.

But when the violence outside fell silent, the violence of the sun did too, and the pink veining faded, and the flowers turned to an unruly, impalpable blot, nestled in the sedate shadows. Then it was only the alarm clock that kept guard, waiting trivially for the light on the nightstand, for the order of various objects, perhaps their integrity, to change.

Because all was passive – or mechanical, in the case of the clock – but ready to serve when the door opened once more.

The glass, almost at once, casts its shadow, faint and translucent, as though rendered in water and glass; then it withdraws it slowly, and later on, but warily, unfurls it again, now in another direction.

When once more outside in the sky, there are clouds and commotion like an underground demolition, the glass takes fright and turns to something clear, concise, and, if possible, tinged with blue.

The alarm clock has gone dead.

Sanctioned by inertia, a fly goes from sun to sun, from sun to sun, but only twice.

The water turns cloudy in the glass and settles. Like a flower, a mosquito has swum across its surface, and now, inside, its larvae plumb the depths.

But this tame sea is a deadly cradle, water empty of nourishment, and in the end, it sends the fragile flotsam to the surface.

The atmosphere longs to loose its gathering weight upon the things, it is a threat to all the days, but it must not be feared.

A stone, a vulgar stone from a ditch, without warning, without encouragement from its compeers, manages what its lesser familiars, the hailstones, white and ephemeral, could not achieve.

It rends the windowpane's chastity, bringing with it the air, which is freedom, though it loses its own, falling prisoner to the room.

Stripped of the unity that helped make it stable, the windowpane breaks hastily loose, and drags its brother, who became a glass, on to his doom. It lays him low with its dead weight, and the shards intermingle amid the disordered expansion of the water, which doesn't know what to do, startled free of its enclosure, and runs all over, particularly onto the paper, its once untouchable neighbor.

The ink, which was cursive, turns painterly and envisages, in blue, bristles, puddles, stalagmites…

From now on, the window resists nothing. It hurries the air along, lets the breeze blow the brittle paper, prematurely aged, off the table, then invites in the north wind, which knocks down the flowerpot and, as if that weren't enough, flings dirt over it and its flowers.

The light, which came only in daytime, and always through the window, returns one night, emanating from the filaments in the lamp in the midground. The objects, opaque under the dust, recover their volume and discreteness.

One of the shoes stepping forth among them lands on the paper, as though to even out the rough spots, though all it does is get it dirty. And so, decrepit and muddy, the paper rises up, crepitating until brought near the glimmer of a pair of spectacles. It descends to the nightstand and there, bathed in a different light, this time from the resurrected bedside lamp, it quivers an interminable while before the round lenses. But it doesn't submit. It is no longer a message.

The purity of the sunlight triumphs over the tenuous yellow, past its prime, still drifting out of the two bulbs.

The sunlight, a stern investigator, finds that everything is there. There's less order: the quilt is wrinkled, the drawers are open... but everything is still there. A shirt is missing from the drawer of men's clothes, and a kerchief and a pair of socks; but dirty, on top of a chair, lie another shirt, another kerchief, and another pair of socks.

from *The Affection of Dimwits* (1961)

The Horse in the Salt Flats

August, 1924

The plane moves evasively through the sky.

When it passes over the ranches clustered around the station, the boys scatter and the men brace their legs to bear the tremors.

It's already on the other side, vanishing, level with the hill. The boys and their mothers look out, like after the rain falls. The men's voices return:

"Must be Zanni... the airman?"

"Can't be. Zanni's taking a trip around the world."

"So, what, we're not in the world?"

"That's right. But nobody knows it except for us."

Pedro Pascual listens and goes along with those who know best; it must be the airplane is going out to meet the *king's train*.

Umberto of Savoy, Prince of Piedmont, isn't a king; but he will be, they say, when his father dies, because his father is a real king.

That same afternoon, they say, the prince from Europe will be here, in this poor, sandy country.

Pedro Pascual wants to see him so he can tell his wife. If only she were there. Pedro Pascual likes to share things with her, even if it's just yerba mate or laughter. And he doesn't like being alone, like a tagalong, for the visit, standing out in front of the yard. He's not sullen; it's just that he hasn't settled in; the Mendozans laugh at his Córdoba accent.

He takes refuge among the bundles of fodder. He works all that land, the boss's land, and has to carry the feed baled in wire so the cows won't go hungry. The hands that grasp and gather light on the plants they have mown along the way, which will serve as medicines for his home. Pearl-fruit, tabaquillo, burro tea, myrtle, vomitbush… He shifts and sorts the clumps and the mixture of fragrances brings back the feel of home, condensed inside an aromatic cup. But the thyme's intensity overwhelms his sense of smell, and Pedro Pascual tries to compare it with something, but he doesn't get it right until he thinks, convinced: *This one is the king, because it brings fragrance to the land.*

That's the king's train? One little engine and a caboose spewing smoke? It can't be, but the people say…

Pedro Pascual ignores it. He's being called by that sheaf of low, blue clouds covering the sky. He feels betrayed, as though they'd distracted him with a toy and called up the storm behind his back. But why all this displeasure and worry? Isn't it water that the fields need? Sure, but… his field lies out past Toad Hill.

The little engine blows its whistle when it leaves the station behind and to Pedro Pascual, it seems like it's startled the clouds. They mill together, change course, open up, as though cracked, prodded by the formidable wind. The sun falls again on the brownish-gray sand and Pedro Pascual feels it light him up inside, because the cloud front looks like it's retreated to take the water to where he needs it.

Now Pedro Pascual comes back to himself. Now he understands everything: the little engine was something like a bloodhound, or like a clown going ahead of the circus. The *king's train*, the train that couldn't but differ from all the other trains fleeing along the rails, is bringing up the rear, more serious, in the distance.

It's different, Pedro Pascual says to himself. He wonders why: because there are coats-of-arms on the cowcatcher, and two flags… And why else?

Because it looks abandoned, with the windows down, with no one peeking out, no one getting off or getting on. The conductor, over there, and a guard, over here, and on the station's cement tiles a soldier at attention, saluting, but to whom?

The populace, uninterested, gathers on the platform, and nobody tries to rush forward. The children are sucked in by the non-occurrence. The men walk from one end to the other, stomping hard, and if they could, they'd raise a racket, but their espadrilles don't make any noise. They talk loud, to show their bluster, but not a single one looks at the train. It's as if it weren't there.

Only afterward, when it departs, do they watch it from the rear, and then the comments come: "It might well be…!"

Before the train becomes a memory, the officious little airplane comes up from behind, not wanting to lose track of it.

Pedro Pascual will end up regretting his curiosity and dawdling, though without much time for penitence.

An hour's walk from the station, past all the goat pens, it greets him, harangues him, blinds him: the water from the sky. It wears him down, bowls him over, as if trying to hurl him down a well. It cows him, puts the fear in him, woven with lightning bolts of a purity like a blade of deadliest steel.

Pedro Pascual steps down from the carriage. He doesn't want to leave his horse, but the tree cover is low, and even crouching, he can barely fit underneath. The meek animal, obeying an unspoken command, stops in its tracks, and the rain pounds its flanks.

Then it happens. The lightning bolt erupts like a white flare and ignites the *alpataco*, the crooked-branched tree that was giving the man cover. Pedro Pascual manages a scream as he burns down to a cinder. He makes a sound, the sound of a man burning down to a cinder.

A few feet away, the horse whinnies with terror, the light has blinded it, and he tears off into the night, and the weight of the cart and the fodder make the wheels sink in the sand and water, but still, he doesn't stop.

The legs of the animal glisten, but his eyes are dull.

He has run all night. He slows his step, sleepy and defeated, and then stops. The shafts make him ache from the weight of the carriage, but he holds out. He falls asleep. A house wren picks at the surface of the fodder and hops boldly along the horse's back till it reaches his head. The animal awakes and shudders and the bird flies around him and reveals the white breast feathers adorning its drab gray torso. Then it leaves him.

The quadruped buckles, more from hunger than fatigue. The load of damp fodder enlivens his nostrils. He sinks in his hoof, straightens his leg, to get traction, then sets off on the hunt.

He sniffs, he tries to get his bearings, though where he is, not the least trail will guide him, and the silence is so imperious that he refuses even to whinny, as if to participate in the all-embracing muteness and deafness.

The sun pounds the sand, ricochets, and sticks in his throat.

The scent of the *caldén*'s fruit beguiles his instincts, but the spines tear into his lips.

The sundown calms the day and grants the animal a respite.

The new light reveals three sets of tracks that lead to the carriage, get confused, and trail away. They came from the feet, nearly flush with the ground, of the pink fairy armadillo, Juan Calado, the beast with the skimpy fiberglass dress. For a night, the bundled fodder would have been a treat for him; parked there, an endless storehouse. But the cart was too high for his tiny legs.

It is also a grisly emblem for the helpless passivity of the horse with the frustrated eyes. There he stands, faint, wasting away, powerless to answer his stomach's urgings.

A partridge breaks free from the mountain; its chirping provokes a fear that displaces hunger as the driving force for the animal yoked to the carriage. The jaguarundis are hurtling through. The partridge knows it; the horse doesn't know, but he has a feeling inside.

The two big cats, one black, the other cinnamon, are playing, tumbling, rolling in a tangle, feinting with their tufted paws, cuffing each other, but harmlessly, saving their claws for the incautious or dawdling prey that will soon come across their path.

The horse risks his flanks and takes off running. The inordinate noise, a noise not of the desert, frightens off the jaguarundis as the horse couldn't have on his own, and he takes off toward the hillocks.

The sand is soft, and the beast's curving flanks are soft as well. He is followed by straight, sharp lines, the geometry of the carriage straining to work its way upward.

And in that war with the sand, the animal starts to pant. Bewildered and wheezing, his nostrils swollen, he has long since given up the search for food, but his foot, like a bolas, has hit on a coarse clump of grass, *solupe*, as it's called. At last he can lower his head from something other than exhaustion. His lips probe greedily until they find the stiff stalks. It's like swallowing sticks, but his stomach takes them in with welcoming murmurs.

Beneath the profusion of solupe lie thin leaves of sweet fescue, and to prolong the tranquil hours of the stilling of his hunger, the edible parts of the fescue are woven below with tender stems of rose moss branching off in supine clusters.

The aroma of the one plant has betrayed the other's presence, but nothing portends water, and the animal returns, another day, to his wonted shelter, to the "islands" of the foothills.

A turbid morass, where the light goes dull, a moribund morass that will be gone with three suns, holds him and holds him like a longed-for corral.

The islands and islets are rife with thirsty animals in transit. Their numbers die down when one group charges another, but it never empties completely.

Their roaring, quarrelsome presence disturbs the horse, but none of them, so far, have turned on him. One day he keeps his distance, suffering the sun on the sand flats, another day he risks chomping at the parched patches of broom.

The hare breaks loose from the islands. The guinea pig digs deeper in its burrow. The fox renounces his hatred of sunlight, and his tail appears in the open field behind his wretched body. Only in the tree branches does life remain, the life of the birds, but they too fall silent: the puma is coming, the short-haired bandit, the rogue who looks small from the front and grows big behind, the better to pounce.

He's not seeking water, he won't eat any rabbits. From afar, he has glimpsed the horse without a master. He proceeds, the wind in his face.

Borne on the same wind, in the opposite direction, is the scent of a wild mare, free, who has never known saddle or harness of any kind. She goes to the islands for water.

The unexpected presence of the male makes her neigh with pleasure, and the horse, still yoked to the carriage, turns his head to look toward her, raising a cloud of flies. Just a few yards away now, the mare trots boastfully, and finally gives in and shows herself to him, with her long mane and sturdy body.

He jerks, jerks with his carriage. This monstrous maneuver startles her, she can't understand how the cart moves when the horse does. She bucks, she slips off as he tries to bring his head close to hers, like a strange, atavistic prelude.

She leaps, eager and apprehensive; the warm impulse coursing through her has shaken her. And shaken, enthused, unthinking, she drops her savage guard and tumbles with a whinny of panic at the first leap, the first swipe, of the panther.

As though his own flesh were wounded, as though hunted by the beast now tearing at the mare, the horse goes mad, takes off in a rush, a mournful clatter, and heads for the sand.

The sand ran out before his terror. Now his hoof steps in the salt bog. It's sticky, ponderous, and sucks him into the earth. He has to get out, but barely reaches the white, sand-flecked surface.

He gathers strength for another push, chewing seepweed, the salt flat's lone daughter, a paperlike leaf hugging a stalk two yards long, furled as if around a staff.

Further on, he chases scents. He sniffs avidly, catches a whiff of something, and follows after it, with his ailing step, until he loses it and it is gone.

Now he smells the scent of pasture, of the thick grass from the corral. He noses around it and gnaws on the bit as if he's grazing. He chews, sniffs, and turns back to get at what he imagines he is chewing. What he smells is the fodder in his carriage, and he walks around and around, dragging it, fervidly chasing the burden behind him. He spins in a deadly circle. The carriage cuts a track and gets stuck, and the horse can no longer move forward. He pulls, his chest swells, he slips. The last bit of life slips out of him.

He's so parched, so thin and weightless, that later, one day or the next, the weight of the bundles will tip the carriage backward, the shafts will point to the firmament, and the vanquished body will hang there in the air.

In the interim, the buzzard comes, in his dark attire, the one who never dines alone.

The cart is cleansed, the bones are cleansed, less from the rain than from the hostile and purifying saline vapors.

The bones are ruins, fallen and scattered, the prison of the skin is gone. But on the tip of one shaft, the flesh snagged in the bridle has withered into a sack, inside which the slender, half-flayed cranium stares up into the sky.

Life skirts over the ruins, the search for the safety of sustenance: a flock of celestial parrots, the males among them almost blue, the females a white barely touched by the sky.

Like them, a pair of ringdoves migrates from the droughted Pampas. In flight, they see the intoxicating brea flowers painting broad swaths of yellow along the mountains to the east.

But the dove with her cool gray plumage knows she will not make it that far with her maternal burden. Below she sees, in the tense aridity of the salt flat, a carriage that might hold out support and refuge. She weaves two circles in the air to begin her descent. She coos, to tell the male she is no longer following. But he doesn't stop, and the family is broken apart.

It doesn't matter, because the mother has found a ready-made nest where she can hatch her eggs. Like a hand cupped to receive water or seeds, the horse's blind, upturned head houses the gentle bird in its depths. Later, when the eggs break open, it will be a box of birdsong.

The Affection of Dimwits

When the tremors start, Amaya thinks: *The thing I've been waiting for so long.* And then, with fervor, with passion: *May it wound me. May it destroy everything, everything.*

She feels alone with the quaking earth. But then her husband starts shouting:

"Go out to the yard! Suspiros! Amaya! Suspiros, go to the yard, now!"

It doesn't occur to her to obey. *Suspiros, Suspiros,* she repeats to herself. *He likes her better, too.*

She waits. The birds chirp violently. A cow moos, anxious to escape. Everything else is silence, and the earth has ceased to shift.

The clamor continues:

"Suspiros! Amaya!"

That's all that's left of the tremors: a man's fearful voice. Nothing has fallen, nothing has been destroyed.

Amaya slides out of bed. Her feet glide into a plain pair of house shoes and her slip falls over her pale knees.

She goes to the girl's room. Suspiros is awake, her head on her pillow, eyes wide open, unafraid, waiting.

"Didn't I tell you what an earthquake was? Remember how everything broke when you were younger?"

Amaya resigns herself once more to her daughter's ways. She kisses her lovingly, picks her up, and carries her to the yard. Why? She no longer has reason to. To heed her husband, who is waiting safe under the pergola.

No, it's just because, as she jokes, *that's the earthquake ritual, going out to the yard*. But then she grows somber: she realizes she had also accepted the possibility of her daughter's death.

No one called Colorada. Where could she be? She is reborn with the sun. She comes back when she's hungry. But at midday, the family performs its duty, with one or two voices calling out toward the fields, in case that's where she's gone:

"Coloraaadaaa…!"

She's reclining in the shade against the trunk of the mulberry. "Dimwit, dimwit," she says. "You're a dimwit." To whom? No one's in front of her, or even nearby.

She hears them calling: "Coloraaadaaa…!"

She says: "Wait for me, I'm coming right now." She raises herself up from the mulberry and steps out into the light.

Under the oilcloth on the table, she touches one of Suspiros's legs. Suspiros knows the routine: she puts out a ready hand, and Colorada fills it with white mulberries.

Amaya comes into the kitchen and forestalls her sister:

"Hands."

You have to wash your hands to sit at Amaya's table.

Colorada resents being bossed around and obliged to wash her hands. She argues, indirectly:

"I'm not red," she says, referring to her nickname, *colorada*.

Amaya feels she's overlooked something and can't afford to be understanding. She grabs a shock of hair and waves it under the other woman's nose, prodding her energetically:

"What about this then?"

Colorada, seeing her own color there before her eyes, smiles softly, points at a portrait on the wall, and replies:

"I'm that one."

It's a family memory: a dead little sister, fair-haired.

Amaya lets the shock of hair go, and her forbearance returns. She remembers: when Colorada was a girl and asked who was in the picture, their father, that lonely soul, responded, to hide his sorrow: "You, it's you. Can't you see it's you?"

Then they grew up, their father died too, and two men came into their lives: for Colorada, one who left her dumber than before, fathering a daughter who would later be lost; for Amaya, the husband walking through the door that leads to the veranda, a little sullen – he has his reasons – and a little discomfited, as well, dropping his eyes for a moment, but only a moment, to be sure that Suspiros is there with them.

At siesta, her husband goes back to bed. She likes the store at these times, because it's empty, shaded, and cool, and the doors are closed to shoppers. Two hours of silence, of not being with anyone. She likes the new merchandise. Trying on all the shoes in her size, smelling the boxes of powder, loosening the glass cap on the perfumes, taking a deep whiff of the colognes the men use…

She roots around in the corner reserved for the salesgirl. There's a package of cookies for midafternoon, a rolled up gray apron, loose papers, crumbs… Amaya looks for the sports paper, with the muscular, young athletes. She doesn't find it.

She makes do with the newspaper. The newspaper's all she reads these days. Her only books lie on the two shelves in the dining room: textbooks from the Teacher's College. One time, her husband – she doesn't know why – burned all her novels. She could have stopped him, maybe. She could buy and read others. But she doesn't want to, it simply doesn't appeal to her.

"Lencinas will defend his degree…" "Crowds of the faithful file

through the vestibule of the Jesuit church to see the heart of P. Roque González de Santa Cruz, first civilizer of the Paraná Basin and Uruguay…"
A photograph: people around an engraved urn. She thinks she recognizes two old acquaintances, though the round hats pulled close to the eyes makes the women's faces look the same.

She likes the stories on the first few pages best, the ones with the letters U.P. in parentheses next to the dates. They come from other worlds.

"This morning, the Graf Zeppelin was expected in Seville. The dirigible met with adverse weather between the Azores and the Portuguese coast. The Duchess of Victoria will disembark in the Andalusian capital."

One bit of news wounds her: "Buenos Aires, 30 (U.P.). – By his own choice…"

The last name is recorded, but Amaya only pays attention to the first, José Luis. And the age, 31 years old, and the fact that he was the poet from that book… which is still almost unread, and that Amaya knows nothing of.

Then she feels a tremor, not from the earth, but inside, a tremor and an anguish that weaken her flesh and make her crumple over the glass of the display case.

She catches the four o'clock bus and gives herself to the city's streets, taking in the shower of compliments. Because she's desperate, and desperation gives her, once the first lapse is over, a strength that makes her body vibrant, elastic, younger.

She maunders amid gallant phrases, incites the men without looking at them. They don't touch her, they graze her. No one gets his hooks in. But it stings like a failure when she walks a block and no brutish, sexual tributes come her way.

All afternoon, she's provoked unknown men, not wanting them, not paying much mind, never yielding, just trying to get them to look back at her. Now she provokes her husband: but in another way, from another angle:

"Thirty-one years old and tired of everything!"

"Is that what the paper says?"

"No. It's what I say. Why would he kill himself when he's still just a boy? For a woman, I know, I don't need you to tell me. Can you imagine? Just for that. A woman makes him disgusted with everything. Maybe even she disgusted him."

Now she thinks in silence and her husband listens in silence; but he looks at her, and she doesn't look at him.

The theme of age reemerges:

"Thirty-one years old... He could have been here, some summer or other. We could have seen him, you and me, anybody could have seen him, and no one would have said he was going to kill himself."

Amaya turns back to silently imagining José Luis's summer in Chacras de Coria. Her eyes are eloquent, but her refusal to speak gives her husband room to reproach her:

"Cacciavillani hanged himself. You didn't say a word..."

"I know why he hanged himself! Because of his ulcers. About this other one, I don't know. That's what matters: the mystery in this thirty-one-year-old kid's death." Her voice grows familiar and concentrated: "He's beautiful..."

Her husband gets angry:

"What a stupid word!"

The woman stumbles, surprised, because the tone is shattered:

"What, what did I say?"

"That: beautiful. It's asinine."

Amaya looks at him, meekly annoyed. Inside herself, she feels the strength of the afternoon, the vehemence of their table talk, disintegrate. She falls mute, and her lips soften, because all at once, she has understood she shouldn't go talking about José Luis to others. She doesn't know why; but without seeking out comparisons, she recalls the clumps of sugar she dissolved in water for Suspiros back when Suspiros was a girl. Dissolved like that, like a sweetness, in her interior, she feels the memory of that José Luis she never knew.

The sweetness subsists in Amaya for days and days, like a hope.

And yet she is easily exasperated.

She chases the flies out of the dining room and kitchen. One lights on Suspiros's buttered toast, Amaya looks sickened, swats the bread away violently, and goes off looking for the Flit gun.

Rabid, she shoots down the flies that writhe against the fine wire mesh stretched over the hole of the window. She sees the reproach on Colorada's face, who says nothing, but is upset. Then she hisses:

"You could have chosen another, less dirty bug: a bee, a wasp…"

Colorada can't bear the rebuke, and explodes:

"No one chooses their children, they just come to you."

Amaya holds back and stops spraying the Flit. She's afraid she'll remember the child that didn't live. She's afraid Colorada will get distracted from her harmless fantasy: that she is the one true mother of the flies, because one flew into her nose and stayed in her head and grew up there, and now all the flies in the village are born there. And when the boys ask her what she's doing with Cataldo, she responds with pure candor: "We're making flies."

But Cataldo neglects her.

Sometimes he says his brother has put him in charge of the shack where they store the wine, and for a week he sleeps on a canvas cot beside the casks. Other times he says he'll scrape together money to get married and sells cane he cuts from the wild canebrakes; then he buys candy and eats it with Colorada laid out on the grass close to the canals, talking to their inhabitants:

"My flies…"

"My worms…"

And they listen close, looking each other in the face to better hear and understand, and neither of them ever interrupts, and that respect brings them close.

It's just that Cataldo is being negligent.

"All those days, Cataldo… where'd you get off to?"

"I was sad. When I'm sad, I don't want you to see my face."

"Ah…"

Colorada understands, and she respects it. She's concentrated because she's trying to give form to a question inside that she wants to ask, and it's taking its time coming together. After a little while, it comes to her:

"So why were you sad…?"

But by this time, Cataldo has forgotten what he's said and tries to earn her forgiveness a different way:

"I was really busy and I didn't have any time."

Colorada takes pity on him:

"Poor thing, Cataldo…"

"Why poor thing?"

"Because if you don't have time, you must be really poor, Cataldo."

"I'm not poor. I just don't have any time."

"Well, that's how it is, then. It's just that Don Teófilo says the poorest people are the ones that don't have any time, because everybody's got time to spare."

"Ah…"

Again their dialogue dies down. Each has listened to the other, and everything is all right. Colorada fiddles with the grass and lets the sound of the water in the canal carry her away. Later, she thinks, she'd like to soak her toes and step in the hot sand at the edge, when Cataldo says so. Cataldo is watching the tree branches quiver. He knows a lizard is wandering around there. He wants to see it, not to do anything to it, just to look. He waits: it'll come out.

"You could take her with you," the husband says, indicating Suspiros with his eyes.

"No!" is Amaya's rebellious response.

But she's upset, because her husband is suspicious, wary, the way he was before.

He doesn't press it, though.

"Leave me some clean pajamas."

He runs the shop in garish printed pants and a pajama top.

From the dresser, Amaya takes out the salmon-colored pajamas with elaborate white frogging and lays them out on their marriage bed.

Suspiros watches. She says:

"The man from the circus had designs like that. But his coat was red."

Amaya smiles at the comparison and thinks her smile is no slight against her husband. But afterward, she grows somber. She pities him, because she knows what he can do. Pity, pity that moves her. She prefers to misinterpret it, to not understand: she embraces the girl and speaks to her, with fire, of how she loves her, of how she loves her lots, "too much," she says. Suspiros lets her, and watches with an empty gaze. Amaya is disconcerted; then she flags.

She returns from the city, ecstatic. But dissatisfied. Someone gave her a phone number. Why did she agree to listen to him? She tries to forget the number, but the digits remain.

On the bus, Amaya runs into the veterinarian, the man from Santa Fe. He's in the next seat over, and his eyes have lighted on her; maybe they did some time ago, sure she wouldn't notice.

Amaya didn't know he was that. She thinks of him as vain, disrespectful. That's his reputation. They call him doctor, even if they doubt a veterinarian deserves such a title, irrespective of how much he studies. Amaya doesn't notice her own arrogance just then, the inner disapproval isolating and distancing her and possibly pushing others away.

She feels something's missing, an omitted courtesy, as if she hadn't answered a greeting, and she waves to him, and the man responds, surprised.

That's all. But during the rest of the trip, their eyes meet, twice.

She is agitated when she enters the shop. She always runs off down the hall. Her husband's verdict: "She has no self-control."

She kisses the girl, kisses her many times… with her mind elsewhere.

She asks the servant about dinner. "You missing anything? I'll go for it. I'm going out. I'm already dressed." The servant, indifferent, says no.

Later, they eat, and the contrast between what happens to her and her surroundings submerges her, flattens her, placates her.

She withdraws into herself, clasps her legs in her arms, and stays a while in a little low chair, in the darkness of the yard, which looks directly onto the fields.

Her ears prick up. She hears noises, like steps resounding from the road. The moonrise lights up the well with the bucket they used in another time. Where she sits, Amaya sees what it was she came to see: against the white wall of the house in front, the moon reveals a man waiting for her. A nervous, silent man, his identity unknown.

And something quivers in some spot in Amaya's body. And she feels the need to open up, to absorb more life, something more. She inhales, inhales deeply, and the scent of the irrigated land penetrates her, and something that seems to come from the pulp of the ripe yellow peaches.

"Mama…"

"Yeah, I'm coming."

But she doesn't go, she lets herself stay there, one arm folded over the cushion under the nape of her neck, her eyes turned to the canvas of the cloudless sky, indifferent to it.

A dog barks, not in the garden, not far off on the road, sounding as if inside the house. But who cares?

The fury is over, the surcease of the foregoing day is over. Now Amaya is a woman unhurried, without pressing needs, indolent and pleased to be so.

"Mama…"

"Yeah, I'm coming."

And the day begins.

Lunch.

The father strokes his daughter's hair.

"You almost ended up without a cat."

"I don't have a cat, Papa."

"Of course you do. The gray one?"

"That one's yours, to keep at the shop so he eats the mice."

The reply unnerves the man, who feels a need to talk, perhaps because no one else is. Amaya and Colorada are eating and ignore everything but their food. Amaya gets up, brings more bread. Suspiros asks for water, drinks, dries herself with the back of her hand, looks outside, and lets her gaze lead her elsewhere.

"An animal! The brute! He brought a beast of a dog into the shop. I didn't like it one bit…"

Amaya stops chewing. She waits.

"… The dog saw the cat. It barked its head off. And everything started shaking and looked like it was about to fall. I shouted at the guy: do something! He grabbed it by the collar, that's true; but then he let it go."

Amaya is already immersed in the episode, she's living it:

"Did it bite him?"

"No. He ran out into the stairwell and clambered up on the piles of shoes up on the shelf."

"Whose was it?"

"What?"

"The dog. What are we talking about?"

"The doctor, the veterinarian. He never comes into the shop. And the one time he shows up, he causes a ruckus."

"Did you get mad at each other?"

"As far as I'm concerned... he's the last person I need... but he wanted to make things right. He offered me a puppy. Because his dog wasn't a boy, it was a girl, and he says she's got two three-month-old puppies."

Amaya lets him talk. He's making some kind of calculation, reflecting on something.

"She's a good-looking dog. He says she comes from good stock. Maybe we should do it."

"You said yes?"

"No. I didn't know right then. I told him there were lots of dogs starving out on the street. I wasn't thinking."

Amaya knows what to do. She talks to Suspiros, without putting a name to the puppy:

"Would you like..."

Suspiros says yes. Colorada too. "Go get it, Amaya, go get it."

The man stretches his hands upward and opens them over the table-cloth, arches his eyebrows, and seems to apologize:

"I'm not opposed to it. I'm not opposed."

Amaya watches her husband gesturing, then turns away from him. *The brute*, he said, *an animal*. Amaya thinks: *A brute, a man who can look at you like that, in the eyes, only in the eyes...*

Amaya will go ask for it and bring it back. But that can't happen before Monday. Until it's ready, you can't leave the puppy alone for a whole afternoon, it'll howl constantly, and that would be just like killing it. Tomorrow is movie day, movie day in the city. Colorada doesn't go, because…

At the Independence Theater, in front of the plaza, they discover the *talkies*, as they're called. Jeanette MacDonald sings with her drawn-out, high-pitched voice. Maurice Chevalier makes faces and belts out happy songs. *The Love Parade*.

When the lights comes up and it's time to go, a murmur courses through the cinema, reaching the husband, who confirms the rumor and lets Amaya know:

"In the balcony over there, look: Borzani, the inspector."

And to Suspiros:

"Look, Suspiros, look: the government."

Amaya imagines the girl will get the idea that the government is a theater balcony with a gray-haired man dressed in black who talks and greets the women in long necklaces that hang out of their dresses.

She thinks she can indulge her husband's occasional dimwittedness and let him go on whispering his little reports ("That one over there, with the beard, is Dr. Viñas, the school superintendent. They say he's got an eye for the ladies.") Amaya pays him no mind, because there is something about that ambience that brings her close to José Luis. She feels a wave of tenderness sweep over her and tells herself one day she'll come to the cinema alone to be *with him*.

"When, Mama?"

"This afternoon, Suspiros. This afternoon."

She can't hold back that long. She goes out in late morning, with Suspiros holding her hand.

She stops on the sidewalk. She never looked closely at the veterinarian's house. It's old, the Gutiérrez family used to live there before he came, but now it's painted and the garden is full of geraniums, poppies, and magnolias.

She queries Suspiros, and her questions have ulterior motives, because right now, she is using her daughter as an oracle:

"You like it? Should we go in? Are we sure?"

For a long time, Suspiros contemplates the garden with its wire mesh barrier. She says yes, moving her lips and nodding her head, then thinks it necessary to express herself more fully:

"Yeah, I like it."

The oracle has responded. Amaya feels confidence and hope growing inside her.

She reaches the open gate. She steps onto the path that weaves among the flowerbeds and onto the porch standing guard in front of the rooms.

She claps her hands.

A voice reveals the presence of an old woman further back, lying in a hammock of wood and rushes.

"Miss…? Good day. Who are you looking for?"

"Hello, Miss… are you his mother? The doctor's, I mean, the veterinarian's. Sorry. Is he here?"

She has blurted all this out, as though appealing to this family relation will bring her closer.

The response doesn't dispel her yen for adventure, for delving into whatever may happen. Yes, she's the mother, but her son isn't there… Will he come back in the morning? Amaya wonders rashly. No, he won't be coming back. The woman's reply brings with it a jarring, unforeseen image: "In the morning he's never here. He's overseeing the slaughterhouse." Ah, the slaughterhouse, Amaya repeats, and thinks of his arms bare to the elbow, blotches of blood caking the hair, holding the mangled bodies of animals. Her initial enthusiasm wanes. She wants to rid herself of this new impression. She looks at the garden.

"Could I take a flower?"

"One? Yeah, why not. Which one? You choose, you can cut it yourself."

Amaya chooses. She snaps a gladiolus stalk and the sap dampens her fingers. She doesn't look at the flowers, but the stalk, with its fresh wound, holds her eyes a few seconds, and she thinks of the scant flow of the clear, vegetal blood, how it purifies.

Now it is easy for her to carry on with their talk:

"I came for a puppy, a puppy he offered my husband."

"A puppy?" The old woman doesn't seem to know about it. "Like a baby dog?"

"Yeah, from your dog."

"But he already gave them all away…"

Amaya looks at the girl. Suspiros waits, trusting: she believes in the promise, passed along by her father, of an unfamiliar man who surely is the owner of a little dog he wants to give them, and this lady has nothing to do with the matter.

"Why don't you talk to him? He'll be around this afternoon. I can tell him to wait for you."

"Yes, ma'am, that'll be fine. I'll be back, of course. We'll be here."

It's as if she'd chosen the wrong house, the wrong people.

"I can make out the colors with my eyes closed," Colorada says.

Unmoved, Cataldo informs her:

"So can I."

"You too?" Colorada is happy to share her gift with Cataldo.

But she puts him to the test:

"Really…? Close your eyes and tell me."

Cataldo didn't think it would go this far. He swallows, brings his eyelids together, and waits.

Colorada doesn't say anything to him, because when she looks around for something to tell him, she can't find anything.

Cataldo complains:

"So...?"

Harried, the girl looks inside herself: she puts a hand under her blouse, finds something, and brings it out.

"What do I have?"

Cataldo tries to reach for it. She swats him away. Cataldo sniffs vehemently, distending his nostrils. He argues:

"We said color. That doesn't mean I know what it is."

"Should I tell you?"

"Yeah, exactly. Tell me."

"It's a spaghetti strap."

"How'd you get it out? You're going to lose your slip."

"What do you care? I want to know the color. Say the color."

"Pink."

"No, white."

Cataldo grumbles:

"I was going to say white."

Colorada gets excited:

"You knew it was white?"

"Yep."

"Really? Then you won."

She stops him:

"Without opening your eyes! Let's keep going."

She takes her time, then continues:

"Do I have freckles?"

"Sure you do. You didn't know?"

"Yeah, I know. But I didn't know if you knew."

"Of course I know."

"From before?"

"From before."

"You notice the color?"

"Never. You've got my word."

"For real?"

"Absolutely for real."

"So guess then."

"You've got reddish freckles."

"No."

Cataldo opens his eyes, confused, to check. He takes a good look at his friend's freckles and inquires, trying not to offend her:

"They're not red?"

"No."

"Not even a little: like brown with a little red mixed in…?"

"I said no."

He gives up:

"Fine, I was wrong."

"Let's do it again with something else."

Cataldo follows along, unnerved. But a long time passes and Colorada doesn't continue.

"Can I help you?" Cataldo proposes timidly.

"No, it's fine. Let's see."

"Is it something far away?"

She says yes.

Cataldo squeezes his eyelids together and says:

"Suspiros, your niece, she's blue."

"Yeah, but that doesn't count. You got that from her name," she says, *Suspiros* being the name for the morning glories that grow nearby.

"No, I swear to you," Cataldo argues, taking the moment to open his eyes. "I didn't even remember what color those flowers were."

He puts as much distance as he can between himself and the game: "What do we take her today?"

Because every day, the two dimwits take her something: a crab with red pincers, a long stalk of Pampas grass in flower, a bay sparrow with big yellow jaws, fallen from the nest...

Amaya is letting the afternoon slip past.

"Mama, the puppy."

"Later."

She's out back, facing the fields.

Ramírez, a day laborer, makes meticulous furrows for the lettuces. The chickens cluck low and twangy, drowsy before the sunset.

"Mama, the puppy."

"Play a while, honey. Tell Ramírez to give you a white fig to eat."

The dog she's mentioning doesn't exist, but who cares? Didn't he use the dog to get closer to her? Is her own life free of lies? Sure, she understands all that, but what is it that has recoiled within her? She couldn't go to the house again, she couldn't look for him. That was what she was doing: looking for him. But what's happening with her, why this need for another person? And what kind of person should it be? A veterinarian? Really, a veterinarian from the slaughterhouse?

She makes a connection: she tries to imagine José Luis... to imagine José Luis as if he were...

"Mama, I ate the honey fig."

"Yes, good. Let me be."

"What about the puppy, Mama?"

"There's more stray dogs than you can shake a stick at! Tomorrow I'll fill the yard up with dogs! Leave me be!"

The girl turns to the prudence of silence. When she notices her mother has forgotten her, she strays and grasps the polished wire of the chicken coop in her hands and in her teeth. She gnaws at it with the tenacity of bitterness.

José Luis. Veterinarian. No, doctor in veterinary science. He must heal the wings of those fallen birds and cure the rich people's sick dogs and cats, for a living, but also from compassion. He must have a house with courtyards and palm trees, full of cages with sick animals, all of them tame, all clean, even if they were sad… All of them entrusted to his hands.

Her husband. Amaya hears him arrive.

"Here it is," he says, and sets a little goat on the floor. It has long, straight hair, well kept, which shimmers like tiny sparks.

It can't be the gift the veterinarian offered. The girl seems swallowed by the same doubt, until her father calls her over: "Come here, it's for you," and she accepts it, running and not stopping until she has it in her arms.

Amaya is suspicious:

"Did you get it yourself?"

Her husband turns to her with his voice, not his gaze, which is fixed on his daughter's enthusiasm:

"No. He brought it, the veterinarian. He said you all went there, this morning…"

Amaya suddenly stands up straight.

"He's there?"

"No. He left."

He looks at her. He's turned serious, he knows why she's asking.

"Do you care?"

"No."

Her *no* is haughty, but also defensive. Then, humbly – he knows why – she justifies herself:

"We should go thank him."

"I already did."

Far out in the field, the two dimwitted ones appear. They're bringing fresh-cut willow branches. They come over cautiously, seeing the whole family gathered.

When they're a few steps away, they stop, looking at the new little goat. Suspiros picks him up so Colorada can see him better.

Suspiros's father asks, "Do you like the goat, Colorada?" and Cataldo answers, "Yeah, it's a gentle, pretty little goat."

The veterinarian bursts in. He's a voluminous man.

"Did the girl like it?"

Of course she liked it. There was no need to ask. Suspiros's father is upset, but the other man doesn't notice.

"You have to take care of it. It was just taken from its mother. Can I see it? Where are you keeping it? Did you make it a bed of straw?"

The father defends himself by letting the man pass. He leads him out back.

Suspiros tries, the way they taught her, to keep the little goat from getting into the garden. But he has a different urge, and is pressing his lips against anything that resembles a teat.

Amaya saw them pass by in the yard near the pergola. She comes out silently and keeps her distance, observing the veterinarian, who gives verbose instructions and speaks frenetically and without resting, as if busy putting the whole world in order.

Amaya feels serene, in possession of all the time imaginable. She waits.

Her husband sees she is there and goes over to rouse her from her enchantment, her absorption, in that man.

"My wife…"

"I know her," he says, and he stretches out his hand to her. "She went to my house. I wasn't there. We've never spoken. I've only lived here a short while."

And he turns back to the husband and the goat.

The clerk from the shop appears. He stands aside, waiting for them to give him the chance to speak.

"What is it? Do you need something?" her master asks.

"Yes, they're looking for you."

"Tell them I'm coming."

"If you're worried about me," the veterinarian says, "just go. I'll wait for you. Nice garden. I'll stay here and look it over."

He's left there with Amaya. He stifles his elation. He doesn't look at the garden.

"You're a teacher?"

"Yes."

"Without a school. Same as me."

"You're a teacher? You're not a vet?"

"I'm a teacher first. But I can't teach. It's not enough to live on. Did you hear Orgaz? No, you weren't there."

"Orgaz?"

"Arturo Orgaz, he came from Córdoba. He talked about us in the Escuela Patricias. I wanted to cry right there in the classroom. Or else beat on everything, break it. I went mad, I wanted to be a teacher so bad, I wanted to sing or scream my lessons."

He lights up, swipes at the air with his arms.

Amaya draws back, admiring his unexpected fervor.

"Why are you here? Why are you working as a veterinarian?"

"They cheated me! I came with the federal intervention. I worked for the party in Sante Fe. They promised me everything and they gave me nothing: I'm a veterinarian in a county slaughterhouse. Have you ever seen it? Are you familiar with the place?"

"No." Amaya stumbles back as though she's been rammed.

"It's on the banks of the canal, in Luján. The blood and offal get dumped in the water. Miles and miles downstream, the people drink that same water."

He stops talking.

He says, "I'm leaving. Good afternoon."

Amaya says, "I'll walk you out," and he thanks her, "I know the way."

He leaves, and Amaya stays there watching him, depressed, but serene. Though he's said goodbye, he turns and asks:

"Have you ever seen a real live monkey?"

"Sure, at the zoo, at the circus..."

He's discouraged, he wanted to offer something new. But he keeps trying:

"Yesterday I brought home two. You can bring the girl over."

He stops and then, headstrong, unsure, he continues:

"If you have another kid, you can bring them both."

Amaya remains calm:

"I don't have another kid."

He nods, blinking, taking time to let it sink in, because he had wanted to get to know Amaya, and he has a welter of things inside him. Amaya knows that.

Then he goes.

"A ferret. A person like that, you'd be best off shutting the door in his face," her husband says.

Amaya muses ironically: *What do you mean, shut the door to a shop?*

How will the customers get in? She doesn't try to defend the man, but she does declare:

"He's harmless."

"Sure, he's harmless all right," her husband says. "He's eaten up with rage, but he doesn't let it out on anyone, because the person he's furious with is himself. He's desperate."

That sums it up, Amaya thinks: desperate. She no longer hears her husband's words while he talks with his mouth full, lifting his fork whenever he raises his voice.

Amaya weighs her options with the desperate man: how not to tame him, how not to do as the others have. How to keep him from giving in. And how to bundle herself in his impassioned desperation, how to make it envelop her. To burn, to burn up. But... does he deserve it? Does he notice her?

"Can we, Papa?"

Suspiros has made use of a break in the adults' dialogue to return to the previous subject: if they can go see the monkeys.

Yes, they can. Colorada, too.

"And Cataldo?" Colorada pleads.

They don't pay her any attention.

At the gate, the veterinarian is calm. Still, Amaya suspects something: she already knows how easily he can lose his cool. She's not afraid, so long as he doesn't turn his agitation against her. She feels like a spectator, someone watching a fire, toasted and seduced by the warmth and the fascination of the flames.

She looks, as she passes, for the wounded gladiolus stalk. She can't make it out. It doesn't weigh on her: now she has, or will be able to have, something more than that sign, that symbol, that memory. She has an uncertainty laden with promises.

"This is my father."

The old man is scraping the soil of the garden with a two-pronged spading fork.

He laughs good-humoredly and with feigned resignation:

"It's thanks to him everyone calls me by my last name: just plain Romano. When I sign my name, it's G.G. Romano. Go figure: a fanatical admirer of the Teutons goes and saddles his son with two names that you can't just come out and use every day…"

Amaya gives him a curious look.

"You want to know what they are? Gandolfo Gildas. Gildas! Can you believe it? You know what it means? *Ready for sacrifice.*"

Romano explains that Gandolfo, also of Teutonic origin, means warrior, a brave warrior… As he does so, Amaya repeats to herself: *Ready for sacrifice. Ready for sacrifice…* And she's not thinking of Gildas anymore, or of Romano, she says to herself gently: *Ready for sacrifice, José Luis, ready for sacrifice…*

Romano walks on, leaves his father behind, and Amaya observes him against the light filtered through the trees, gesturing frantically, euphoric, and yet so near to falling, to collapse, even to crying like a frightened child. And again, compassionate thoughts flow toward him: maybe he doesn't know, maybe he has no sense of what he's fated for, even if he knows what his name means… Maybe José Luis doesn't know…

Romano encourages Suspiros and Colorada to go on without him, pointing them toward the right, behind the wall, where a little door hangs halfway off its hinges.

Amaya can tell he wants to talk to her. She slows her step. He stops her, brusquely. He's no longer the festive man of before. He points over to where his father goes on poking at the unearthed roots.

"You know what else is his fault?" he says bitterly. "Me living here."

"The lung," he says, and points at his own body. But there's no room for doubt: his father is the one who is sick. "The slaughterhouse, the cows, tuberculosis. So here… well, you get it."

Amaya says to herself: *Something else that's wrong, something else that's happened to him. Listening, always listening. But all I care about is my own story.* The words she uses are different:

"That's nothing strange around here. Lots of people are sick. They cover it up. They come from all over. They say the air is good. Those who don't know better say the air is getting contaminated now."

Romano's disenchantment is evident. Without affection, without courtesy, he reproaches her:

"Yeah, but that's not what we're talking about. You don't care what I said about myself. You don't care about my dependency, my exile."

Amaya defends herself again with what seems like a commonplace:

"No one understands his neighbor, no one."

Really, what she's saying is: *No one understands me either, no one.* But all Romano grasps is, *No one understands his neighbor,* and he replies:

"No one listens. Everybody's deaf, that's why you end up alone."

He turns his back and heads inside, leaving Amaya to follow him as if it were a simple matter of fate.

The animals are behind the wall. Not one, not just the two monkeys. Amaya finds herself before all the crates and cages she had imagined in José Luis's courtyard. No one had warned her about this, and in her chest, something is pounding feverishly for Romano.

It's not exactly the same, no, not at all. This was a garden, that's clear, but someone let it dry up and the ground is hard and almost level. There's nothing green but the two trees that rise up behind the brick wall, and the sun seems to shine down not to give life, but to deplete it.

The dog, leashed to a cable run stretched from one end of the enclosure to the other, barks, upsetting the silence that has settled over their curt dialogue. She barks affectionately, seeing her master, and leaps up at him, posted on her back legs, slobbering from pleasure, her tongue hanging from one side of her mouth. Romano lets her stay a moment, then pushes her away. The dog follows him, doting.

Suspiros and Colorada have found the monkeys' cages and are keeping their distance, looking while the monkeys look back at them.

The veterinarian grabs one of them by the scruff of its neck, the way you pick up a puppy, and the creature struggles.

"You'll have to tame him. After that, they're really good. By the time this one's six months old, I'll be walking down the street with him on my shoulder."

He tries to get Suspiros to touch the coarse yellow coat. Suspiros refuses. Then Colorada. She won't do it either.

"What about you, Amaya? Are you up for it?"

He called her Amaya. She looks him in the eyes.

Yes, she's up for it. She pets the monkey's flanks, he nestles in her human hands, and as she pets him, she looks into Romano's eyes, which have come to rest on her again, intense, anxious, with an adolescent allure.

In the other cages, dark birds, quiet, glum.

"What are they for?"

"They're laying birds. I use their eggs to feed the vipers."

"Vipers?"

Brick, mortar, and glass: something further off that didn't call Amaya's attention. They coil up inside, press one against the other.

"My idea is to make an antivenin and sell it to the Department of Health."

Immediately, Romano starts mocking himself, but somberly, with a glimmer of his previous ardor.

"My idea. I've got a lot of ideas. Look."

He leads Amaya to another cage, of thin, octagonal wire. Shifting, climbing, immune to the laws of equilibrium, they run a few inches, pause, look, sniff: six or seven white mice.

"I'm thinking of raising them and then selling them. It's easy here, and it's cheap: but who would buy them? There's no medical school, no one does experiments. I'd have to send them to Buenos Aires, to La Plata, to Rosario, to Córdoba, I guess, and come to find out, you need special packaging. You believe that? I know how to raise them. There's no point, though. I could do the experiments myself. But I'd need a researcher to guide me. Get it? So what can I do?"

He interrupts himself abruptly. He looks up, as if to let the light shine in his face. He smiles, bitterly, but he smiles.

"Come on."

He takes her hand and tugs.

Amaya obeys and at the same time looks around for her sister and daughter, to see if they're watching. They are walking from cage to cage, rapt, oblivious to everything that isn't the animals.

Against the far wall is a ruin. Bricks, straw, a thick pole sunk in the ground, and chained to it, a small fox, undeveloped, trying to huddle, to avoid being seen, cowering into the earth, but knowing from experience there is no escape, that his captivity offers no hiding place.

"I caught him, without hurting him. He tried to get away from me. I got him by the scruff of the neck, with both hands, and he must have thought I would kill him. He gave up kicking until I put him in the sack."

Amaya looks at the man's hands. They don't frighten her. They could choke her to death. In certain circumstances, perhaps, she would let them.

Romano baits the animal. He takes a stick and pricks him in the side. The fox gets angry and bites, stripping off the bark. He leaves his hollow in the straw and gets to his feet, not valiantly, but in a half-crouch, barking like a dog, with the same voice, but shriller, more ridiculous, more terrible and poignant.

Romano is amused.

Amaya feels her daughter and sister close by, there to witness the derision, which they do not join in, but suffer through.

"Why don't you let him go?" Amaya asks.

Romano's amusement comes to an end.

"Let him go. Sure, maybe. I hadn't thought of that. I could sell him to a zoo, but he's worthless, and he'd probably tear off my hand if I tried."

His whole broad body retreats toward the unhinged door next to the cages. As if he were announcing: the visit's over.

Amaya takes her child's hand, and the girl turns back to take leave of the captured animals.

In a green dress, the dimwit trots along behind them.

Where there's shade and you can breathe, between the porch and the tall plants overlooking the garden, Romano stops the woman, grabbing her bare arm.

"I want to see a plaster figure with you."

"Where? Come on, there's still time."

As though to say: *I'm not gruff, I'm not offended.*

"Not here. In the city, at the studio."

"What studio?"

"The sculptor's. His name's Cardona. You know him?"

"No. But I can't go to the city."

"Not today. Tomorrow, the day after. Can you do it?"

Again, he tries to meet eyes with her. Their eyes understand each other.

"Yes."

They agree. On a certain bus, the following day...

"Talk to me about the sculpture. I might need to make an excuse."

He talks in front of Suspiros, in front of Colorada, and they don't understand a word:

"It's a little country boy, like the one who washes the streets with a pail. Just imagine, a sculpture wearing espadrilles. Can you imagine how it pains me? The attitude, you know? Shrunken, soft, beaten down, hungry! That's right, he's forgotten to eat, he's stranded. It's a shame!"

He's gotten worked up again. He raises his right arm, which trembles with rage.

Amaya squints her eyes and shakes her head softly.

Romano thinks it's sorrow, for the boy from the country. He lowers his arm and falls silent.

The three women return to the house, climbing the cobblestone paths, then descending over furrowed trails of hard-packed soil and dusty ones that give way beneath their feet.

Can you imagine how it pains me? Amaya remembers the man saying. But she is pained, too, pained in a different way, by that strong, inordinate man who wants to make money off white mice and viper venom; cruel with the fox he didn't strangle, compassionate with the poor derelicts whose dolorous image the sculptor's fingers bring to life.

Suddenly she feels tired, very tired. Tomorrow… She wants to convince herself that no, it's not tomorrow that wearies her, it's today, the day she's just been through, she thinks, the kind of day that consumes you, because you live through so much, and all at once…

They always tramp around a bit. But not today. Colorada has somewhere to go. She takes Cataldo's hand and leads him into a vineyard, they jump a gorge and pass over a broad, fallow field full of weeds with hot clumps of earth that burn their feet. They follow this path through the lowlands to the veterinarian's house. They climb up the low brick wall.

"Here it is."

"Yeah." For Cataldo, it is clearly not a revelation.

"Have you been here?"

"Yeah. The big guy was carrying a basket and something was shrieking. I came over on the other road – it's easier that way – and waited to find out what it was. Two monkeys. They're there." Cataldo speaks calmly, looking down on the yard littered with cages. Colorada watches him. She follows his explanation and then inquires, prudently, with affectionate respect:

"Did you invite me to come and I forgot about it?"

"No." Cataldo doesn't take his eyes off the interior. "I never told you. It's sad. Animals that don't eat each other don't need to be in cages."

"Ah…"

"Could you handle being caged up?"

"No. You'd let me out."

"Yeah. I'd let you out."

Silence, and a new meditation from the girl.

"Vipers don't eat each other. Should we let them out?"

"They scare me."

"Me too."

They look for something to do. It takes them time to figure out what. Now it's Cataldo who proposes:

"The fox."

"He bites. I saw it."

"Doesn't matter. He's got a little mouth. He won't bite much. And he's not poisonous."

"Amaya told him to let it go. The man promised."

"He didn't let him go."

"No."

"The mice."

"OK. What if the dog catches us?"

"I know what to do."

He clambers down armed with a long stick. The dog runs from one end of the wire to the other, but only her barking reaches him. Cataldo lifts the wire latch and pushes it until it flips over. The door opens and the white mice run out and scatter. In an instant, they've vanished through the holes riddling the wall. Only one stays behind, ignorant of its opportunities, running swiftly over the mesh of the cage. Cataldo hits it with the stick and the creature, more frightened than before, darts off and discovers the way out.

"Help me."

Colorada gives him a hand and Cataldo climbs over the wall.

When the sun goes down, they are sitting on the ground at the end of a vine row, eating grapes.

"I'm hungry. They go better with bread."

"You want to look for some?"

"I don't feel like it."

"Fine."

Somebody comes up through the rows. The two dimwits stop speaking or moving, knowing they're intruders. They wait, hoping to pass unnoticed.

The farmhand is going back to the house, hoe on his shoulder. He sees them and ignores them. *With what little you get for grapes*, is what he thinks.

In the hand holding the hoe he has a kerchief, with knots like little ears on either end. He remembers it and turns back. When he's reached the two dimwits, who look up at him from below, still chewing their pink berries, he drops the hoe, undoes the kerchief, and takes out two crusts of bread. He offers them in his hand, a single hand coarse from working the soil:

"Here. They're better with bread."

Cataldo takes the crusts and passes one to Colorada. He starts to eat the bread and grapes and looks askance at the farmhand, asking himself why he won't leave, since he's not kicking them out.

The man wipes the sweat from his neck with his kerchief, slips it into his pocket, picks up his hoe, and goes on his way.

Later they lie back in the scrub between the vines and Colorada looks for fennel, to chew on the succulent seeds.

Soon she starts to laugh, low, as though to herself, absorbed, absent.

"What's with you, huh? You going to tell me?"

"I feel a tickle."

"How? Who's tickling you? Where?"

"Here," Colorada says, and lifts up her skirt. "Between my legs."

She opens her legs and shows her thighs, all the way up. She doesn't stop smiling, now broadly, now softly, as if waves of itchiness were coursing over her.

Cataldo offers to help:

"You want a hand? Want me to scratch you?"

Colorada agrees and lies down on her back, her skirt pulled up over her belly, her knees spread apart.

Cataldo scratches softly on the inner walls of her thighs, and she wriggles with laughter.

"Hold still, I can't do it with you like this."

All at once, the laughter stops. Cataldo scrutinizes the girl's face. Colorada has rested the back of her hand over her mouth, going hic, hic, with tears running out of her eyes.

"What about now…?"

He doesn't answer.

He waits.

When she's calmed down, she asks:

"Didn't you see you gave me the hiccups?"

"Oh…"

Colorado sits up and goes on scratching herself before pulling down her skirt.

"How'd it happen?"

"What…?"

"The tickling, down there…"

"I remembered the mice."

"Oh…"

"Don't make me remember, or else I'll…" And she starts laughing again.

Cataldo, instead of worrying as he had before, laughs and laughs, he falls to the ground laughing. It passes, for her as well as for him, and both of them are left feeling cheerful.

"We could keep one."

"One… what?"

"A white mouse."

"Why?"

"For Suspiros."

"True. What do we take her now?"

"I don't have anything. Another toad?"

"The house is already full of toads. Amaya's husband stepped on one and went crazy. He said a bunch of bad words."

"That red rock?"

"I don't like red stuff."

"What if instead of taking her something, we bring her here?"

"It's late. The sun's going down."

"There's games you don't need much light for."

"Well. Amaya did go to the city."

"We could hunt bats."

"With big canes."

"Suspiros will like knocking the bats down."

"Yeah, with big canes. She'll like that."

The father's using a flashlight, but he still trips over the furrows and vegetables. He shouts:

"Suspiros…! Suspiros…!"

Tripping, whining, guilty, the servant follows him:

"Ramírez was watering. He saw her."

The man jumps the barbed wire; the woman slips between the strands. They tread over the produce at two of the farms and skirt the threat of the dogs.

Ramírez collapses early onto his cot; during the week, he's no friend to the nightlife. His farmhouse has gone dark, save for the embers outside where he grilled dinner.

The mutt keeping watch awakens him before Suspiros's father calls.

Yes, Ramírez saw her. She passed through his fields with Colorada and Cataldo. She didn't come back…? How could that be? Colorada neither?

Ramírez buttons up his pants, puts on his shoes, and thus shows them his willingness to help search.

It's 9:00 at night. Amaya comes back, her face, neck, hands covered in kisses. They didn't see the sculpture of the boy, they didn't go to any artist's studio. By 8:00, Romano decided to leave her, because he wanted to attend a teachers' conference.

Amaya still feels that humid pressure, with a slight scent of tobacco, in her mouth, violating her warmly, in a succession of never-ending waves.

Unusually, there's no light on in the doorway or the courtyard. But there is in the bedrooms, in the dining room, in the kitchen. Open, well-lit rooms, full of furnishings and everyday objects. But now, though she's never felt this before, Amaya envisions her home like a house suddenly emptied by misfortune.

She stays in the courtyard, afraid to go in, afraid a stranger will leap out from some corner to tell her what's gone wrong.

She doesn't imagine tragedy striking anyone in particular, she doesn't want to assume such a thing. It's something else, a retreat from her, an exodus, she imagines, as if everyone, even her sweet dimwitted sister, knew what she'd been up to. She feels exposed, denounced, singled out by the silence.

But it's only for a moment.

Then she thinks of Suspiros. She thinks, apprehensive about doing so, afraid of breaking something with her thoughts, afraid of naming her, because it might bring some evil down upon her.

She lights a lamp on the veranda, spilling clarity onto the tiles in the courtyard, and this action replenishes her strength and allows her to call out, still softly, hearing herself:

"Leonardo… Leonardo…"

And to pass through the bedrooms and open the window that looks out over the back yard, heavy with shadows:

"Colorada… Colorada."

And to look in the kitchen where no fire is lit for dinner and there's no point in calling for the servant.

Mute, afraid of lashing out, she runs along the walkway and scans the street from end to end, and when someone comes up and then down on the uneven footpath, she takes cover in the unlit doorway and lets him pass without seeing her. And she stays there, one hand held high, braced on the flaking, whitewashed wall, waiting for whatever there is to wait for.

Then the servant comes, covered in mud up to her knees.

She has to find out if Amaya came back, if Suspiros has returned to her. That's what the boss wants to know, while he's out there trampling the fields and poaching half the people from the various houses, who come along to help.

Amaya presses her to tell her where.

And the servant cries:

"I don't really know right now, Miss. They went that way" – and she stretches her arm out in a cardinal direction, toward no precise place or distance.

Yet the way Amaya shakes her, her merciless rage, hands her back over to the night.

The scornful words rain down on her:

"If they sent you here, woman, it's because they want you to go back. Idiot, use your head, idiot!"

It gets worse. The woman's understanding grows cloudier and she can no longer continue. She throws herself to the ground and cries. Amaya rocks her, trying to stand her up, begging her in the end, but it's pointless.

So Amaya goes alone.

Feeling her way in the shadows, she reaches the edge of the canal. Further down, much further, scant lights like fireflies scrawl straight lines in the air. She understands: the men thinks the same thing, that down there in the water...

She stands there, weak, terribly weakened, but straight and wide-eyed, hearing the water she doesn't wish to see.

She looks up, moistens her lips, gnawing at them softly, and utters her sacrifice:

"I renounce that man. He will touch me no more. I promise you. But let her be alive. Even if she's sick, even if she's wounded, let her live."

No, Cataldo hasn't gone back to his family. That's not unusual: he spends so many nights in the old shack...

His brother, intelligent and strong, to make up for the burden the dimwit represents for the family, stands at the head of the search party.

From afar, he calls his name, as all of them call his name, "Cataldo, Cataldo!" And also with the name Cataldo will know is coming from his brother, his strong brother, his protector: "Blackie, little Blackie, I'm looking for you!"

Cataldo hears and stops lashing at the air with his cane.

The moon reveals to him, walking through the last patch of vines, not his kindhearted brother, but a troupe of people he doesn't recognize.

He throws away the cane, grabs Colorada by the arm, and takes cover behind the old storehouse.

But then he remembers, and slides over toward the oven left over from the old house. Gently, he calls out:

"Suspirita…"

Suspiros doesn't answer. He's confused. He looks as far as his eyes can see. She's gone. But she was there, not long before.

When they knocked down the bat flying out the storehouse, awake after sleeping on one of the joists, they told Suspiros about it, then went on chasing those fleeting, airborne shadows. Suspiros didn't finish it off, Cataldo didn't know why, and she retreated to where the oven stood, to watch the long canes flailing, wielded like slender stilts, but up high, which always finished with grousing: "I let him go," "He got away."

Cataldo didn't know why Suspiros ran off so quickly. The bat was in the dust, and it was moving, as if preparing to escape, to fly away. But that was all. And the girl got scared by the animal's silence, having it there, loose, at her feet, unable to escape, suffering without a shriek, without complaint, like people, or dogs run over by cars.

Suspiros isn't next to the oven, or on the other side of it, either. Cataldo guesses how far the unknown group has come, then flees.

The men stop before the inert night cloaking the storeroom, and don't even bother to look around.

They're about to turn back:

"What do we do? They're nowhere around here."

"Not a trace."

Only the father, seeming uncertain, mulls over what next to do. He says, "Suspiros, Suspiros…" And he repeats, as though with so soft and solitary a voice, he won't discourage himself further: "Suspiros, Suspiros…"

From the oven, from inside it, a leg emerges, but no one notices.

Then, soft and silent, Suspiros climbs out, advancing toward the voice that calls her name.

Amaya imagines the conversation. She polishes it, always in the same direction, since it depends on her thought and her will.

She will say to him, *Do you believe in God?*, stiffly, because they've always talked that way, and he will say no, because there's no other way it can be: *No. I don't believe.* She will ask him to respect her religious convictions and he will say yes, he can do that, he is capable of respecting the faith of others. That will be the moment to explain to him her pledge, the pledge she will have to keep, because the girl was brought back to her…

Her husband walks past in his frogged pajamas, lost in his own affairs.

Amaya gets up from the chair. Her arms retain the feeling of her weight stretched out halfway across the table.

She turns toward the kitchen. She heats up the milk in the aluminum milk can. Over the flame, which exudes a domestic aroma, she stirs a long time with a spoon. And the vapor warms her up and dampens her hand.

José Luis. He's still with her, he's still in her. She didn't make her pledge for him, but for another man. She doesn't have to expel him from within her.

The milk whirls on its own, dragging her hand and the spoon along, as if they were weightless.

José, José Luis.

Deprived of its chance to exist, the dialogue dissipates in Amaya's memory.

He's not looking for her, as if he expects her to do everything.

She runs into him on the bus. Suspiros, between the two of them, impedes the words that Amaya wouldn't have agreed to say there, because if she brought it up, it would only be so he would understand... He is restrained, but his consternation shows through, the fact that something, or everything, is eluding him.

Another time, he's standing by the front door to the pharmacy, arguing, exasperated. He pulls on his shirt collar with his left hand. He's perspiring.

Amaya says:

"Excuse me."

He blubbers as he steps aside.

When she comes out, he's vanished.

She asks her husband:

"So the veterinarian... he never showed back up?"

"Yeah... he buys pomade, brilliantine... Always stuff for his hair."

Amaya smiles. Different habits now, maybe, different penchants.

She wants to find a loose thread to pull on, to see if he remembers her:

"He never asked after the goat? He didn't want to see it grown up?"

"Never. Nope."

With a soft nudge from her right hand, Amaya sets the burnished wheel of the Singer sewing machine in motion. At the same time, she presses the pedal and the hissing sound of the machine drowns out the family once more.

They follow the carriage, just to follow it. Winter's ending, they like walking in the sun, and it's good to have an excuse to go somewhere else.

With the revolution, Romano lost his job. He didn't make much anyhow. He signed up for the rural school, but it disappeared from all the lists of openings.

Now someone's given him a bit of coin to set up a hennery for pure-bred chickens. The other guy's put up the land, down the canal from Chacras; he's bought the initial breed stock, an incubator, wire for the pen, corn, and Romano will do the work, putting all his time into it. He won't have any helpers. He'll get a third of the earnings when they sell. In the meantime, he can fatten up his pigs, as long as he doesn't use the corn or the feed pellets. Some condition.

The two dimwitted ones follow the carriage, just to follow it, to see where Romano's going with his empty cages, the bed, and the trunk.

Then the rumors start flying:

"He's going to make a pile of cash."

"Big hens, white and red ones."

"And *belichas*," they say, referring to a native breed.

"They say he goes armed out into the fields."

"With live ammunition."

"He knew how to make something of the land."

"But us, with the vineyards, well, just take a look around."

They don't look around. They think of what they've already seen, and fall quiet. Big graves, between the vine rows, for the half-ripened grapes. They think of what they will see, what it's said they'll have to see: vine-yards uprooted and the wine running in the ditches.

"There's too much of it, they say."

They talk about the grapes, the wine, without mentioning them by name. They talk about the government without identifying it. They talk about federal regulations they don't understand, because they destroy all they've built, all their parents or grandparents planted.

"There's too much of it, they say."

"That's what they say."

Maybe she's careless, Mrs. Ignacia, and that's why it's so easy to step into her life and be in her home, whiling away the endless afternoons.

Mrs. Ignacia's husband belongs to one of the conservative factions – which is it, the blue or the white? Amaya isn't sure. He's a dynamic man, with slight white streaks in his temples and a penchant for sports coats and silk kerchiefs knotted around his neck. He has tennis rackets, though they always stay in their case. He represents something important in the government. He also does business: he sells tractors and things like that in the Calle Lavalle, in front of *La Libertad*, but he doesn't deal with it personally, he has others who work for him. If he wanted, he could be a teacher at the Colegio Nacional. *Where did he do his teacher training, in Paraná or Buenos Aires? Teacher training? No. He's just an accountant. But you know…*

Sitting in canvas chairs beneath a canopy of wisteria, their eyes wander as they recount all the joys of that summer house, lined up beside others like it against the foothills. Mrs. Ignacia recollects frequently: "It wasn't like this before." It might seem she was surprised that she got so rich so fast. It might seem she was begging pardon for it. But really, it's just sincerity: the evocation of other times without whites or blues or tractors.

Maybe she's careless, and that's why she forgives any unpleasant memory Amaya might entrust to her:

"What else could you have done, my woman…?"

Amaya can step out with her and visit the Confitería Colón, the pastry shop her husband never took her to, and not on account of the price, she thinks. See a movie – *Lluvia de millones*, *The Unfinished Symphony*, *The Scarlet Pimpernel* – and later pass the time rehashing it.

There's no rush, no last bus pulling away. Her friend's husband has an official car, and they meet back at the hour before dinner.

That twilit, superfluous time unfurls in coming and going along one sidewalk or the other on the Calle San Martín. They pull away from them, they run ahead, the two girls, Suspiros and Mrs. Ignacia's daughter.

The mothers disregard them. Everything is secure for them, they are blessed with security: the nest egg, the home, the husband, the daughter, the broad sidewalk brimming with people who appear to have nothing to do...

But one time, Amaya sees a flatterer bend down with a greedy face as Suspiros passes. Amaya loses her temper and tries to reach her without hurrying her step, without Mrs. Ignacia knowing what has happened. When she has her daughter in arm's reach, she turns her around, and Suspiros shows her a face glowing with joy. Amaya looks, looks, what can it be about that thirteen-year-old girl, and then she notices the subtle and delicate beginnings of breasts beneath her nearly transparent blouse.

With the tip of his finger, her husband traces out the newspaper insert from the tobacco company *Cigarillos 43*. "Monthly raffles, certified by a notary public... Prizes from 5 to 5,000 pesos."

Inattentively, Amaya observes the photograph at the top of the page: *The Aguilar Spanish Lute Quartet...* That was what was on last night.

Mrs. Ignacia and her husband went to hear them. But that lies outside Amaya's tastes. She doesn't envy them. She'd like other things.

"Why don't we buy a car, Leonardo?"

Her husband removes his finger from the insert. He looks at her as if that question had upset his composure.

Amaya, without forcing it, without getting upset, makes her case.

"We could do it, couldn't we?"

"Yes, but I have other ideas."

And his fingernail goes on trailing its way down the column dated the nineteenth.

"It's for him. He takes it out, he brings it back. Now he's wondering about those hills, if they're hiding something…"

"Water?"

"No, minerals. If the man shows him signs of them, he'll buy them up."

"The hills are for sale?"

"Sure. Even a good ways out. Once we went to the goat pens. You've been there…?"

"Yeah."

"Farther than that, even, much farther, my husband says."

"And with a wand…"

"With two."

Amaya thinks of a stage magician, in his tuxedo and turban.

He's not like that. He's in white pants, a short-sleeved shirt, and sneakers. He's a well-built man with long, flaxen hair that falls whenever he moves, unless his hand is holding it in place.

She sees him with Mrs. Ignacia, in front of a tall drink made with grenadine.

Amaya is shy, because she doesn't know how to talk to him and her friend at the same time. But he doesn't make any special impression on her.

Colorada comes over with her hand closed, shaking it now and then next to her ear.

"What've you got?" Cataldo asks.

"Two flies."

"Oh..."

"Suspiros is a good girl. She gives me back the flies when I drop them."

"Yeah, she's a good one."

Cataldo agrees, without adding anything.

"Something wrong, Cataldo? You upset with me?"

Cataldo shakes his head.

Colorada keeps trying:

"And your worms...? It's been forever since you've told me about them."

"I don't have any more worms. They all left."

"Ah..."

That's enough. Colorada doesn't ask anymore.

But Cataldo has got to reminiscing:

"When the doctor saw me..."

And then he comes out with it:

"It's time for me to go into the service..."

He gestures into the air, as if explaining something. But he doesn't finish the phrase.

He's twenty-four. They called him up four years back. He went to headquarters, but after the physical and psychological exams, they turned him back over to his family. He'll never have to serve, but from time to time, he revisits that intermediate moment between the checkup and the possession of a soldier's uniform and arms.

"You gonna go, Cataldo?" come the shy words, voiced by Colorada's grief.

Cataldo presses his chin into his neck and nods brusquely. He keeps looking down, as if to say there's nothing to be done, and sees, close to his pants leg, Colorada's hand weaken and open up. Two flies escape.

That night, Cataldo dreams his friend proposes:

"If I have to stay here alone, Cataldo, I want you to help me get married."

"I'll help you, Colorada, you know I will."

"You have to tell him, you have to be the one to tell him."

Cataldo dreams they are walking behind the carriage loaded with the cages, the bed, and the trunk belonging to Romano, the veterinarian.

And in his dream, Cataldo is dressed as a soldier, and is telling her yes, he'll help her marry the veterinarian up ahead of them in the carriage.

In the morning, Cataldo walks along the canal and reaches his destination. He wanders around Romano's farm, glimpses the big man between the wires. But he wavers.

When he sees Colorada, he says:

"You can rest easy."

He knows what he's talking about. She doesn't, but since there's no reason for her not to rest easy, she responds:

"All right."

And the two are in agreement.

He's a layabout, Mrs. Ignacia thinks, and announces her conviction to Amaya.

The dowser lives easily in the room that's been provided for him and no one interrupts his rest. Twice, but only twice, he's been seen out, on the jagged, shadowless hills.

The rest of the time he spends looking for water in the fields where the shovel finds it without much effort. But he prefers using his two wicker rods, which he claims to feel vibrating when he finds whatever he's looking for down under the soil. Then he stops and says: "Dig here." Infallibly, they find dampness beneath the dry crust, more of it the deeper they dig.

When he walks through the village in shirtsleeves, the boys follow along, and he's pleased with his retinue. At night he goes to the movie theater beside the plaza, where the films have no end or beginning, because the reel is always broken, the film goes in or comes out wrong. It doesn't matter. He enjoys it.

He's a layabout. But Mrs. Ignacia's indifference will put up no resistance to her husband's enthusiasm for the dowser.

Now, Amaya feels good, like before, under the trees close to her friend's home. She wouldn't mind a bit, she thinks, if he weren't there. He lacks allure... All she likes is that he's easy, always ready for a laugh.

He's in the deckchair and Suspiros is chatting with him.

Later, the dowser approaches the yerba mate the two women are drinking from and sits in a chair made of bulrushes. Suspiros sidles up to him on the ground, watching him from below while he speaks with Mrs. Ignacia. Amaya notices her gaze and is pricked by apprehension. She keeps her eyes on Suspiros's blouse.

"Gaspar," the girl says.

And he turns his head with a jovial smile, as if to say, *I'm here. I'm listening.*

But he goes back to talking with the two adults.

Amaya calms down. She looks at Gaspar good-naturedly. *Gaspar,* she thinks, *it's so simple. Like saying my name. Like saying José Luis.* And in her mind, she utters José Luis's name, without withdrawing completely from all that surrounds her just then.

"Why is your name Gaspar?" Suspiros asks, drawing on what childishness is left in her.

He laughs. *There's something beautiful about his laugh,* Amaya thinks;

but then she recollects her husband's steely phrase: *What a stupid word, beautiful...!* That was how it all began, more or less.

"Why?" he laughs at her curiosity. "You never heard a Persian name before?"

"No," Suspiros says, fascinated by what might follow his question.

"Yes you have. You've heard one and said one, too: Gaspar."

Suspiros isn't satisfied.

"What does it mean?"

Amaya interrupts, as if at the behest of a presentiment:

"It doesn't mean anything, people's names are just names, that's all."

Gaspar silences her gently, stretching his arm with his upraised hand toward her, as if plugging a leak:

"They do, though. They do mean something... Mine means, *the one who guards the treasure.*"

Amaya feels engulfed in a déjà vu. *Gildas! Does he realize? Does he know what it means?* She's afraid of repetition, of confusion. The possibility inflames her.

But this is different, she thinks, trying to convince herself. And she forces herself to be there with the rest of them.

"Can you find gold?" Suspiros goes on interrogating him.

"If it's there..." Gaspar says, and with his answer, he rests his eyes on Amaya.

Amaya doesn't respond to that stare, which for the first time has lighted on her alone.

Gaspar goes on explaining:

"But I don't look for gold, Suspiros."

She can talk to him. She can be alone with a man without him harassing or pouncing on her. Mrs. Ignacia leaves them. She doesn't pay any mind. She doesn't care.

The two of them converse, and sometimes Suspiros comes and posts herself at her mother's feet and looks at Gaspar's mobile lips. Amaya pats her child's head. She thinks, this could have been her family. But she takes it back: Gaspar is some six years younger than her.

When Gaspar tries to interpret what happens to others…

"It's the passing of the days that destroys beauty. The passing of the days obscures what's good, because there's little good and life is made up mostly of vileness, blundering, monotony."

Amaya would like to tell him that with him, the days are never tarnished, they never grow ugly. That it moves her to see a man unashamed to use the word beauty, without feeling less of a man. She says nothing. She listens.

"Failed marriages… No. The failure is general. The person who gets married feels chosen, but at the same time, feels the pleasure and the responsibility of choosing. And then so many things get turned around… It turns out that the opportunity to choose and being chosen doesn't end there."

"Yes. There's something to that," Amaya avers. And all at once, she feels depressed.

To choose forever? And what if the election had brought the two of them, José Luis and her, together…

It almost seems as if Gaspar is offering his answer:

"There are marriages that are sweet…"

Sweet marriages: the notion sticks with Amaya.

"… in old age, in some of those marriages that have survived, that sweetness flourishes. Have you ever seen that, Amaya?"

She nods, and yet it strikes her that a great distance separates the harsh conception of life Gaspar espoused at first and that measured final observation. Why? For her? She doesn't like him recanting his thoughts out of courtesy. But an inexplicable exuberance takes hold of her: as if he had divined her spiritual communion with José Luis and lavished it with respect.

"Tomorrow I'm going to the city. You'll have to mind the store."
The task disconcerts Amaya.
"The whole day?"
"No. In the morning is all." And he adds, suggestively: "I'll drive back."
"What... You bought a...?" She doesn't get out the word "car."
"A truck," he informs her. "It'll haul three tons. Six thousand, nine hundred pesos. In two years we can pay it off, if we get enough work hauling."
Amaya looks at her husband, calculating. She turns to the window and sees the rarefied blue of the sky. On the trellis in the yard, the *cereza* grapes are ripe. Some of the leaves have gone yellow. She had noticed them before; she thought they were burned by the sun. Now she sees it's autumn, that autumn's on its way. Her friends will be returning to the city.

Rocks and weeds surround Romano's hennery. Fewer on the canal side, where the border is cool from the shade of the willows.
Cataldo looks out, sometimes from the field of rocks, holding onto the wire, sometimes from the ravine, sitting in the fork of a tree.
A manservant comes at dawn and leaves with the fading of day. But the veterinarian moves about as if he's the only one working, furiously active, energetic, and efficient. Cataldo watches him from the distance. Sometimes he sees him with a shotgun.
That shotgun has a story. Cataldo doesn't know it, others do. The police know it.
A man who had gone into the chicken coops one night took some shot to the leg. He ran off and hid in his farm. He didn't want help, but his wife brought a nurse over without telling him. The nurse healed him, but

wanted to know: "What happened, you got into a tussle…?" The wounded man looked down. "I have to inform the police. That's the law." That was worse, and the man clammed up. The nurse gave word of what had happened. The police got the man to talk. At the station, seeing up close the little crestfallen man he'd emptied his shotgun at that night, Romano's memory went blank. Later, counting the New Hampshire hens in the third corral, it hit him: the little country boy in espadrilles, the little country boy who hadn't eaten, Cardona's sculpture.

Romano prods the two four-hundred-pound pigs and the smaller one. All three are yellow. On the shore, the rubbish brought up by the water gathers against the roots, and the breeder lets them loose a few times a week so they can eat the rubbish and save him money on fodder.

Cataldo sees him coming and steps away from the tree to take off. But he turns brave and stays there waving his arms, as if in defense. Really he is just steeling his spirit for what's to come.

Romano drives the pigs downward and cuts a willow branch, stripping it patiently into a switch for the way back. But his eyes are focused on Cataldo, who is twenty feet away, vacillating, ready to escape, anxious about something.

He addresses him:

"Any chance of knowing what you're up to? I've seen you around here all the time, lately."

He needles him:

"You want to eat some chicken? A little hen…?"

Cataldo shakes his head, then blurts out:

"No."

That's enough. He's started talking. Now he'll keep going.

"No. It's about something else."

"And that is…?"

"The thing with Colorada."

"What Colorada? The one who goes around with you?"

"Yeah. About the marriage."

"You're getting married?"

"What do you mean, are we getting married?" His tone becomes clouded. "You're the one that's getting married!"

The expression on Romano's face – half-surprised, half-scornful – does him no good. It is as if Cataldo has already passed into another stage in which Romano has given his word he will marry Colorada. That is why he rushes him:

"You promised! You promised!"

The stocky Romano is no longer crouched down, readying his willow rod. He has stood up now, and the rage has risen up into his face.

"What did I promise, you son of a bitch? Say it, what did I promise?"

And he hurtles forward, the branch raised high, trembling and thin as a whip.

Cataldo slips agilely down the ravine. Romano follows him. Cataldo runs up the other side, scurrying over a little trail with his hands and feet, and the veterinarian tries to do the same, but he has trouble, because his weight makes the brittle soil crumble.

At the top, the dimwit is waiting for him with a stone. When the big man peeks over the edge, Cataldo steps back, leaving him an open path. Romano comes up and brandishes his whip. Cataldo places the stone in front of his right eye and closes his left. He sees his hand with the stone lined up with his enemy's chest. He cocks back his arm, brings it forward, and hurls the stone. Romano feels the blow to his chest like a wound. It's not so bad. But he drops the branch and brings his forearm up to protect his face. He thinks something else is coming that will destroy it.

Cataldo flees.

As he runs, he says to himself:

"Now he's been warned."

"She asked me to, right in front of you."

Her husband grumbles, but he admits it. Besides, at the time, he himself had assured them they needn't worry, because he was happy that day, proud even that Mrs. Ignacia's husband had invited him over and would share his table with them.

"You'll have to come around, Amaya. I'm asking you... There's so much that only a woman can see."

Mrs. Ignacia will come around, of course, once in a while on the weekends, and a woman will stop in from time to time to air out the bedrooms. Gaspar will stay a while, too; but you know, a man just isn't the same...

You can't really call the house vacant, with Gaspar inside, even if Gaspar was generally out, with his wicker rods, detecting minerals... It wasn't a secret: no one was going to refuse to let him dowse with his implements, nor would his master have any competitors out to buy those dry hills, bare and lonesome... He'd also sell machinery to plow the land in Luján and Maipú, where the vineyards were growing scarce. That was the commercial zone assigned to him.

But this Gaspar, so fruitless with his dowsing, had another mission: to keep his eye on emigration. Vegetable patches of half a hectare, or one, or two, little vineyards that crept out behind a family's house, were squeezed between the expansion of the villages; but it drove the farmers to despair, as they saw prices and yields stagnate, while their children grew and needed more things; they were little use there, and they began to dream of the city.

His master, the civil servant, couldn't be seen there looking into who was leaving, what their needs were, and the effect it all had on prices. Someone else did that for him, and that someone was Gaspar. The purchase was formalized in a notary's office in the city, through intermediaries. The lands were useless, and the families of the farmers turned them over for a few pesos, thinking that everything was finished there, that it was time to move to the capital, without knowing very well why, maybe to set up a neighborhood store, get the girl and the children to work there… Useless lands, acquired for mere pesos, in bulk, by the hectare; someday they'd be worth something, someday they'd be priced in square feet.

Amaya catches wind of something. But Mrs. Ignacia doesn't let her suspect:

"A handout from my husband, so they can leave, so they don't protest against the government, which does its work, even if they don't see it. They're ignorant."

Mrs. Ignacia thinks the land is worthless. That's what her husband told her.

"You know, Leonardo. You were there that day."

"They could have left behind a caretaker!"

Amaya has an answer for him: *Gaspar's there.* But that's exactly what she shouldn't say, even if her husband knows.

Amaya adopts a new affectation without noticing it: on those evenings, she wears flats and flared skirts. If he is there, she always imagines, they will walk a lot, on the path that extends from the villa and flanks the foothills. In fact, they never go further than the eucalyptus stands that form the vast backdrop of the property.

She doesn't always find him there. Sometimes, he's asleep by four in the afternoon, face down, with the stove lit, one leg hanging out of bed, dressed, uncovered. Amaya has seen him from the hallway.

"They'll come in August. I'll be gone by then."

"Really? What about the girl's school?" What she means is they can't leave the city, where her friend's daughter will have classes until the summer starts. What she means, almost, is there's no need for Gaspar to go. Besides, why should he?

Gaspar laughs at her confusion:

"No, it's not them who are coming. Laborers are coming, to make the pool." They will install a swimming pool. They have four hundred square meters set aside, overgrown in summer with short, spongy grasses, muddy now, because the ditch running past it has overflowed.

"And you, do you have to go?"

"I have to sometime."

"Does that mean your work's done?" Amaya keeps on. "There's no advantage to being here?"

"Yeah, but... I need to keep going."

"Keep going just to keep going?"

"Yeah," Gaspar confesses in a low tone.

Amaya doesn't understand; but she begins to open herself to him:

"Everyone who makes me feel good leaves..." They are standing under the eucalyptuses. Amaya leans on a silvery white trunk. The water roars tumultuously in the ditch. Without knowing, Amaya has been staring at the soil strewn with slender withered leaves gone brown, soon to rot.

"I had a lover..."

"Let's walk," Gaspar offers delicately.

And they walk between the smooth trunks of the trees.

"I had a lover. He was thirty-one years old. He killed himself."

He falls quiet. Amaya thinks it's more and more certain that she could have had José Luis.

"Give me matches."

His dear brother gives them to him.

"What about money? You want a twenty?"

"Not now."

Cataldo wants matches, that's all.

He makes a little fire and waits amid the budding vines or in the bottoms or behind a half-destroyed house of mud brick… He's studied the man's habits. When the veterinarian goes to the village to see his parents, to have a home-cooked meal, or to bring back something or other, the rain of rubble comes down on him. Sometimes Romano manages to spot the imbecile, peeking over a wall, running off into a stand of poplars… Other times he doesn't. But he knows it's always him.

A pebble, two, three, swiftly. They hit him in the face, on the back, they make his legs dance when he turns and tries to stop and face off against Cataldo where he grabbed him before. The veterinarian's pockets are stuffed with rocks, but he almost never gets the chance to use them. He knows who it is. He could go to their house and tell them, *It's that half-wit of yours. I'll kill him…* But he prefers to stalk him. Not on the street, not in the fields. He can't use the shotgun there. He's done it before, though, and he was within his rights. Eventually, the dimwit will go back to the chicken coops, maybe even go in. And then…

Cataldo, with his little fire, just embers, so it won't smoke, is waiting behind the bulrush awning over the tomatoes. When he has the man in his sights, he hurls two, three, six stones, direct, thudding, and he sucks up his snot and tears, lamenting to himself alone:

"She's yours and you won't take her, moron."

Another rock, another sniffle:

"And I love her more than you do…"

Amaya sees he is washing clothes. She sees them hanging on the line.

"Give me the sheets. I'll wash them."

"I have lots. They left me a drawer full of them. Embroidered. You want to see?"

"Give me something else, then. Whatever needs doing. Just say."

"Find me a woman who will wash clothes. I can pay her."

"I'll bet!"

It's a blow to Amaya's good mood.

But Gaspar reconciles with her effortlessly:

"Don't get mad." He gives her a friendly smile.

Later, because they've fallen silent, despite everything:

"I wish I was that kid that killed himself."

"You do…?"

"Yeah."

At that moment, Amaya could cry. She can, so she lets herself.

"For you, I wish I was like him. Obviously, as far as other things go, I'm happy how I am," he says with easygoing modesty.

Amaya thanks him, in her heart, for moving her one moment and then giving her this soothing joy.

"I could be a nice memory, Amaya," he says when he sees she's recovered, and it is impossible to say precisely whether his tone is naive or premeditated.

Amaya doesn't want to know. She is just thankful that he is as he is and that he says things that flow through her.

She feels soft, docile before a voice that seems still not resolved to say everything.

"The girl's got a fever, don't you see?"

"Fever?" Amaya gets scared, and puts a hand on her forehead. "No she doesn't."

"There's measles going around."

"Measles…? She already had it."

"Look at her eyes."

"What about them?"

"You can't see a thing! You're as dumb as Colorada!"

Amaya seethes, and feels sorry for her sister.

Colorada curls up on her side, as though expecting a blow, but it has already struck her. She's understood.

Everyone harbors a private bitterness, and from that moment no one eats comfortably.

Her husband has something else, a fury of suspicions.

"And don't you go anymore!"

"To where?"

"You know what I mean."

"What is it, Leonardo? What's going on?" She begins undoing the knot in Suspiros's napkin. "María, help her to bed, now please."

Colorada feels useful, being called by her real name, María; she livens up and takes Suspiros away. She doesn't know Amaya only remembers her name when she feels a wretched compassion for her.

"In front of the girls, Leonardo, why?" she asks, desperate after his ultimatum.

"Because whoever it is, you're not going anymore!"

"That's impossible," she says, almost imploring. "We promised…" She implicates him in the promise.

"I didn't promise anything, and you're nobody's servant, I don't care if he's the president."

"But I'm not serving anyone, I'm just watching, that's all."

"So…?" he says, and gets up.

Amaya scoots back, pushes away her chair. A sign that she won't argue any further.

The man bites his tongue. He goes to the bedroom. He lies down and rolls on his side, so his back will be turned to her when she comes in.

Cataldo is filthy, filthier than in the summer, and that's something, because the filth is harder to see in winter. Filthy from so much hiding and waiting, sprawled out on the ground, stomping in the mud, crawling under bridges…

These are things Colorada doesn't notice. Amaya tells her:

"Say something to Cataldo. Otherwise, I won't let you keep seeing him."

A surface precaution: don't get her sister too dirty. For the rest, no other warnings are needed. Cataldo can't have children. They've known that for years.

After the warning, Colorada notices something, it's true: his nose isn't the way Amaya says noses ought to look, or his hands, or his heel, coming out of the back of his espadrille... But she won't say anything. And that's what their harmony is based on: never pointing out their shortcomings, never throwing their clumsiness in each other's faces, never hurting each other...

But:

"You're going, Cataldo."

"Yeah, you know that. My uniform'll be here soon."

And since he sees she's sad:

"But I'll get it taken care of before I do. I'll make him come round, one rock at a time..."

He smiles, content.

Colorada doesn't react, she doesn't know what Cataldo is talking about. She's still leaning over.

Cataldo understands: it's because he's going. He should prove to her it's not his fault:

"It's because of the war. They need me. The war in Abyssinia. The gringos are there to kill, that's all they care about. And they'll make it here soon. This Mussolini's in charge of them, you know?"

Colorada is frightened by this *there to kill*, and that look from his poor friend recalls to Cataldo the responsibility his dreams have laid on him:

"You won't be left alone, because I'm going to handle the thing, you know? You want me to?"

The imbecile would like to know how it can be that he'll leave and she won't be left alone; but she's too defeated, too crestfallen, and she doesn't try.

Gaspar passed by in the agent's hardtop Chevrolet. He usually comes back in it after driving around for days. It was eleven. He'll eat something, maybe, he'll sleep. Or he'll stay there, under the eucalyptuses, waiting for her to arrive.

Amaya hurries through lunch in the kitchen. On the bed, she sets out Suspiros's pleated smock for school.

She calls them to eat, and urges on her husband, who's dawdling. But she regrets it. He looks at her with renewed distrust. Amaya is drained, she's frightened. She's always afraid in certain situations, she knows well why.

She dresses Suspiros, gathers her notebooks, takes her to the door, and watches her go.

Her husband is in the corridor, his wool vest buttoned up the front. He glances at the newspaper, so quickly it's clear he's already read it cover to cover.

"Where are you going?" And he looks at her as if he saw every part of her, but he only notices two things: the flared skirt, the flat shoes. Also, though he ignores this, the eager face and the longing to flee.

"Around here. I'll be there and back in no time."

One step.

Her husband has abandoned the newspaper.

He doesn't hurry. She won't move. Not even when he hits her. She won't shout, she won't put up resistance. Not even when she's fallen onto the tiles and he's kicking her.

She won't move. He has time to step forward slowly and let the memory burn him: the troops beneath the spring shower, taking the main street into the village; the nighttime shooting drills in the neighboring hills, flashing like lightning through the murk; Amaya, deranged with joy, stumbling the whole day long, and those escapades, *Where are you going?, To the camp, to see the tents, the machine guns*; the departure, in trucks that pass without cease, crunching and crunching those tenacious nocturnal beetles that fall down from the streetlamps... And that whimpering of hers, beside him on the sidewalk, which seemed like nothing, at first...

She won't move. He knows. Not when his hand reaches her, nor when the hand falls on her.

And in turn, Amaya knows he will beat her and beat her. It will be the same.

Pummeled, but dry; livid, but dry, dry she has taken cover in her daughter's little bed, curling up on the mattress, with the door closed.

The servant brings her lips to the keyhole and whispers her merciful accord:

"Ma'am, Ma'am... Do you need anything?" she asks, waiting for an answer that doesn't come. "Do you hear me? Do you need anything, ma'am? A tea...?"

Then there are little raps calling her:

"Mama, it's me. Let me in, Mama."

It's a serious voice, concentrated this time, Suspiros.

Amaya goes over to the door.

"Are you alone?"

"Yes, Mama."

She opens.

"How?" she asks, astonished.

"There's no class. Papa said it's in the paper."

And she explains, but testily, as if she were very tired:

"The epidemic, Mama. Measles."

And she asks:

"Can I lie down, Mama? Can I? Will you let me…?"

Then Amaya notices the thing her husband mentioned: the febrile glimmer in her eyes.

TEN DAYS OF SCHOOL CLOSINGS. FLU AND MEASLES EPIDEMIC, the papers say, to keep from alarming anyone. But they themselves hint to the contrary: *Congress has approved obligatory diphtheria vaccination for the entire province.*

"Diphtheria," the doctor says, despotically. "Your daughter's not the only one, ma'am."

Amaya lets him leave, with his rash indifference. When he's out the door, she says to her husband:

"Let's call a different one."

He accepts and goes out to find one.

Amaya hears the truck motor: her husband will take a while.

She goes back and contemplates the girl in her fevered sleep. She remembers that she has the prescription in hand, and calls to the servant.

"Go to the pharmacy. Have them fill this."

She's alone. Sucked in by the silence.

Suddenly, the tears come, a silent sob that doesn't bow her over.

"My fault," she blubbers, associating the idea of punishment with what she and Gaspar have done.

She thinks of God, but she doesn't want to make a commitment. She asks him, that's all, she asks him. She begs and prays.

That night, with the second diagnosis, she yields. She falls on her knees and promises.

Cataldo said he would hurry, and he's wasted two afternoons.

He gives excuses:

"He isn't bringing the pigs."

He looks for the right moment:

"Now, now that the worker's gone. But not yet: when it gets dark."

Something thunders in the air. Cataldo looks up and there are no clouds. A plane with three motors cuts through the twilight. It roars over the willows and leaves Cataldo perplexed:

"They're already here… That's Mussolini, for sure. So I…"

Then his courage stirs him. He climbs over the fence and enters the henhouse.

From his shack, the veterinarian observes the invasion. He readies the shotgun, but he doesn't bring it. He goes outside and hurriedly gathers stones.

Cataldo is meditating on his demands, and looking for phrases, he forgets about the danger.

The first stone strikes him in the groin. *Right here*, he thinks, because he wants to run away, but all at once, his leg gives out. But he doesn't hesitate, he turns. A second one hits him in the back, it feels like someone's shoved him. With effort, he tries to make off among the whirl of hens.

Romano follows him at leisure. He has him trapped, and he's waiting to pin him against the fence, because with his leg impaired, he won't be able to climb it.

And when Cataldo gets there and can't, he falls to the ground and curls into a ball to better bear the blows.

Romano stops twenty yards away. He wants to make him suffer more, from fear, before he finishes pelting him. He aims, slowly, over and again, leaving him wounded and bruised.

Every stone that strikes shakes the dimwit's huddled body. Every time, he crumples further, and now his face is turned to the ground. When he rubs against the dry grass, Cataldo remembers the matches. Hiding his hands even more, he takes out the box of Victorias, strikes one, it flares up, and he sets the scrub alight.

He crouches and crawls, and under the rain of stones, ignites the edges of the chicken coops.

Romano pounds him more and harder, but with his excitable disposition, he gets distracted, turns to the flames, starts stomping them and fanning them out with his hands. He digs into the earth with his fingernails, pulls out clumps, and throws them on the fire, but the soil takes the grass with it, giving the blaze more fuel.

The dimwit, wits dulled further by the flames, stops lighting matches and starts gathering stones. He puts two fingers in his mouth and whistles shrilly. Romano turns around, surprised, and just then, something strikes his ear, which starts burning as though it were singed. Another whistle. He understands: the dimwit is calling him so he can hit him in the face. He puts up an arm to protect himself, and runs off, tripping, because he can't see well, there is smoke and there are shadows and the dimwit is striking him implacably from behind.

Cataldo knows fire. *Over here, it will swallow me. Over there it's going slower.* At the same time, he thinks: *He lets the pigs out somewhere around here*, and he finds the way out.

Romano goes into the shack and picks up his loaded weapon. He steps out pointing it wildly, trembling. Then he sees that the fire, hissing like a cauldron, is devouring everything, and fear fills him, and he drops the gun.

A moment's reaction, just a moment's, is enough for him to try and save something: he frees the pigs, and opens the coop that houses the white hens.

The hens overrun him, and in a whirl of feathers, he grows confused among the pigs roaming confusedly through the ashes.

He heads to the road. Beside him runs a pig, and a chicken flies past his head.

The fire burns out in the fallow fields. But the smoke has risen into the night and it, more than the fire, alerts those nearby.

The scent of charred birds, of feathers and flesh blended together, begins to spread, and the hungry people from the farmhouses emerge into the darkness and sit down, silently savoring the scent of six hundred chickens roasted all at once.

The dogs catch a whiff, and it raises their spirits; but later, without hope, they will lie down with the men, their stunted maws between their outstretched legs.

"I want to go," Amaya says, and rests her fingertips over the small coffin, at the height where her daughter's lips may lie.

The carriage is white, and at each of the four corners is a chubby angel with golden hair.

Next to the open hole in the earth – *so big*, Amaya thinks, *with such smooth sides* – a priest is waiting.

Later she sees that the priest is speaking and making familiar gestures beside the casket.

From among those gathered, only one howl can be heard, a howl from a dimwit, punctuated by hiccups.

Amaya takes all the roads that are not lined with houses, for hours and hours, one day and the next. She returns when the cold lashes her, or sometimes even later.

She ruminates.

She says to herself: *I have lived. Now I will think.*

She imagines she is lucid, but she contradicts herself.

I have thought a lot about what I was doing. Now I should live.

She goes over her memories of the girl.

Now I won't hurt her. Even if I went with every man I came across, nothing will happen to her again.

I'm free.

She feels she's been released from her pledge: she offered Gaspar in Suspiros's place, but it was Suspiros that she lost.

And she runs into Gaspar.

He looks at her, and he wants to hold her with his gaze. She stops. She observes him, she looks up at the eucalyptus. Again, she contemplates that gentle man, with sorrow, but empty of desire. She says no, shaking her head. And she goes on her way.

Later, on another afternoon, she says over and over: "My affection, José Luis, is like the affection of dimwits: my affection endures."

And even: "You have to forgive me, José Luis. You have to forgive me for Romano and Gaspar. You are the one I was looking for."

from *The Absurd Ones* (1978)

Aballay

In the evening sermon, the friar said a rather difficult word that Aballay didn't manage to catch, about the saints who climbed up on pillars. Questions are plaguing him, but he saves them for when he has the chance to ask, at one of the bonfires, maybe.

They are visitors here, both of them, the priest and him, with the difference that, when the novena is over, the other man has somewhere to go back to.

The chapel, which rises above the scrubland in the middle of the low hill, with no dwellings or any other permanent structure adjacent, opens for the Marian feast days; that's the only time the priest, who comes from a faraway but equally devout parish in the city, comes around to lead the services.

The pilgrims set up camp, and the merchants, too. The nine days pass with prayers and processions; the nights are filled with golden racks of ribs, guitars, yerba mate, and *vino carlón*.

Aballay has seen a shotgun wedding between two Laguneros – descendants of the Huarpe Indians – as well as various newcomers' baptisms. He wandered in mainly from curiosity and the need to see how he got along with people, but he kept his head up and didn't meddle with anyone. He counted four soldiers.

‿

Meantime, the candlewicks burn down on the altars, and outside people feed the fires, which blaze in the temporary brush shelters, built for those dates alone.

The priest walks along the path running through the bivouacs, passing out his blessings and good nights. Each group clamors for him as he passes, and he pays honor to a family shown up from Jachal. They grill baby goat, the grandmother fries pastries, a man pours wine, everyone is peaceful and subdued. Songs are sung early in the neighboring shacks.

Facundo's name comes up, because of a recent action.

Didn't they kill him years back…?

Aballay was a shadow in the footsteps of the soutane, and now he is an inert mass out in the open. He waits.

One of the men from Jachal invites him over. He waves him off. His hunger is for something else.

But the priest intervenes, and Aballay obeys him. He doesn't add to the conversation, nor does the priest urge him to speak up, maybe he's used to the silence of the humble and dour.

But at a certain point, when the stars have climbed over the horizon, Aballay surprises him, touching his sleeve, and letting a query slip out in a soft voice:

"Father, could you hear me out…?"

"In confession?"

Aballay thinks it over, and says after a pause:

"Not yet, Father. But let's talk now, I'm asking you, just you and me."

With time, they pull away from the tumult around the bonfires, elude the revelers from the canteen, and vanish among the resting carriages where the children have lain down to sleep.

⌒

Then they talk, and when the matter that has troubled the unknown man comes to light, the father is pleased with his skill as a holy intercessor. This is the sign that his words sink in and are capable of sowing doubt. He tries to temper his speech with a simplicity of language, of expression, insofar as possible.

"No, son: I didn't say they were saints, but that their lives were saintly. That custom was known among anchorites or hermits."

"With due respect, those weren't your words."

"No...?"

"No, Father. You called them something else."

"Well... Stylites. Could that be it?"

"Could be."

"All right, then. It means more or less the same thing. Except that the stylites were a special class of anchorites... You know what that word means?"

"Yes and no."

"Let's just say no, and I'll explain it to you. The anchorites were recluses, they withdrew voluntarily from other human beings. At most, they kept a faithful animal as a companion. They traveled through the deserts or lived in caves on the tops of mountains."

"Why?"

"To serve God, after their fashion."

"I don't understand. In the sermon, you said they were on top of a pillar."

"Yes... a pillar, or a column. That's what the Stylites did. This strange custom of theirs was only possible in the ancient countries of the world where there were monumental temples, with pillars holding up their roofs, built before the coming of Christ. When the old religions disappeared and men abandoned the houses of worship, over the course of centuries, they were destroyed. In some cases, the pillars were all that was left standing. The Stylites would climb them to expose themselves to the elements and be free of temptation. They would stay there through wind and rain, through illness and through hunger."

"How many days?"

"Days…? Eternities! It's said that Simon the Elder lived thirty-seven years that way and Simon the Younger sixty-nine."

Aballay enters into a dense silence.

The priest nudges him:

"So…? What do you think, now that you know the scale of their sacrifice? Could you imagine?"

These questions leave Aballay unaffected. He has many other pressing ones: could they sit down in such a narrow space, or did they have to stand, crouch, or kneel; why didn't they die of thirst; did they never come down again, for any reason, not even to answer the call of nature; was it really believable that they didn't fall to the ground when they slept…

The priest answers, knowing these questions may be the goading of an unbelieving hick bent on stripping him of faith in what he's preached from the pulpit. No matter, he tells himself, there's an answer for everything.

"How did they eat? They did so moderately, though some, depending on where they'd settled, enjoyed the blessings of nature. They might have had wild honey or fruit from the trees. Others, especially those who walked in the desert, are said to have eaten spiders, insects, even snakes."

The repulsive creatures he's just evoked deepen the priest's growing worry. Worried for his safety, he tries to get a sense of his location. *It's the depths of night,* he thinks, observing the thickness of the surrounding brush. They have gone far from the encampment, the mass of carriages and draft animals. He considers himself and this seedy man he's never seen before, who looks anxious and unruly, who might or might not bring danger. He recovers his nerve, tries to calm himself down, and tells himself he should enjoy this possibly naive provocation, which has brought the memory of his readings back to him, if for no other reason than to communicate them to a lone parishioner in such extraordinary circumstances.

The priest explains that they may well have been able to sustain themselves through the charity of others, but Aballay says: "I thought they were alone and that they escaped from the rest of the people?"

"The desolate and faithful made pilgrimages to ask for their help before God, and from those pious persons, they would accept certain very pure foodstuffs."

"Were they saints, then? Could they consult with God?"

"We all can."

Aballay takes another turn in the narrow alleyways of his soul, and his attention strays from the priest. The priest lets him go, supposing he will react on his own.

Then:

"You said in the sermon that they withdrew to do penance."

"I said more than that: penance and contemplation."

"Contemplation… maybe they did see God, then?"

"Who knows. But contemplation isn't just a matter of trying to know Jesus's face or his divine splendor, it's also about giving your soul and your thoughts over to Christ and the mysteries of religion."

Aballay has grasped this, but he's keen to clear up the first point, specifically:

"You said: penance. Why do they do penance?"

"For their faults, or because they take on themselves the failings of others. Concretely, in the case of the anchorites: they climbed up a column to be closer to Heaven and to take leave of the earth, because that was where they had sinned."

Aballay knows what a great sin it is to kill. Aballay has killed.

Tonight, Aballay has decided to take leave of earth.

It's true that the plain, which is the only place he knows, has no columns; he has never seen any apart from those of the portico of the church of San Luis de los Venados.

He remembers that to escape his mother's discipline, he used to climb a tree. He admits that he's trying to do the same now: flee from his guilt, and find a place to climb to.

It wouldn't work anymore. Not even if he hid out in the leafy heights of an *ombú*. They'd find him out, they'd stone him, even if they didn't know exactly why, just because he was acting strange. Nor would anybody offer him a crust of bread.

He's resolved, conscientious, he's made a deal with himself to abandon the earth and live a life of penitence. He killed, and savagely. He'll never forget the gaze of the mestizo boy who saw him kill his father, one of the scant memories left to him from that alcohol-soaked night.

But his remorse won't let him be still. He has to walk. To go (from one place to the next).

The friar said they *climbed* the column. Aballay is a horseman. Very early, at the first light of day, Aballay *climbs* onto his sorrel horse.

He pats him gently on the neck and asks: "Will you hold me?" He supposes his companion has agreed, and as they go off at a soft trot, he readies him: "Keep in mind it's not for a day… it's forever."

⌐⌐

The first day, the fast was voluntary; the second, it was a torment, obsessed with eating without finding a way to do so.

He enjoyed it at first. A day's deprivation purifies the blood, he told himself, by way of consolation.

Then the hunger came on hard and heavy and he started losing hope of getting help and being able to carry out his resolution.

A cloud of smoke oriented him. He made it to the ranch. They had slaughtered an animal and were roasting the offal right there in the yard. There was no need to ask. But he drew their attention with his refusal to settle in among the overseer and his kin. Still, they passed him a generous serving skewered on his own knife.

He knew that time was different from the others. He had received that hospitality that is offered without question to wayfarers. He'd gotten it before, too, in different places. But from now on, he would have need of it every day, and his changed condition wounded his pride.

He felt hemmed in by the straits he foresaw and those that penury had begun to reveal to him.

From now on, he'd have to use imagination to sustain himself, and wherever his wits failed him, or he glimpsed some risk of breaking with his plan, he would rely on the teachings in the priest's tale.

Farms weren't common in that lonesome country, and he didn't see himself as a hanger-on. He would get hold of tools and provisions; he had a little cash left to pay for them. Would he hunt? Sure, but how would he cook the meat? Eat fruit? Nature didn't abound in them in those parts.

He'd always been nimble in the stirrups or hanging off the cinches, so it was easy for him to fill his cup with water or even, when he felt like trying his luck, to drink it with his lips skirting the surface of the arroyos.

He had experience sleeping on the horse, and the horse had experience of him doing it. But if he didn't unburden the animal, he wouldn't get any rest, and soon enough, he would die. So he lassoed a bronco, made it his second mount, and passed from one to the other, to let them catch their breath. The second didn't put up resistance to the rider or the routine; he must have had an owner before.

If he'd adopted the law of life on horseback with absolute rigor, he might have been reduced to the most ignoble practices in regards to the call of nature. He'd had the good sense the night they were together to ask the priest, who never found out the motive for that lengthy inquest on the customs and constraints of those who live atop columns. The friar said he couldn't imagine a penitent so severe that he would forbid himself to climb down to earth for a purpose so plainly justified, though no doubt there were some whose mortification led them to excesses.

Whatever the case, Aballay planned to stay clean. Wasn't he repenting to clean his soul?

⌒

Aballay rummages in the branches of a bush, looking for something to eat. He surprises a woodpecker, which stalls before taking flight. He slaps it out of the air. He picks it up, careful not to hurt it. He sees its desperate agitation and looses it from its horror.

The bird shoots upward now, and the man is happy to see it free.

But a stubborn memory pierces him: the mestizo boy's stare, when he killed his father.

⌒

Stubborn as well, determined to return, is his vision of the men on pillars. Generally, it is blended with his impressions from the day, and tonight is no different.

Aballay is a penitent and he sits on a pillar. Not a pillar like the one at the church, nor a pillar from a cemetery gate: the stone pillar of a bridge, thin and tall, with him on top.

He's not alone. There are other pillars and others doing penance. They are ancients, saints, and for him, they are strangers. They don't talk, because they are not allowed to, and if they did, he wouldn't understand their language. They, like him, are draped in ponchos.

In one part of his dream, there is peace, then it turns to a nightmare: the birds arrive.

They walk on his head and shoulders. They peck at his ears, his eyes, and his nose, or they try to drop food into his mouth. They make nests, lay eggs... and the whole time, he is mortified from fear of the void, where he will fall if he moves a muscle.

Aballay wakes up groggy. He orders his horse: "Take it eeeasy...!"

⌒

He comes upon a shop. There's no point in riding up to it: there's no grate built into the wall for him to make his purchase from his horse.

With time, he finds another. Before passing him his jerky, the shop-keeper sets a condition: "Cash in hand." Aballay pulls off some of the copper bits and coins of various denominations that give his belt its glimmer.

He comes upon the yard of a staging post. There's gambling. Cards, knucklebones. In the ring, the cocks slay each other at first sight, or blindly, if they've clawed each other's eyes out. People place bets.

There is drinking and eating.

Aballay has tied the bronco to the post, and he wanders through the different groups on his sorrel horse, to take a look. He takes a look as well when he passes by the grill. But someone accosts him: "You don't play, you don't eat." Aballay understands. The man who accosted him is about to throw his bone. Aballay pulls another coin from his belt. The bone takes flight and lands on the ground on its edge, meaning Aballay has won. The loser pays up: contemptuously, he throws his coins on the ground, between the sorrel horse's legs.

Aballay looks at the money that could be his, if he stooped to asking someone to pick the coins out of the dust and bring them nearer his reach. He could grab them himself, sliding down the animal's belly, holding onto the cinches, but people would laugh, and he'd have to fight. With vague sorrow, he considers the two futilities before him, trots off to the post to untie the bronco, and goes.

Since then, on account of that gesture, which the witnesses had trouble puzzling out, but which had something to do with repudiation, Aballay's fame begins to spread.

He is unaware of it. If he were more observant, he would have seen the sudden glow in the admiring eyes of the servant girl who brought him yerba mate with sugar one morning.

The ones he brews himself are bitter, and he drinks them in the morning, to still the insistent rumbling in his gut. He doesn't abuse the exemption apparently granted him by the examples the priest had given, save for cases of extreme necessity or insurmountable demands – though for him, yerba mate is one of those. He doesn't even set foot on the ground to light a fire.

He has the necessary tools. He chooses uneven terrain to serve as a table whenever he can tie up the horse in such a way that it more or less rests against the edge. Over a mound no higher than the saddle, he makes a little fire and boils the water. When the plains are too level, he descends into those wide, deep channels in the earth opened up by forgotten currents. Then, he finds his flat spot from below.

Drinking mate slowly at sundown, he admires the calm bronco's submissiveness. Without troubling his master, he nibbles at whatever plants are within reach. In the meanwhile, his partner, free from his duties, wanders through the tender grass and sprouts at his leisure. Aballay has his legs crossed on the quadruped's back, which serves as a chair. He laces his fingers to form a hollow the size of the delicate gourd. He sucks, with long pauses, at the handmade metal straw. He is absorbed, not in his thoughts perhaps, but in the mystical languor of the warm, green juice. And, though he is not in the habit of talking alone, he exclaims, one time, aloud: "God is my witness!"

Startled by the noise, which breaks the supple silence, the bronco reacts with a neigh and a shiver. Its trembling clears Aballay's head.

On a trail, he comes upon four docile Indians. Generously, they offer him fish, which has started to stink. It's raw, they carry it across the countryside in rush baskets open to the sun to sell in the market in the village. Aballay doesn't accept it, but he returns the favor, giving them two fistfuls of salt from his saddlebags.

Right away, the Indians set up camp, start a fire, gut and grill the fish with the pearly scales.

Now it smells passable to Aballay's incurable hunger. He waits, splay-legged, on his horse.

The four fishermen are jubilant and try to force him to come down and join them. He refuses, but accepts his portion.

The Indians crouch while they eat. One of them observes him from the corner of his eye. He realizes it's not that the white man doesn't want to, it's that he can't climb down from his animal's haunches, and he transmits this disturbing conclusion to the rest of his clan: *man-horse*.

Bulges sleep in the night. Aballay and his horse are one; the gentle bronco is the other. They are nestled in a mass of weeds, it's the best thing they've found as far as they can see. There's no light from the moon, a blanket of clouds obscures it.

Aballay is perched on a pillar. The sun is burning his mouth with its aftertaste of spoiled fish.

There's an old man. His column is more splendid, but their thirst makes them equal.

He's old and looks like a saint, but he doesn't have a saint's composure. He lacks endurance. He opens his poncho at the neck to cool off. Everything occurs in silence, until the old saint shouts: *Water!* To Aballay, it didn't sound like water, but that's what he gathers from the man's gesture; what he imagines is thunder, on the heels of a lightning bolt…

Aballay falls, he thinks the flash of the lightning bolt has knocked him over, and when he lands, he awakens, and the rain is soaking him. For an instant, he enjoys the water, which gives succor to his burning mouth. But then he finds his body has touched the ground.

Though the downpour pelts his eyes, he tries to look up, or at least lift his forehead, in a confused motion that not even he knows the meaning of: is he begging forgiveness, making clear his fall was unintended?

Muddy and unsettled, he leaps onto his horse and decides, according to his judgment and at his own risk, that this descent need not be counted, even if he worries otherwise. He recalls that he himself chose the yoke that now weighs on him. He will heed it with the most docile obedience.

⌒

The days of the dust cloud have proven demanding, and the distress has taught him to use his wit to secure his sustenance.

From the signs, he deduces the dust isn't windborne, that it's horses, not wild ones, but cavalry from the armed forces. That's bad for Aballay; he might get recruited, or bayonetted for no reason; he could lose the horses, they could be requisitioned or simply stolen.

He takes cover in the distance and leaves behind the last traces of people, ending up in the brutal pampa.

He draws on the examples given by the priest, who told him of the penitents in times long past who didn't have it easy when they took to the desert: he spoke to him of eating spiders and even snakes.

He feels for the jerky in the saddlebag and senses hunger not too far off. This gives him ideas: serpent-lizard-*pichi*. Probably there were no armadillos running around in the deserts where the saints of old dwelled.

It's the way they shoot off in all directions, plunging into the caves, clinging desperately to the roots, that makes them so hard for Aballay to hunt them on horseback. But he ventures toward the ruts (those he makes, hanging from the animal when it rushes off; those the animal will make if its leg sinks into the holes the *pichi* digs for its dwelling).

He fails repeatedly. He perseveres and learns.

Later, when he has to cook them, it's like boiling the water for his mate. Except that you have to kill the creatures. He lays them on their back, stabs them to death, and makes a cross-shaped cut to open them up. For his lunch, he cooks them in their shell, which serves as a pot, in their own abundant fat.

And so there's food to spare. But he needs water, and that makes him turn back..

⌐

Utterly bedraggled, he's returned. He hasn't seen himself for some time. The eyes of the others are wary of his presence, not because it's unusual for vagrants to come through, but because they don't care for them, they might turn to crime if their misery gets extreme.

At a farm, they know who he is. They don't recognize him, they've never seen him before; but they've heard his story, which has spread, unbeknownst to him, in diverse and contradictory forms that nevertheless exalt him according to a certain conception of the good.

"He bears his cross," they whisper to each other, with a reverent demeanor.

Aballay, who has pricked up his ears to hear their murmurs, thinks the truth is strictly otherwise: he has no cross, no medal, not even a prayer card.

He accepts some tattered clothes, which are offered to him as alms.

It's a warm day.

He looks for the arroyo and submerges himself, in abundant ablutions.

He doesn't have a comb, and he plans, as soon as possible, to stop at a shop or a staging post to get one, and to replenish his salt, yerba mate, and jerky.

Riding one day at a slow trot, at prayer time one afternoon, he strips and files down a dry branch with his knife, and then another, shorter one. With a strip of leather from the bridle, he ties them into a cross. With another, he ties it around his neck and lets it hang outside the shirt he now wears, thanks to the charity of the farmhands.

Where five houses cluster together, he hears thundering sounds, but they are not aggressive, he soon learns, when the cries of enthusiasm and demonstrations of joy rise up. Passing alongside the store, he sees their origin: among the scattered planks, with a border of logs, the hard, compact balls, carved from *quebracho*, maybe, thrown by various men, look lithely now and freely for their path, now strike one another like bandits. Bocce: he's tempted to join in. Probably they'd let him place a bet. A depressing memory pulls at him. Could he throw one? How nice it would be…! From the horse…?

The comb, the jerky, the salt, and the yerba mate use up all the money in his belt. All he has left is one coin, the most valuable, the silver *patacón*, which had been the centerpiece of the glimmering garment, when all the coins were still there. He keeps it in a slit, like a pocket, in the hardened leather that firmly and gracefully envelops his waist.

He doesn't join in the game, only in the spectacle of the game, but without mingling with the men. Since he's stuck around, they remember him when it's time for the barbecue:

"Go on, go for it."

He wavers, so they continue:

"What…? You want some, no?"

Aballay nods, but barely, without fully assenting, because he can guess what will happen next: they will try to get him to come down and gather around the grill, and once more, it will be a duel between himself and his resistance.

And so it is, until someone sees the crucifix and asks his neighbor: "Could he be the one...?" They agree that it could be him. Then they step forward to pay their tribute – bread and wine, to start with – to that strange pilgrim who, so they say, never gets down from his horse.

⌒

And so Aballay's spring ended, and his summer passed.

The winter made him think summer had been a heaven for him and his life in the open.

Past the fields, the sun was rising, but Aballay couldn't manage to wake up. It was freezing, and he was freezing. He was gripped by vague sensations of living in a state of wonder now grown brittle. He didn't bother to move, and a benign drowsiness overtook him.

His lethargy lasted a long time, the proximity to a gentle death, but his blood responded to the first hints of clement air.

When he became aware of the risk he had waded through, he made the sign of the cross, kissed his wooden icon, and looked down at his bearers, wondering:

If I died on horseback... who would take me down? Could death accomplish it...?

⌒

From his wagon, the rag-and-bone man shouted at him: "Gaucho!" and Aballay didn't realize the man meant him, or else didn't care to be addressed in that manner, as more than once, it'd been done to disparage him. He was going to ignore him, but the other, shouting to make himself heard, was only trying to ask if he had feathers.

Aballay restrained himself.

"Feathers?"

"Ostrich feathers. I'll buy them, or I'll trade merchandise for them, quality stuff."

This meeting, this proposal, convinced Aballay he'd found a calling that wouldn't require breaking his vow.

He had to head off toward the central plain, less arid, more solitary, and go south, to places odious for the danger they posed: of treading the turf of tribes hostile to whites.

He stalked the rhea. Not to harvest its flesh (which would be impossible without stepping down). Aballay didn't want to take its life, he wanted to take its feathers.

He learned to wait patiently, to employ a watchful eye, to yield to immobility (to avoid alerting the long-legged creature to his presence).

He tried to chase them down, to snatch at their wingtips or tail feathers when he came up beside them. But they didn't give: if the sorrel horse caught up with them for a stretch and he got hold of the feathers, the strides of their long legs threatened to drag him off, or the ones he'd tear out were scant or tattered.

He rued his ineptness with a bolas, but then, he didn't have one anyway.

He tried with the lasso. He learned that pulling an ostrich over wasn't the same as capturing it. The big bird kicked with frightful energy and scared off the horse.

And finally, in front of the shopkeeper's grate, he saw his dreams of barter had been a deception.

No one ever told him that was woman's work; he'd taken it for granted he'd be dealing with a man. And yet there, in the front of the wagon, was a woman.

In considerable straits at that particular moment.

No one noticed Aballay, nor did he step forward, nor even utter a single word. He simply stood to one side to assess the situation, and noted that those inside the wagon were trapped: another woman, more delicate in appearance, a man, maybe her husband, and two or three girls.

He could see that for the driver, pulling that wheeled mass out of the muddy water was the job of the oxen, and she shouted at them imperiously and prodded them harshly with a skillfully wielded cattle prod.

Aballay waded into the mire, to see how deep it went. Then he unraveled his rope and tied it around the yoke. He came round to the front, and with his main horse and its companion, began to pull, with caution, but steadily. All this without dismounting from the sorrel, which roused the driver's attention, then her admiration. She joined in to help him.

The first attempt did little, given the weight of the wagon and its load. They lessened it: one by one, Aballay helped the five passengers out, without letting his horses rest, and they set to pulling once more.

Around twilight, free from the prison of silt, though it had left its marks on their boots, clothes, and faces, they relaxed in front of a vigorous fire on dry soil. The pot of corn porridge sat in the cradle of the flames.

Aballay could see his fate – which he hadn't sought out – would be to provoke confusion tinged with admiration.

Given his attitude, the driver acceded without resistance or comment to his refusal to dismount to eat the warm food, and later, to rest in a natural position. She acted with inborn prudence and trusted she would find another occasion to pay him back for his help.

Aballay slept on the bronco.

When he awoke, knowing the affection his sorrel horse felt for him, he didn't worry over its absence; it had been left to run loose as usual, and he supposed it was out grazing, to recover from its strain the day before.

Aballay, too, was savoring his own green aroma, in successive rounds served by the postboy along with some flatbread to eat. Then he went off to find the laggard.

When he found him, he was lying down, untroubled, unmenacing, unbreathing.

Aballay started thinking, and wondered whether he might merit dispensation to step down from his horse. After deliberating, he decided against it. Hanging down from the bronco, he removed the sorrel horse's bridle and let his hand linger tenderly on the animal's smooth, glowing coat.

A feeling of helplessness seeped into his will, a desolation that so dazed him that he couldn't think of what to do to keep from killing the bronco with his weight. He was in the same place as at the beginning: to keep from setting his boots on the earth, he needed another horse to alternate with.

Undecided, he followed the wagon.

Further on, when they were stopped, he had his chance:

"Might you give me…"

With these few words, the driver made him a gift of the little mule, the pack animal that brought up the rear of the wagon on long journeys or else stayed out front, just past the postboy.

⌐

He joined in their crossing, unmindful of the scorn of the man moving from one side of the country to the other, with his effects and his family of four women pulled along by the slow, stately troupe of oxen.

Aballay was fine so long as the driver put up with his peculiarities. If he didn't care to give them up, then he would incur obligations. And so he ended up relieving her, driving the wagon for half a day or more. All he had to do was jump from his horse to the box seat, without the sin of dropping to the ground.

At night, the shelter of the box seat eased the transit toward sleep, with less shivering. Eating became a surer thing as well.

Aballay tormented himself with two questions: why is she watching over me? Is this penance?

To the first, he sought an answer from his benefactor:

"Why…?"

"Because you help me," she said. (She was less stilted with him than he was with her.)

She didn't convince him, and he fell silent.

Then the woman deigned to answer:

"Because you remind me of a son I had."

They spoke as equals, at equal height, in the course of the night. To see eye to eye, he would mount the mule and she would sit in the bottom of the box seat when the wagon was at rest.

When she passed Aballay a bowl or a spoon, disquiet would overcome him. In his hand, the spoon represented ease, and that was when he asked himself if he was truly doing penance.

He called it *living freely* and knew that was like *living on handouts*, but he also suspected it was living in vain.

He thought once of going to find the priest or another older, learned man he could depend on for advice.

As though from the darkness, an answer to his doubts, something like a justification, emerged: living to pay down a debt was not living in vain.

They might have calmed him down, these thoughts, if the boy's face hadn't cut in every time. There was no making peace with the boy!

Aballay disappears for two days.

When he returns, there's a bundle on top of the mule. It might not mean anything; but the woman attributes something, still uncertain, to its presence.

If Aballay entrusts her with it, as he is doing, it could be seen as compensation for his part of the costs of travel. That's not what she thinks, even less when she unties the bundle and finds: bacon, gin, salt, biscuit… and besides that a roll of percale, perfume, a kerchief…

Something in the driver goes weak.

Now she almost understands… Maybe it's not a present for them. Aballay is leaving, and he's paying up; no, not paying, atoning.

She can almost understand it, seeing it this way, though Aballay has yet to explain anything.

He won't tell her he gave up his silver *patacón*, the one from the slit in his belt, held onto for a special occasion. Or for a moment of great need (to do what he's done, for example).

Just as the wagon and the driver vanished, the winter vanished, the years vanish.

The bronco died, and the sorrel horse and the mule. He always managed to replace them, never with anything better. At best with a stray; at worst, with a tame one. On the lookout for the latter, he would lasso loose animals that didn't have a brand, looking for the old ones, which were said to be more sedate. He needed a favorite one to ride, and then an alternate. For a while he got along with a donkey for the second. All he needed was an animal he could sit on. He never got hold of a seat, blanket, or packsaddle.

Suspected of cattle rustling, more than once, he caught an officer's eye.

Aballay and his animals were dragged down to the barracks.

The soldier told him, "Get down, the chief wants to see you."

Though Aballay had courage enough not to obey, it didn't suffice to utter the humble words that formed in his mind: *If he wants to see me, he'll have to come out.*

He bore the man's tone, with his anger, with the filthy words. He reckoned on receiving a few blows and jerks, but the soldier decided to give him another chance:

"You've got to go in, let's do it the nice way."

"Long as I can go in mounted, I'll do so."

"Oh, it's you, the crazy one...!" The man in uniforms recognized and mocked him, but without daring to go further.

He went to get the commissioner to arbitrate in the dispute. He came back out, no less imperious after being thwarted, and acted as though addressing an absent third party:

"By order of my superior, the accused, Aballay, must appear, no discussion."

Though he did feel compelled to add, in a different tone: "Go on in, you've got to have it out with the boss. But pass through the yard; you can enter with your horse."

The commissioner, to keep from putting himself on a lower footing than the subject under investigation, pretended he was about to leave, and mounted his own horse. Only then, as though graciously deciding to take the matter in hand, called out: "Let's get it over with! Tell me, Aballay, what kind of nonsense you've gotten up to..."

But he was indulgent. He knew (or thought he knew) who it was he had before him.

⌒

After a period of wandering, he came across a group of horsemen.

There were three of them, and they looked like trouble. They had a similar suspicion about him (though the crucifix around his neck could throw them off), but something seemed to change their minds.

"You looking for work?"

"Depends…"

They were rounding up laborers. Two were farmhands and one was their overseer. They were setting up a ranch for a landholder and gathering men to clear the terrain.

Aballay said no, it wasn't for him.

"Stuck-up gaucho," one hissed, aggressively.

Again? Aballay asked himself, unable to keep the fury from filling his eyes. The one who'd badmouthed him held his stare, and pranced past him on his horse to underscore the provocation.

The foreman had no time for this pointless squabble. He called the man over: "Pereira!" and chided Aballay:

"Who are you anyway?"

Aballay responded: "A poor man," as if his words were faintly crumbling. He looked straight at him, and there was no longer ire or pride in his face.

Then the storied wooden cross and the features of the itinerant rider made sense to him. Respectfully, he brought his hand to his hat and uncovered his head.

And Aballay knew, at long last, that he'd returned to the hospitable territory the wagon led him away from.

⌒

There were other times when he ran into people on foot. *Poorer than I…* he concluded.

A day could pass without him seeing a single person, and maybe the same was true for the stranger; but when they passed, it was rare they'd say anything beyond:

"Hello…"

"… take care, my friend."

And each would proceed on his way, lost in himself, closed off in that wide-open (and lonesome) world.

He could tell you about the exodus – who knows where they thought they could earn their bread – of families that had nothing but their children. Dusty troupes, with the father at the head, and the kids bringing up the rear; one, maybe still nursing, under cover of the ample shawl of the mother, who was usually dressed in black. The most sprightly, if he wasn't weary from starvation, was the dog.

"Hello…"

"… take care, Sir."

What stood out was their respectfulness, and not just because they called Aballay sir. One man saw him on horseback, and got up from the ledge where he'd been resting. He took his hat in his hand and knocked off the dust against his leg.

"You know me?"

"I've heard mention, Sir."

Aballay left him standing there and thought. The rambler was the type who'd gone downhill till he had nothing left, not even his faith in himself. It occurred to Aballay they could make the journey together, and that a man condemned to the ground and a man who couldn't touch the earth could do a lot for one another. Aballay told himself that traveling with a partner would entail chitchat, and he wasn't much of a talker. And he proved this later when he left, without revealing these notions of companionship.

In the distance was the outline of what looked like a man in a black soutane, with a poncho that hung down to his feet. He was gesturing, calling for him to hurry over, but Aballay didn't feel pressed.

He waved a long stick to prove his point, and was brash about commandeering the other horse, which to his eyes was going to waste.

Aballay endured his parley, noted his envy, guessed at his dexterity with the stick. He told him he had no interest in an ally, and this exasperated the man, and when Aballay saw this, he decided to leave without adding another word.

The rogue swung his weapon, trying to knock off the horseman's head, but he ducked down and saved himself, and drove his horses nimbly onward.

"God be with you then!" the feeble bandit fumed, in the purest of language. "Go on then, God be with you!"

"That's what I'm hoping for," Aballay consoled himself.

⌒

At a later stage, his health deteriorates. He doesn't hide it, nor does he make it known.

The smallholders, the women, do what they can for him: an herbal tea, some chicken broth, warm goat's milk… They don't dare give him medicine: a man in his state should be in bed, they think, but this man, no.

Nor do they dare say a prayer for him. They take it for granted that Aballay's departures are filled with supplication.

But it's not so, not the way those women imagine it. Aballay does pray, in his own way, and not for the restoration of his health. He's always done it the same way. His prayer is like a thought, which continues after the doctrinal phrases are uttered. He has never used prayer as an occasion for complaint.

Today, racked with fever, when he's huddled in a gulley, shivering from cold, he notices, as night draws close, the majestic painting in the sky. It fills his spirit and inspires the urge to do what has never occurred to him before: to pray on his knees, without breaking his vow, without crouching down on the earth; kneeling on his horse.

He tries, with devotion, with vehemence, with tenacity, but he can't do it; he's risking a nasty fall.

He presses his legs desperately into the animal's body, trying to keep from slipping, to confront the infinity of shadows swallowing him.

He dreams of the petals of peach blossoms.

He dreams he is interpreting his dream: that must be my succor, time in the sun, for the flower opens in spring.

One day, seeing a peach tree with blossoms bursting on all its branches, he remembers that dream with relish, and sees the certainty of his prophecy.

~~

A woman asks him to save her son.

Aballay doesn't understand. Should he help her take him to a place where there are doctors?

No. He should bless him, and the boy will get better.

Aballay is startled by this reputed power; they are confusing him with a saint.

It hurts him then, when he says: "If I could..."

~~

The old man, draped in a white poncho, vexed him.

From among all the pillars of the roofless temples, he had climbed the broken column nearest to his own.

He brought with him an odious silence, very different from the one practiced by Aballay, because for Aballay, keeping quiet was a custom and not ostentation.

The old man showed up with a combative silence, as though determined to make Aballay leave.

Aballay felt watched, and though he didn't affect to be better than anyone else, he didn't give in, and he watched over his neighbor.

He noticed if the old man descended more than was allowed, and he noticed as though nourishing his spite.

If he suffered from the rain or cold, he resisted, and looked to see if his rival was weakening.

If the hail fell, he counted not how much struck his own head, but how much pounded the other.

His behavior was churlish, he had to admit it, but he ascribed it to the other's ill-spirited vigilance.

In any case, each passed his time eager to see who would fall first.

They remained attentive to the signs: if one slumped to the side when sleeping, if the sun made the other woozy, or if he had an attack of chills.

Maybe that white poncho is bringing him favor, making him look like a saint… Aballay adduced reasons to scorn the old man's advantage in the offerings piled up at the base of the column.

A hundred years' rivalry passed before they reached their deaths. The power of expression left them both in the same instant, and little by little, they dried out. Then they crumbled like two old loaves of bread.

This nocturnal fantasy left its mark on the rider: it carved deep furrows of acrimony and melancholy inside him.

⌐

He always thinks of the mestizo boy who pinned him with his gaze.

Years pass. One day, he catches sight of that gaze.

He knows that the boy, now a man, has come to collect.

He has followed him, the boy. He catches him in the canebrakes.

He could be a young saint on his stately horse. His eyes are impassive, but decided. Like Aballay, he is dressed in rags.

He tells him:

"I've been looking for you."

"A long time…?"

"My whole life, since I grew up."

He doesn't ask, he tells him:

"You knew my father."

It would be pointless to ask him who he is, and who his father was.

He tells him:

"Get down on the ground, Sir."

Aballay decides that this isn't reason enough either. And it seems to him he shouldn't reveal why: it would look like he was dissembling his fear.

As his reflections make him waver, the other goads him:

"Sir, I've come here to fight you."

Aballay makes a serene gesture, showing his agreement, and the young man continues:

"I know you're said to never come down from your horse. I'll have to knock you off. I was just offering you the chance to face me man-to-man on solid ground. If you don't want that, we'll do it your way."

Slowly the man unsheathes his *facón*, the knife draped across his back, as long as the quest he's just brought to an end.

Agile and rapid, Aballay lurches forward and sharp-eyed, energetic, determined, he cuts a stiff, thick stalk of cane more than a yard in length. He takes his position, holding it cocked like a lance, his triangular knife blade tucked back in his belt.

His opponent is startled:

"You don't have a decent knife…? You're not even going to use the one you've got?"

But Aballay utters no more words, he waits.

He doesn't wish to kill, but he'll defend himself.

They fight. He whips the man with the cane; the wounds are superficial. He tries to strike the hand that holds the weapon, so he'll drop it. His contender rushes past him, swiping in arcs that hit and sting. He turns and swings with two hands, trying to split his face open. Aballay sidesteps him and his facón hits the cane, cutting it into a perfect point. Aballay instinctively holds still and doesn't buckle. When the boy stumbles, the unintentionally sharpened tip plunges into his mouth, ruining it. The man slips, gasping futilely at the reins for support.

From above, Aballay studies him for a second. He has failed and done the thing he hoped to avoid: killing a second time. The profuse blood, drowning the man's wails and muffling his bellows, provokes his compassion and nausea.

He dismounts to help him, and makes it over to the vanquished man, but then, his law makes him stop short: he is not to set foot on the ground, and he has done so.

In anguish, he looks up, and resolves on his own that this time, he may stay down as long as necessary.

This moment of vacillation lasts long enough for the avenger, from below, to raise the tip of his knife and slit Aballay's belly.

Aballay falls, his forces drain quickly, and the first thing to abandon him is the suffering from the wound.

He sees that his body will remain bound to the earth forever now. His thoughts blurred, he babbles excuses: "Under the duress of a greater force, it has…"

Aballay is dying, stretched out in the dust, with a pained smile on his lips.

Fish

For Lumila, the whispers of the night recoil, then disappear. They make a hollow in her mind, and she falls asleep. No matter how tenaciously they catch on the underbrush, exhale like sighs, or screech, or mimic lamentations or danger.

She sleeps beneath the night, Lumila, a slight and fragile rest. It breaks, and her eyes open wide at the behest of what comes from within her: a presentiment. Her man won't come back. So long an absence is suspect.

She won't sleep more until she sees him; she is dying to see him, even if he shows up unwell... or in pieces. She shrinks from this last thought, and huddles: let him return, from that faraway roadhouse in the country, even with a few cuts on his face or body.

All the silence – which is not silence, but murmurs clotting in her consciousness, because the sounds she longs to hear don't come – gathers together into a ball that lodges in her stomach.

She wants to cry, now more than ever, but she stops, careful to listen, because any sound of horsemen, even in the distance, consoles her. She doesn't need to guess at the nature of the sounds, she deciphers them effortlessly, those of the birds and the pests and the air. She tries to sweep them away, to let through only what she longs to hear. She tries to recover pleasing memories, ones they have in common, to distract herself, and remembers that other horror from her childhood: the enormous bird with the fish's body.

"With no legs," her husband likes to add, and he assures her he's seen it.

"So how does it perch?" she's always asked, hoping the monster is a lie.

"It perches on the water."

"There's no water here."

"There used to be, as much as there is in the sea."

"But you weren't born then, Gabriel..."

Cornered, because he's never made clear whether he saw the bird, dreamed it, or has described it from secondhand accounts, the man argues back:

"It nestles down in the smooth sand, all this that used to be at the bottom of all that water."

Lumila's trained ear perhaps couldn't distinguish the hoofbeats of the returning horses, muffled in the shelf of sand, were it not that the irons click constantly against the shells of mollusks, which cover with bluish white those vast extensions of what they say was once sea, where that couple has settled in poverty.

The horse stops. Lumila's points of reference dwindle, and time passes. Did he come alone...? Has Gabriel been injured...? She waits, chewing the edge of the sheet. Lumila can't go out to look with her own eyes, she's bound to the bed.

The animal gives a cautious whinny, which confuses Lumila's impressions: it seems to be trying to alert those inside, or else it feels alone, and wants to call those familiar to it; fortunately, it appears to have roused the person riding, letting know he's reached his destination.

Then comes the rugged sound of a falling bundle (or a dead body hitting the ground). For Lumila, the wait continues, but now more desperately. Because she imagines they've killed the man, laid him across the saddle, and let the beast loose, sure it will make its way home.

Still, she is intrigued, because she can't investigate with her own eyes.

Later, after various preliminary sounds, the master of the house, looking devastated, fills the doorframe, his face clouded before the serene shimmer of the candle.

From Lumila comes a rabid, solaced cry and a feeling crashes over her, making her complain – a vapor of alcohol has invaded the room: "It stinks...!"

The man crawls toward the bed, climbs in as best he can, grabbing the iron arches of the bedstead, nearly crushes the passive woman as he reclines, and without further preparations, sleep shoots him down.

～～

Lumila wakes up with a thirst eased by what's left of the water in the bowl. She'd like more, but she won't ask for it from the man sleeping so serenely, so silently, by her side.

Dark velvet butterflies whirl around Lumila and finally cover her eyes, delivering her to a peaceful nothingness.

Once more, her thirst expels her from its domains. But it's dawn now, and she craves yerba mate and nourishment as well, because Gabriel missed dinner yesterday and naturally, impeded as she is, she can't prepare it alone.

This thought – that he was missing – intimates to her that something different is happening now. It's strange for the sun to rise without his warm, aromatic mate greeting her, because even if he does stray at times, she has to admit he's trustworthy, hardworking, and compassionate with her, and alone, she can barely get along.

Now she remembers everything, and she examines him with a protracted stare and a jealous and wary soul. He's still dressed, curled up, on top of the covers. And now that she can see him better, she notices his left hand almost suspended in the air, half-resting on his chest, the fingers curved, as if where the heart lies, an ember was burning, and he was making ready to dig it out.

Then Lumila understands.

⌒

She has swallowed her grief, which ran untrammeled for hours, and her tears have lessened the dryness in her mouth.

With the coming of day, all that is living in the land has been reborn.

The bleating, without losing its inherent humility, begs insistently for the freedom the warped fence posts of the corral negate, blocking any trot toward the scant grass and tender straw that serve as sustenance for the meager flock.

The hens and rooster have turned to their routine, rooting with their beaks for bugs to peck and roots to shred.

The dogs loaf around, without a flock to drive to the open field.

The horse, tied neither to the fence or the hitching rail, has dared to dig into his portion of fodder in the lean-to, weighed down only by the now-useless saddle and the reins that drag the ground and get caught in his legs if he steps on them.

The morning thrives, and that moment of general contentment arrives, as if every living thing obeyed the magic of that star with its burning eye above all, which stops, for a moment, motionless and vigilant.

The goats have softened their moaning.

The silence abounds and inundates the farm.

Lumila's plaints and hiccups cease. She yields.

And there the two of them are, on the bed, one utterly dead, the other with half her appendages possessed by death.

⌒

Lumila has ignored her most intimate necessities, which now manifest themselves, impatient and exacting after so much procrastination.

She knows she will be faced with an extraordinary effort, because she relies on her husband even for that, and now she'll have to do it alone.

She gets ready to climb down from the bed. She leans on her left arm and tries to follow suit with her left leg. But it doesn't obey.

She tries again and fails.

Her left leg defies her, just as long ago, up to the present, and perhaps forever, she lost control of her arm and leg on the right side of her body.

She curses and then flinches, less from her state than from having uttered profane words.

She asks herself if she's dying bit by bit and looks at her hand, which is still useful, imagining the moment when it will fail her.

Between so much sorrow and dread, she wets herself, and is ashamed as if it were the first time. She makes excuses, upbraids herself; she whines, and seems to try to explain that she wanted, was trying, to go relieve herself in the proper place:

It's because I'm so clean that this happens to me...

She reacts, called upon by the need for sudden, immediate change, for an end to the suffering of near-total paralysis that has afflicted her unexpectedly. She lifts her head, tilted to the side, to read the prayer cards lying on the nightstand, and, panting fervently, she prays and beseeches, prays and beseeches, begs... "A miracle, Lord, restore my Gabriel to me."

She gazes intensely at her pale, prostrate husband, with trepidation, should what she has sought suddenly occur. As she waits, Lumila asks herself in what way life will return to him: through his flesh, or through his understanding... If his eyes will open first (they have remained closed through her plight, perhaps because he perished in his sleep). Or will he manifest himself in words, and if so, what mysteries will he reveal? And will he suffer on returning...

Nightfall.

Her necessities torment her, tearing her up inside. The heat won't die down. She is sweating from the sultry air and her valiant attempts to free herself from the bed.

It must be fear… Fear of the dead, even if he's my man. Fear kills, and it killed my one good leg.

She needs to see something living near her, in her vicinity. She calls the dogs:

"Trusty, Lion, Bingo…"

There's no need to continue: "Whitey, Patches, Ginger…"

All six of them are already there, shaking off the dust from a long nap in the yard or under the eaves. *They must be hungry*, Lumila thinks, and continues: *Same as me.*

But contrary to custom, and despite their aplomb, they don't go beyond the door, not even Whitey, so affectionate she usually jumps up on the pillow without permission.

The hounds' reticence leads Ludmila to another intimation: it is not Gabriel, but a dead man who is now on the farm, and if his presence disconcerts even the dogs, what sort of night awaits her…? How will she bear the darkness with a cadaver in her bed…?

The urge to light the candle overcomes her, regardless how much strength it takes. She talks to her working hand as if it were a friend, begging it not to collapse, to save her, not to leave her in the blackness… Nervousness makes her waste matches and energy until, in the end, a flame rises up. Lumila says her thanks, and when she sees the images around her once again, in the light, she decides to request another miracle. It already seems to her she's asked for too much, and she's afraid of causing offense and incurring punishment. *He was my husband*, she thinks by way of justification. *He was good with me, even if he was a nobody to all the rest. Poor little Gabriel, he never got any credit.*

The temptation to pray for her son to return presses in on her. He's gone to the city, to the factories. She could say in her prayer: *My son, Lord, Gabriel's and my boy, born in wedlock, baptized and everything...* She falls short, not daring to begin again: *It would be a lot to ask, too much of a miracle...* And she burrows into her thoughts: *It could be he'll come back on his own... that he'll sense my call.* She asks herself what he must be like now, after ten years. If he'll remember her, if he'll know somehow his father's not alive. And she concludes that if his father's died, then he's a spirit now, and a spirit can speak with the living, and maybe Gabriel's spirit will let their son know that she's alone and she needs him desperately... Could he...?

⌒

Despite what she'd imagined, the night doesn't add to her terror.

In a certain way, the shadows shelter her, extending her the mercy of obscuring what lies by her side. She has a sense of it, there's no escaping that; but she doesn't feel it, or else she already feels it, or wants to, as something alien, which she resists touching.

But then she recalls, like a dereliction, that she hasn't given him a kiss goodbye on the forehead. She forgoes it, speaking to someone who isn't him:

"There will be time. He's still here, he hasn't left."

She defends herself to him now:

"I can't move, I can't reach your forehead. I don't even have water, you know, and I'm dying of thirst..."

Then she moves on to more immediate worries. She needs to drink, she needs to eat. She needs help from beyond but must resign herself to smaller miracles than those she's been beseeching, and she solicits them abundantly, by the handful: for Don Casimir to look in, or for the offal vendor to pity her. For Inés to help her out, to think to stop in. For the patrol to make its rounds. For the mad dentist to come. For someone to come… someone…

But, for now, no one comes. There's no lack of possibilities: Don Casimir, the lacemaker, the travelling salesman and lovestruck Arab, only comes to those parts every few months, and irregularly. (Reborn in Lumila, like a picture, is the memory of that finespun lace she could never afford.) The offal vendor won't forgive their debt, and once a week, they hear him blowing his horn – that's how they know it's Tuesday – but always from far away. (From the cane lattice in the hallway, the wire mesh basket for the meat hangs empty.) Inés only takes the road when she's headed to the village, because she's heard the Health Department trailers with the doctor are finally passing through. As for the police patrol, they only bother to go past the farms where the chief can get a bite and wet his whistle and even then, it's best if they get a suckling pig on their way out the door. And the dentist, with his hardtop Ford and his treadle drill thrown in the back… He insists on taking the ramshackle roads and never notices the shacks he drives past, unless someone comes out from to wave him down or chases him on horseback until his car gets stuck in a patch of brush. Lumila, in her long white smock, hands immaculate, gaze fanatical, evokes him, saying, "He's so kind, but so mad…" over and over until she comes back to herself, says, "My soul, so alone…" and flounders in her helplessness, which nothing can relieve.

Sleep overtakes her, and she dreams she's a little girl walking barefoot over the sand, looking for seashells, and the sea licks her feet and covers them in foam and Gabriel is courting her and she refuses him because she's thirsty and her lips are loath to kiss, they covet the water, and she doesn't want Gabriel because he… has died.

She awakens. It's true: he's dead, long dead, cheek by jowl with her. She screams. She needs to scream.

From the yard, the dogs hear her, and they follow her lead, imitating her with rending howls.

Save for one. He slips off, humbly, to the bedroom and lies down at Lumila's feet. It's Trusty.

Lumila is laid low by tenderness and cries sweet tears.

But later, drained, she slips once more into sleep, and she dreams of the lake or sea that was, and there's a storm that batters the canoes woven from rushes of the fishermen throwing their nets, and the bird with the huge wings and the body of a fish breaks into her room on the farm with a caw and a clamor.

She awakens. No wings are flapping. No rare bird profanes the sad, secluded space where Lumila's angst abates, because nothing's happening, perhaps, save in her nightmares, or because Trusty is guarding her, so devoted.

Devoted, that's what we should have called you, she thinks, and pronounces the new name with a tender tone.

She foresees the coming day. As she sleeps, the daydreams and desires pile up, and in them, her home is flooded with people who care for her in her mourning, and no doubt they will manage to furnish a grave to the deceased. But no one slakes her thirst.

⌒

When it's time to pasture the goats, she grieves for the flock, which has no way to get out and graze, and is left with the dry boards in the trough... At the same time, she covets the milk in the nanny goat's udders, which could give her drink and nourishment.

She endures the dawn and the sorrowful bleating. She lives with, or tries to ignore, her obligatory companion in the bed, because – she comforts herself – it's better not to witness what is happening on her husband's skin.

She forces her senses and her imagination to abide. At odd seconds, she hears the little bell of Don Casimir, the lacemaker; other times, she's dazzled by a glimmer of sun on the curved tin roof of the offal vendor's cart as he comes around the corner toward their home…

None of this happens. No one comes.

The Zonda does come, the cruel wind, hot and dusty, unliable to human will.

It drones, dances, whips, hurls its winds dense with soot and sand, crushes blossom and branch. In the immensity, it sets to shaking the scattered houses of the families that tend the goats, so far each from the other that even in adversity they find no strength in unity. It invades them, ripping off their roofs.

At Lumila's, it is worse. The bedroom door has been open since Gabriel's return. She can't close it.

Brutally, the wind chokes her with dirt and hurls her about while shattering the flimsy furnishings, the full-length mirror, the tranquil treasures for ornament or devotion in their wonted place on the top of the dresser.

The door lurches on its hinges till it comes loose. The window struggles not to splinter.

Lumila hides under the blanket, chokes, uncovers herself, and covers back up. She repeats the process over and over.

The reprobate is known for visiting his infamies on them for twenty-four hours without reprieve. This memory brings the woman to the outer edge of desperation.

But this time, after midday, its furor wanes, and little by little, it sees fit to let the air be breathable again.

Lumila emerges in a mask of earth furrowed by tears. She contemplates the disaster; she imagines the devastation, perhaps the deaths, among her animals; she asks herself if that loud noise in the morning wasn't the shed being torn away... and she tries not to look at the man.

She can't help it.

The chaos of the wind has knocked him from the bed. Lumila already sensed it some time ago. There was missing weight, a missing form by her side. But she didn't hear the noise, it was covered by the rumbling of the air.

She doesn't dare admit that she's relieved. She no longer has him attached to her, she won't see him unless she bends over and looks in that direction.

And yet, in another way, his presence lingers:

"It stinks!" Lumila sniffs with disgust.

It stinks. The burning heat of the Zonda has sped up the decomposition of the corpse.

The woman is bitter, and creaks with impotence. But she takes care, from respect for the dead, not to inveigh against *that man*.

⌒

Famine makes the packs of dogs split up. They run off into the mountains to resume their ancient calling of hunting for food. Only two stay behind: Trusty and Whitey.

Ginger and Bingo, fast friends and allies, drift quickly from the uncertain gain of the scrubland to human territory, knowing that where there are people, there's extra food, at least at times.

They sidle up to the farms they came to on occasion with their master; but the others of their species are hostile, and chase them off.

When they catch sight of Inés's home, her house dogs face off with the invaders, but the dustup is nothing more than a bit of snipping, because the owner recognizes the visitors and obeys the code of country hospitality. He brings peace and lets them in, convinced that his friend, Don Gabriel, must be wandering nearby, maybe rounding up stray goats, and that he'll bring up the rear soon enough.

Inés has observed her husband's actions, asks him why, he states his reasons and she respects them, though she doesn't share them. For a moment, she suspects something strange is happening at Lumila's. But she won't talk for now. She tells herself she'll do it later, when her husband figures out he's erred on his own. Not to be sneaky, just to keep from bucking his authority.

⌒

Not the next day, but the one after, Trusty, now the only pet worth mentioning that has remained close to its owners, even after jumping over the fence, plagued with hunger, and getting rammed by the billy goat, walks with a disturbing restlessness. Only briefly does he return to the master bedroom.

He curls up now in the nook his bones have hollowed out in the floor of the room, and the disordered voice of the woman, halting, so close to his ears, disturbs him.

Lumila, at the extreme of weariness, no longer knows heaven from earth, and begs for another miracle: for the use of her disabled leg to return – not the other, she no longer asks for that, she's already given that one up for lost, but the one that gave out on her first day as a widow.

She decides an old man will come to see her, that the old man will grant her what she has wished for.

She imagines his face, radiant like rays of sun, with the pure beauty of light blue eyes.

She opens her own, to see him.

At that moment, from one side of the roof, a dark creature with broad wings breaks away.

A current of fear runs through the woman's chest, formed of all she's heard about the bird with the fish's body. But as her mind is not wayward and she regains her lucidity, she hurries to apprehend this first moment in her life when she will meet the legendary monster.

The spell breaks. She thinks: *If it was him, he's shrunken terribly.* And her gut tells her that one, at least, was nothing more than a bat.

The winging of the dark *dog of the air* upsets the dog on the ground, while Lumila picks up the thread of her appeal for miracles, and confused now, unsure whether she has received the benediction or not, she tries to use her left leg.

It obeys her.

Her eyelids fall half closed, and behind them a wave of benevolent peace descends.

She proceeds as cautiously as she can, employs all the forethought left to her, to try to move again, and this second attempt bears fruit.

Then she's possessed by the impulse to run, to make it however possible to a place where liquid can sate her. With the half of her body that functions, she works to free herself from the high bed, hoping to walk, or roll, or drag herself to the well, for when she gets there, she'll know how to lower the bucket to the water.

But from the sudden effort, or from her dreadful physical condition, she staggers, falls, and cuts herself on a piece of the broken mirror.

She sees the opportunity escape her, and she faints, lying supine on the ground.

Emptiness intertwines with half-thoughts, among them, that someone is kissing her wounds, and the feeling of the kiss horrifies her, regardless of who it comes from.

Her weakened senses stir and she finds her dog passing its hot tongue over her wound. Then her impressions change, she feels secure, and she smiles. She's sapped and remains on her back. She's resting now, and she says to him, with affection and gratitude:

"You're my dog, and your name is Trusty. It's a good name, I always knew that."

But the avidity with which he licks her bleeding flesh, opened by a sliver of mirror, alarms her. She finds herself opposite a maw, a pair of eyes, that force her to grovel and shout:

"Trusty, you're the one I rely on... don't fail me."

But the redoubtable canine's glare grows savage.

"Don't hurt me, Trusty!"

She says it in terror. Meek, as though kneeling.

Obstinate Observer

Rubén, aged seven, returns from school at lunchtime. He eats and disappears. He ignores the order to take a nap and the summons to play with the boys from the neighborhood.

He plants himself a block from home, alone. Sitting on the sidewalk, on the edge of the ditch, he stares, long and intently, at the building before him, on the other side of the street.

It's a one-story home, squat and decrepit. No one enters or leaves through its doors, no ladies peek through the windows, there are no cages with darting canaries. It's sat vacant a long time.

It offers nothing especially distinct, squeezed between the grocer and the tailor's shop. The façade is unfaded, of a light, celestial blue, and Rubén likes the color, though it is not the cause of his coming here.

In mid-afternoon, he leaves his watch for a mug of milk and homemade pancakes. Not too clear on the duration of his absence, his mother complains: "Where were you?" But what absorbs her are the vicissitudes of her demigods on the radio play.

Rubén repeats his escapade, his abstract contemplation, day after day.

"Where'd you go off to, lazybones? What time are you going to do your homework?"

Later, the boy senses that the situation could get worse: his mother shoves the problem off on his father; his father talks about conduct and issues vague threats.

It's not rebellion that makes Rubén stretch out the hours: he's held there as though captive before the mute wall on the other block, until the crepuscule clears away the powder blue of day. He suffers, in succession, censure, shouts, and slaps; then he gets them all at once, or in a jumble.

One morning, he senses he can't take his route to school, but must instead turn toward his observation post. He takes up his place on the sidewalk pavers and sets down his unused notebooks beside him, along with his school supplies, his spinning top. He watches, unguarded, but expectant; he knows he has to wait.

A neighbor lady notices him and shakes her head on her way to the grocer.

A schoolmate, one from the afternoon class, stops on his way to buy bread and asks him:

"Did you go to school?"

Rubén lies brashly, to run him off, because he prefers to tend to this matter on his own.

"Yeah, I went, but they kicked me out."

He leaves the meddler stupefied and abashed before a delinquent of the kind that could merit such a punishment.

Rubén ignores him.

Around eleven in the morning, while the people wander past indifferently, he discovers, on the front wall of the house that draws him there, a crack opening noiselessly, like a black bolt of lightning hurtling downward. A rumbling begins, and behind the wall, raining down amid the scudding dust, the beams tear loose then disappear, along with the panels of corrugated zinc: the roof has caved in.

While the pedestrians shout and flee, Rubén takes a step back, in dread, but without averting his eyes.

Then the sky-blue wall collapses and the catastrophe comes to an end.

⌐

Rubén, now nine, can't follow his history lesson.

In other subjects, his grades are satisfactory. Not in this one. Not that he dislikes it: to the contrary, the heroes and their exploits excite him, but, being passive and ill-inclined to any strenuous activity, he never dreams of being like them.

He doesn't get distracted on purpose; but there's something forceful in that teacher's allure. Not what she teaches, not what she says, but her, simply her. It doesn't happen with the other ladies who instruct him. Just with this one, who lacks any special charms beyond her head of hair, and isn't even nice to him. Her severity and sternness don't bother him since he's given up being a good student.

As soon as she enters the classroom, Rubén is filled with doubts. Something demands he remain anxious, vigilant, throughout the forty-five minutes. Why? Is he afraid of her? No. Something outside her upsets him. What?

Every day, he yearns for class to end, for the year to come soon to a close, for the cold to lift, at least.

When he returns from recess, if she doesn't show immediately, he clings to the hope that she won't: that she's sick, that they've hired another teacher in her place... Her appearance portends another forty-five minutes of agony. Even if nothing happens.

Lately, he feels the tension rise when she moves to a certain corner of the room, explaining the day's chapter or quizzing one of his classmates.

He asks himself why she ends up there. Why? For what?

What is there in that place...? It must be that it's the intimate corner, with no doors to let the chill filter in, whether badly shut or flung open at odd moments, or for any other reason; because there is the stove radiating its heat, warming them all up, more or less. Rubén understands. Nonetheless...

Today the teacher has unfolded maps over the blackboard. She shows them the routes of the armies in the mountains. On the far right, the point closest to the cozy corner of the room, she shows something on one of the posters. She stands there in her white smock, holding a long pointer that glides over the brown, blotchy illustrations; she stands there, making reference to something, something Rubén can't grasp because his mind is beset, he doesn't know by what; but whatever it is, he feels it's about to explode.

Then a long flame shoots up behind the instructor. It's her white smock, which has brushed the stove and caught fire. There are tears and cries of fear, and the terrified teacher flees to the schoolyard while the flames grow, fed by the air, spreading to her clothes and now to the long mane of hair falling over her back.

⌐⌐

Rubén, aged seventeen, questions himself.

Friends his age, his fellow students, boast of their flair for courtship, or else fall seriously and demurely in love. He hasn't, not yet.

There's a girl he finds charming, the daughter of a soldier, who has come to live in the neighborhood; his attitude toward her is contemplative, not heated. Indecisive, his attraction shifts between her and one from the teacher's college who has danced with him on the occasional Saturday at the high school parties.

He doesn't believe he's in love: neither inspires that rapture or tenderness he imagines is borne of of true infatuation.

This doesn't particularly sadden him, because of his placid nature, unenterprising, unenergetic, or his habit of waiting, in thrall to vague intuitions, for things, finally, to happen.

But with a certain woman, his behavior dismays him – and consequently, he upbraids himself. She's barely more than a girl, beaming, simple, with a pleasant face, even a pretty one, it could be said. She's tired, she's pregnant. She's the wife of an electrician, not much older than she, and they live nearby, so he runs into her often.

Rubén doesn't recognize in himself any feeling that he could call love. He respects her, and his principles, which he examines with thorough anxiousness, would forestall the least attempt to get something from her, to expect something.

But why is it, lately, when she goes to the square, to sit in the sun and knits things for her baby in the offing, that he chooses to take a walk along that very path?

Inevitably, he blushes when they exchange a timid greeting, from afar, though the girl shows no sign of discomfort or suspicion.

Rubén wonders whether he shouldn't fear – as happened before, especially when he was a boy – that what he senses, indistinctly, is the presentment of disaster.

He doesn't give in to his incomprehension, nor does he manage to perceive any message he could pass along to the woman or her husband to keep them safe, if danger is looming. They would think him ridiculous.

Today he has left home without remembering her, without a single thought that alludes to her. But then he sees her on the corner and feels he shouldn't go on downtown, as he had planned. He stops.

She's waiting for a bus, she is in the right place. He will follow suit. He greets her with a smile, barely nodding. She responds with the same delicacy, and Rubén can see she favors him. He finds the moment touching.

A bus pulls forward. He doubts she will step forward rashly. She doesn't.

Once she's in the bus, a man politely offers her his seat, deferent before her evident pregnancy. Rubén stands up, grasps the rail while the passengers press in on him, and curses himself for obeying his destiny.

Suddenly, the young lady bursts into worrisome cries, saying something like *Oh my God, help me!* and he understands, now the dread has passed, the baby will be born in the bus. This is neither exceptionally untoward or strange, you see it in lots of cities... The passengers can help (they already are), and he will call for an ambulance and medical assistance and alert her husband and tell him to run, to run... and that everything will be all right.

That is why – he discovers, pleased that this time, it's been to do good – he had to be there.

⌒

Against custom, Rubén leaves his office just past 6:30 in the evening: he is distracted by the burning city streets, and glad that the sun still shines golden above it, it's summer and the shop doesn't close till eight.

Nonetheless, he recalls, he has not gone out for recreation. For what, then? There's no mystery, inside him or out. All he wants is to return home. Why, if his home will be empty? At that hour, the maid has left; his daughter will be out shopping, his son-in-law still at the office...

Well, that is why he's returning at this instant: to be alone, in his widower's solitude, for an hour or two, until his daughter shows up to start dinner.

The neighborhood seems changed, more animated, he notices. Ordinarily, he doesn't pass through until close to nine, when the little shops and garages in that residential zone have lowered the rolling blinds and turned off their neon signs.

Where he turns onto the block, the Fiat and Volkswagen workshops are humming. He sees, tied to a tree in the courtyard, visible from the street through the gate, the source of the persistent barking he's heard through his bedroom window for days now. It's the first chance he's had to lay eyes on the guard dog, he must be new at the job.

He's a yellow dog, of medium height, and when he sees Rubén making his way slowly up the sidewalk, he stops his barking and commotion and stares at him raptly, at him alone, with mournful eyes.

Rubén watches calmly, lamenting the situation of that sensitive animal bound by a chain.

He can't shake the impression. He knows it's only natural, given his condition, that the dog has a certain mournfulness in his eyes. Yet he feels that stare has been prepared for him.

Back at home, he looks toward the roof to see if there is a flag there. *A flag...?* he wonders. *Why am I looking up there for a flag or some fluttering fabric?* He is perplexed, and he goes on questioning himself. What color then...? Should it be dark? After a slight hesitation: *Why am I asking myself about the color of a flag that isn't there, that doesn't exist...?*

He puts the matter aside, choosing to leave it in the street no sooner than he enters his home.

He can have his solitude as he wished, free from the voices of others, free from upsets, without any thought in particular.

They eat dinner, the three of them.

His daughter leaves afterward to clean up the kitchen, and the men move to the living room, where the television is.

"Papa, do you want a coffee? Want me to make it...?"

"No, honey, thanks. It keeps me up, and I want to sleep tonight."

But when he retires, though the night is calm, rest refuses him its sanctuary.

He recalls the yellow dog, perhaps because he doesn't hear it. He, at least, must have gotten some sleep.

Around one – the cuckoo in the dining room has just announced the hour – Rubén turns in the sheets, cross at his sleeplessness.

Just then, he comprehends, without impatience, without bother, that he has to wait until five. To wait... for what?

He resigns himself to ignoring the question, to waiting. He spends the remaining time shuffling through his memories, ploughing the night in stretches marked off by the chirp of the cuckoo: three, three-thirty, four, four-thirty… In a few minutes, it will be five.

When he senses there's almost no time left, he gets up, without turning on a light: the light coming through the window suffices to dilute the shadows. He settles in the most comfortable chair, the one reserved for reading, turns to face the bed.

This comfort gratifies him, he stretches out his body: his wait is as lucid and serene as his gaze.

Then, when the cuckoo calls out five, he observes, from the chair he has sat in, himself, dying in his bed.

Italo in Italy

Monday, 5:00 p.m. in Rome.

"I'm foreign…" I tell the fresh-faced woman in the thin, open blouse, who has seen me enter and greets me while I choke on the hot air from the streets.

"Oh, I know," she says with a complacent smile.

"… but my family's Italian," I say, trying to justify my modest ability with her language.

"I understand."

"I'm from a very different country," I continue to explain, not yet mentioning Argentina or describing my present demanding life in Scandinavia, hence without exciting any curiosity in her with regards to my person.

"Sure, you're looking for sun. It's still a long time till you'll be able to take your vacation to America."

"Correct," I say, displeased she has seen through me.

"Well, we've got plenty here, we're boiling in it."

"But I'm not looking for sun in the city."

"You want sun and sea…"

"… and hills," I say, using my hands, making shapes, the way they do. "One village on the rocks, another for the fisherman, not too many tourists…"

"… fish on your plate, red wine in your glass, am I right?"

"Right."

She says, now animated, clearly eager to drag me into her project:

"I've got it. You like sardines? You can go to the capital. I'm not talking about a big city, I mean a little fishing port next to the sardines' favorite waters. A village in the provinces, in Sardinia. Hills… You can't even imagine…! And seven temples." And then, like an overture: "You know those temples, like the ancients had, the Greeks…"

She unfolds maps. Her scrupulous office worker's finger traces out on the colored sheet a route that starts precisely there, in Stazione Termini.

⌒

Another day, a Thursday.

But it's morning, and the sea is there.

The sun is there, ruling over space.

It seems immobile; and yet, if I take the dare and look straight into it, it spins or shimmers, and that trembling strikes me as a presage. Dazzled, my eyes hurt, and I let them rest on the blue of the waters, and it seems as though the star's quivering had descended to their surface. It clashes and raises violent spume, but in other places it undulates, describing harmonies in gold.

I don't see a flag warning of hazards, or even a flagpole. Maybe I'll take a dip.

From the rows of canvas tents – medieval and martial in appearance, fringed in green and red – a sunburnt man motions to me, curt and vigorous; stripped bare to the waist, in rolled up pants, barefoot on the sand.

He guides me over officiously; but when I've heeded his call, he figures me out, and he's no longer interested. His money-grubbing belittles me.

After shedding my garments, I find I've brought along the money I should have left in the hotel. It's an absurd sum for a day at the beach: ten thousand lire and three hundred new francs. Why francs? I remember: I paid, I got money back during my layover at Orly; I changed it out, changed it back, made a stack with the brand new bills, folded them twice, once in the middle and once over Voltaire's nose.

I slide the money into one pocket of the pants I've just removed, which I will leave behind in the canvas tent. I try to be trusting: nothing will happen here.

I reach the water's edge, where the limitless mechanics of the sea caress and withdraw, lurch again, recede playfully... The sand, lit with glimmers, is the color of hazelnut, smooth, scoured, and passive.

There are no swimmers, save for far out. Observing this, I recognize that I prefer company and that my plan to take a solitary rest was absolutely insincere.

I see that there are hills (I don't see temples), that there are arid spaces, stands of trees, slopes covered in red and yellow poppies.

I walk to where I saw people before. I stop before I get there. I refuse to be a hanger-on.

I look back at the sea: it's still choppy. I feel a bit of fatigue and lie on my back. The sun in my eyes bothers me, and I roll onto my side. My perspective is different from down there, at the level of the beach. I notice a girl's body, so natural, so trusting... Between the two of us, rising in the foreground, her sandals... Far off (I see now), where two hills meet, with third rising behind it, the pagan columns sit serenely...

I have slept, and I am starting to wake up, where? The confusion is agreeable, because it brings no worrying symptoms with it. The sun shines down on me lustily and abets my recollection. Only in this landscape can I feel I've arrived to where I wished to go. It is satisfying.

Something begins noiselessly (or the sea drowns it out). When I note this, it is already in motion.

Two girls are there, standing, in their minimal bikinis, there as though they'd just come to a stop. Four boys are in front of them, as if they too had just come to a stop in that moment.

They could be, but profuse with life, in human form, the columns of the temple on the hill, responding to the waters' ancient summons.

This idealization pleases me, but it's fleeting. Then I suppose that the girls are foreign and the four boys, in swimsuits, are Sicilian.

Briefly I consider the girls' contours, but what seduces my senses most is the mystery of the sudden immobility of boys and girls alike.

It lasts only briefly, but long enough to imagine the boys are captivated, staring at them, and the girls bewildered by the admiration they've provoked, and feel themselves possessed, though from a distance, however scant, by the four adolescents' devotion.

In the stillness, it is as if they are touching, but none makes a single gesture: it is the pure veneration of bodies.

I reach the sea. We struggle, I to swim and not sink, the sea to refuse my wishes. As I advance, I grow disoriented, and I don't see the shore, or the boats, or the bathers. Suddenly I am struck by a vision of debris washing up on the beach, those things the sea has destroyed and expelled. Intermingled is the memory of other waters, another time, another fringe of sand, where one by one, the bodies of those slender Nordic women were brought up from the cruel sea, their long, fair hair dripping water...

A wave crashes over me; as I fall, I glimpse the shore and paddle toward it.

Upset, emerging from danger onto the dry, hot sand of the beach beyond the shoreline, with the taste of sand bitter in my mouth, I am overcome by impressions of that sea in Valencia. I hear the helical rumbling of the rescue helicopter making pass upon pass, and relive my envy of the pilot and his privileged view of the three women in the sunlight, beautiful and dead ...

Which is my tent, and where is the guard? It's not this one, because mine had two ears.

He comes over and I wait for him. He says, by way of introduction: "My coworker went to have lunch."

He waves me past. So this one was mine.

I find my things, and something tells me to dig quickly through my pockets and to count the money again. The lire are there, all the ones I had. But two hundred of my new francs are gone. I calculate their value in dollars. It's a stupid way to distract myself and put off what I have to do: complain, declare the theft. I walk out into the sun with the urge to shout, *I've been robbed!* The man with the missing ear is a mere step away, as though waiting for me, and I do tell him, "I've been robbed," but without shouting.

Instead, it is he who raises his voice:

"Me...?" His voice trembles with wounded pride. "You come here to me to tell me you've been robbed? You think I'm a crook?"

"No," I defend myself, in defiance of my thoughts, because in fact, he's the one I suspect.

His chest puffs up, he poses on his short, solid legs, stretches out an arm, and says, in this grave, Olympic posture:

"The police station's over there. Go if you want."

A moment ago, there was no one around the tents. Now we have a crowd.

A man in street clothes has stepped forward without uttering a word. Perhaps it is not, as it is for the others, the simple hope of witnessing a fight that has drawn him. He doesn't intervene, he lingers. The one-eared attendant notices something as well, perhaps that the witness is dangerous, because, still blustering, though now a bit calmer, he says:

"You are ruining me."

"What am I ruining?"

"My reputation, with the spectacle you've staged here…"

"But I've been robbed!"

"Sir, I didn't rob you."

"Who did, then…?"

"I don't know. I didn't, Sir. If my friend took something, I'm sure he was just borrowing it."

"What do you mean, took…? Borrowing…? I'm not putting up with this farce any longer! Where is the police station?"

"Just a moment, Sir," he says, raising a dignified arm to placate my fit.

I'll give him time, but I don't want to get wrapped up in this mess, let alone in front of the crowd, which keeps growing and gawks at our dispute.

The inexpressive onlooker is still there, not far away.

"We're poor, Sir. He's my friend. We grew up together, in poverty, always. Filthy poverty! This is the first shot we've had at a stable job. Maybe he did do it, but don't destroy things for us, Sir."

He's gone from aggression to begging.

"All right then, where is your friend?"

"Eating lunch, I'm sure of it. It's that time."

Then he changes his demeanor, he's self-assured and overbearing, and he advises those gathered:

"I think all of us should do the same, and bury the hatchet here once and for all, no? Let's eat, that's for the best!"

He addresses me in particular:

"Go to that trattoria," and he points. "You'll find good pasta, *fritti*, sardines, drinks, and when you've calmed down, we'll talk again. I'll go have my meal as well."

I challenge him:

"Are you trying to swindle me? You thought you were smart, accusing your friend."

I gesture toward the spectators and warn him, with bold self-assurance: "They'll be my witnesses."

As proof, I grab the mute man by the shoulder, and he nods.

My impression has a deep effect on the attendant. He exclaims softly, with a fist placed theatrically over his heart:

"I do not snitch, Sir!" and adds, in a more tenuous voice: "Doing so is deadly."

(I think of the Mafia.)

He sees he is trapped, but he looks up, with beguiling vivacity:

"You, Sir," he orders me, "are not to move from this spot. Wait for me. I will go and find my friend."

He departs, but then turns back brusquely:

"I swear to you, Sir," and he makes a complicated sign with two fingers over his forehead and chest: "When we were boys, my friend ate one of my ears. If he is guilty, I'll eat both of his."

I am persuaded.

The people say *oh*, and they start to pull back: the festivities are over.

I conclude that here, an oath is sacred, and the tent guard has sworn so effusively that all have figured, *His word is sufficient*, that justice will be done.

I'm unconvinced, and I realize I'm losing my witnesses, now even the silent man is gone.

In the opposite direction from those departing, a boy comes pushing a bike by the handlebars, opening a path in the crowd, and the first thing I notice is his lack of immaturity, of callowness. He approaches the attendant and whispers, and the attendant leans down to hear better. A message from his accomplice, I imagine. Or a sentence from the mafia, since he's committed treason, ratting out a comrade.

Once the secret's been told, the attendant stands up straight, and brazenly pretends, as though they hadn't been talking, that he's only just now aware of the boy's presence.

"Finally, Giuglielmino, you're here. Give me the bike, I need to eat lunch too."

"What do you mean, eat lunch?" I interrupt.

He tells me in a near-whisper: "I said lunch so he'd lend me the bike."

I don't believe him, but I accept, I let him go.

He starts to pull away and still, taking his leave blithely, he gives me an order and a promise:

"Just go eat. We can see each other after."

"Ah, no," I shout with vigor. "We'll both go."

He observes me disconsolately; lets go of the bicycle, which falls in the sand; opens his arms, and says:

"But Sir… what bad luck I have with you. You don't get it. You going there won't turn out well."

"I don't care! You aren't leaving me on this beach. I don't trust you one bit."

"Sir…!" He tries to imply I've offended him.

But then he turns lenient and friendly, extends his right hand, and introduces himself."

"My name's Turì." And he invites me: "Come on, let's go, it's up there."

⌒

Up there indeed, in the opposite direction from the beach, we climb the hill on a ragged slope that leads to the densely packed houses on the village outskirts. They are charming, made of whitewashed stone.

My buttocks hurt from sitting on the bicycle tube and I am bathed in sweat from the sun that I myself chose to relax under, not knowing circumstances would arise that would place me beneath it with my head uncovered.

The air and the countryside have changed, the tensions have slackened. I snigger at my posture on the frame of the old bike that the one-eared kid – a tame, chastened bull – pedals arduously, trying to haul his weight and mine, jerking and swaying. To keep from rolling off and getting covered in bruises, I stretch out my legs and lift them up, trying to help him keep balance.

He's strong enough to chat as if we were just out for a ride and were well on our way to becoming friends. He doesn't notice my surly expression, which it's not easy for me to keep up. I try not to let him win me over. To win me over or to beat me.

This is surely not lost on him, because he repeats his arguments to convince me of his sincerity, and plaintively intones:

"Oh, God! What a terrible mess you've gotten me into, Fungo."

With my back to him, I can't see the indignation that must be spreading across his face, and if I shift on the crossbar, we'll fall to the ground.

"So who's Fungo?" I ask, though it's not hard to figure out.

"Fungo...? My friend!" He corrects himself: "The guy who says he's my friend. I hate him. He ate my ear!"

Now I believe him, and conclude that a longstanding anger is consuming him, but I refuse any attempt of his to soften me through compassion. I just show naked curiosity:

"How'd it happen?"

"In a fight. I said what his sister was, someone told him what I said, he swore he was going to eat both my ears."

I neglect caution and turn to look at him, in case I saw him wrong before, but no, he's just missing one, the other ear is in its place.

He clarifies:

"Right, but he couldn't. The weakling couldn't do it."

"So what was the sister...?"

He stalls a moment before answering, and then, in his very cavalier manner, says to me:

"Think about it," and starts to whistle, as though waving the matter aside.

I want to keep our talk going, to find out why the other didn't manage cut off his second ear or eat it, but I'll have to wait until he decides his whistling is finished, and now, we're entering the village.

A boy greets him, happy to see him.

"Ciao, Turì," and he waves his hand.

"Ciao, caro," he responds affectionately and raises his hand, letting go of the handlebars, so the machine veers under my weight; but he saves us from tipping over, he's very fast.

And then:

"Hey, Turì. You want to try?" It's a boy wolfing down some sort of dough wrapped in paper.

"If I didn't have things to do...!" he exclaims with jocose resignation, presumably winking and pointing at me as the one to blame for his forbearance.

I'm starting to like him, this Turì. In half an hour, he's drawn me toward him. Half an hour, by my reckoning, and a glance at my diver's watch confirms it.

My taste for my vacation, my tourist's nonchalance, has returned. I tell myself the 200 francs are worth less than being with these people and feeling included in this adventure, which can end whenever I wish, and I come to terms with forgetting the money.

Two or three boys are following us now, it's nothing for them to jog along, because the bicycle, with its double load, is traveling slowly.

They court us without a word, until one of them inquires:

"Hey, Turì, he's a foreigner, isn't he?"

"Obviously, Flaminio. Don't you see him...?"

"American?"

"No."

He keeps on:

"He's not a Yankee? No dollars?"

"No, come on, look at him!"

I could answer myself, but I don't. I prefer to spectate (I paid a hefty admission fee, two hundred new francs).

Then the boy, now properly informed, attacks: "Sir, a hundred lire..."

And the other two: "Hey, Mister, how about a hundred lire for us."

Other naked feet dash out of a door, the poor boy is frail, and convinced, perhaps, that I've been handing out money the whole way, he begs and laments:

"For me, too, Sir, a hundred lire. Why not for me, too?"

If I've paid a wad of bills already, without meaning to, what's the harm in adding a few coins? Smiling, with an implicit promise that they will receive what they've asked for, I feel in my pocket and realize I'm still in my bathing suit, that the money remained in my pants, and my pants inside the tent, wrinkled and exposed on the sandy ground.

I swallow, and the diversion I'd enjoyed since deciding to put aside the thought of my robbery goes sour. I feel like an utter victim, though this time of my own negligence.

I've not been left empty-handed, I reflect, I have more than enough at the hotel, and yet, that doesn't mitigate my displeasure.

But the geraniums and the shirts and colored blouses hanging from the balconies and windows where the neighbor ladies yell back and forth win me over:

"There he is, the foreigner!"

"The foreigner, Maria!"

"Look at him, look what he's like!"

Maria, Paola, Fina, Rosanna, Lucia... I feel as though feted, in the frank voices of those women who spread the word that I've come all the way up to their village.

A pleasant illusion, ephemeral: deep down, it's not lost on me how they say *the* foreigner and not *a* foreigner, and they must know I'm here not for festivities, but for punishment, a payback arranged by this Turì, who has acted as an informer.

But if that's how it is, why is Turì still luxuriating in the greetings he receives as he passes by? Why don't they condemn him, with their eyes, if nothing else, for taking me to the thief's redoubt?

The number of boys has grown, and they keep following us, though they're not begging. It's a bad sign. I sketch out an interpretation favorable to me: they've stopped clamoring for their allotment of a hundred lire per head after seeing my face when I stuck my hand in the pocket of my bathing suit. They know I have no money on me. They're smart, and only curiosity makes them persevere. They want to see where my daring or Turì will take me; after all, he's one of them, and there's a reason they admire him and he's so popular. They must be thinking he'll play a trick on me and cleverly thwart my operation.

As we continue upward, a young woman comes down, running next to the walls. I think I know who she is because suddenly, Turì starts humming, as though nervous, without harmony. What I've discovered is not her, I think, but her fire.

"Greetings, Giannina. Are you going?"

"It's for the best, don't you think?"

They exchange a *good luck*. Both wished for the same thing, and now they are taking opposite paths. I notice they've spoken courteously.

"Who is… Giannina, you called her?"

Turì, concentrating, without any show of hostility toward her: "Fungo's sister. It's because of her that I lost my ear."

I didn't look closely enough at her, I think. She was worth it.

"Why did she say it would be best if she left?"

"We're there…!" he interrupts me vivaciously, perhaps to elude explanation.

Turì lets the pedals go. We step off, and I stretch to bring life back to my sleeping legs.

When it happened, was it mere spite that led Turì to insult Giannina's honor…? The spite of an adolescent who loves a slightly older woman who refuses to hear him out or understand? Turì, who just said *It's because of her that I lost my ear* – could he not admit, *Because of her I saved the other?* Why do I imagine it that way? His expression upon seeing her held no rancor. Either she stopped her brother from cutting off both or else that love has left its marks on him inside as well as out.

There's no proper door on the house where Turì pounds an iron knocker: it's more of a portal, so wide, perhaps, to accommodate without impediment not just the mass, but the magnitude of the matron making her appearance.

In the meantime, the children have gathered, along with women with babies and dogs.

So it had to be: we stand there, the three of us, in front of the portal, with no need for introductions. An empty half-circle divides us from the spectators, whom I take to be half the town, minus the men, who must be working.

An insubstantial greeting, mine terse, Turì's subdued, receives no response from the massive woman. She studies me bodily with a frown of offended dignity, I imagine because nothing covers me but a short swimsuit, and there is no doubt we are at a family home and not out on the beach. Only now do I give any importance to my appearance. Turì is wearing long swim trunks and has thrown on, albeit loosely, a button-down shirt.

All this scrutiny doesn't keep me from observing the flimflammer, whose demeanor is passive and expectant; nor does it keep me from watching the matron, who spies on me greedily, with a single eye from the side. If she has another one, she's thrifty with it, because she keeps it covered with an eyelid. They make quite a pair: the One-Eared Man and the One-Eyed Woman!

They are talking, but it's hard to understand them. Their Sicilian is heavily tinged with dialect and beyond that, I'm having trouble fitting in: I feel explored, perhaps condemned by the many judges there. Or else I am afraid, not of the danger Turì hinted at before we came up, but of being scoffed at, of playing the clown.

I begin to capture their words when she starts insulting him:

"Are you not ashamed of talking about my son with a stranger?"

I don't plan on letting them trip me up again with their argumentative chicanery, so I don't respond to her derision, instead stating:

"Ma'am, I don't speak dialect, but you'll be able to understand my Italian. So listen: I want my 200 francs back, and I don't know whether your son stole them or not. If you can't tell me anything about that money – and remember, Turì's the one who brought me to you – then I will go straightaway to the police station, with or without the bicycle."

She makes a show of shrugging her shoulders and waving me off, and then, without even turning her eye on me, yields slightly, answering not me, but Turì, in dialect:

"My son isn't at home, and he's not coming to eat, either."

I announce, very decided:

"That's no concern of mine. I'm going to the police station."

Turì persists in his patient diplomacy: "Wait, my man, wait a moment. What's the rush? Everything will get taken care of." He's speaking casually with me now. But I know him, and I don't take offense, this is his natural self coming out. I even believe he will try to take care of it, because he obviously fears the police.

As he's managed to prevent me from leaving, he sets to reasoning frantically with Fungo's mother. He tells her the risks in store.

He compels her to acknowledge me, and she speaks to me for the first time:

"Mine is a good house, with good people. My son doesn't do the kind of things you're saying. He'll come and he'll set the record straight. But..."

(Her verdict:)

"... if he has stolen, it needs to come out. My husband's in there..."

(She points her fat arm inside, but her husband doesn't appear; she's almost certainly a widow.)

"... and he'll put the hurt on him, he'll kill him, maybe, but he'll get a confession out of him."

The assembly of women and children has understood everything perfectly: the son must confess; the mother has said so, and she is clearly the authority in the family.

Now there's a pact. Just as on the beach, once the deal is made, interest drops off and people return to minding their business.

The only laggards are a few dogs out dozing in the sun and a couple of uninformed cadgers who run after us as the bicycle speeds down the hill, with me sitting on the frame as before:

"Give me a hundred lire..."

"What about those hundred lire...?"

Turì is jubilant, he could even burst into song, and that puts me in a better mood.

Bent over on her balcony, a woman calls to me:

"Stranger…"

(And when I look at her, she heaps curses on me, on account of the coins:)

"… Swallow them with your bile!"

She continues to smile as she says this.

A pain about the money, that I don't have it to hand out to the boys… so they'd stop thinking of me as a foreigner, a scoundrel, a cheapskate.

She hasn't humiliated me.

(Between the bars of the balcony, the blossoming stems of geraniums emerge; next to her mother's legs, a girl with sky blue eyes, aloof from those wars, peeks out.)

～～

Before we make it out of the village, Guglielmino intercepts us. He's on another, newer bike, painted green. I suppose he wants his back, and we'll be condemned to walk.

But no, the boy alerts us energetically:

"I saw him, but when he caught sight of me, he went the other way."

Turì is unmoved and doesn't hasten to act. Instead, he takes time to expound to me his philosophy:

"Why rush? Why look for him…? He'll go home, right? His mother's waiting for him there, and that's that."

I almost accept his soothing conclusion, but something has happened there in the square. A person hurried off and a woman shouted: "Stop! The foreigner's here." I didn't recognize him, I don't see her.

I question Turì:

"She said: Stop! The foreigner's here."

"Who?" He's surprised. "Who said stop?"

"That woman."

"What woman?"

How can I point her out? That part of the street has emptied out; the square is empty.

Turì lavishes me with his tolerance:

"My dear Sir, you're confused. A woman was singing, in dialect, that's why you didn't understand her."

I refuse to let myself anger: but she wasn't singing. This is pure chicanery: modulating her voice was part of the ruse.

Turì suggests:

"What if we have a glass of wine...? My treat."

Since he sees my annoyance, and I don't hide my inner struggle, which he comprehends, he tries to distract me:

"It's hot, the wine's cool, the bar is nearby."

I don't accept, and we get back on the bike.

The houses in the village outskirts thin out as we descend, and the sea breeze embraces us, changing the temperature and perhaps our thoughts. Turì, tenacious, picks up on it:

"You're really not thirsty? Not now?"

I say yes, but not for wine. "A Coke, maybe..."

My censor, Turì, has worldly instincts, and says witheringly:

"Sure, a Coke, even I drink one now and again."

I shoulder the insult and recant:

"Or maybe a coffee."

"Maybe an iced coffee," he suggests.

At the counter in the bar, I conform to the customs of the region, which must have their reason for being, I suppose.

Then I agree that we sit. There are tables, and the dining room is cool. I accept an almond milk, also cool, and then another, and we chat.

A rest in the shadows suffices to reinvigorate my distrust. (Why is he holding me up so long? Has he forgotten about his job?)

I try to pay, forgetting that I have no money. Turì watches me root in vain through my pocket, and hands a bill to the waiter, unhurried, because I can neither beat him to the punch nor refuse his gesture.

The one who's hurrying is I, because I remember my things are back in the tent, and I take it for granted that, with one attendant gone and the other vaguely investigating me, the tents must be unguarded and open to looting.

I tell him this as we walk toward the door, and he rejects my worries, trying to put me at my ease, his attitude suggesting such trifles are below him:

"Sir…! In places like this, we all know each other, we live in peace, no one covets what isn't his. Criminality is unknown here. If anyone kills, Sir, it's out of love."

We walk outside, the sun assails me, and I come to a stop, nearly blinded.

I've paid no attention to what Turì is doing, until I hear him clamor:

"I've been robbed! I've been robbed! Reprobates, thieves!" and other niceties as well.

I'm half-amused, half-perturbed. I suffer his howling, then try to calm him down and get him to answer me:

"What the hell did they take from you?"

"The bicycle, don't you see? And it wasn't mine, as you well know."

I find a wicker chair under an enormous yellow parasol. I give him time while he blasphemes those who have gathered round, insults those known and unknown to him, appeals to the powers above, disavows justice; and finally, after seeing him trot a half-mile up the street dodging autistic drivers who curse him or don't pay him any mind, I force him into the seat next to mine and make him take a sip of coffee.

"Linden blossom, that's what he needs," the waiter says, with neither compassion nor respect for Turì.

Turì looks at him askance, piercing him with a homicidal glance, and says:

"Poison! None for me. I'd serve it to you, though, if you like, you piece of trash."

Clearly this is a manner of speaking. They don't take offense, and nothing indicates an urge to come to blows.

Turì forgets his rival and sips his iced coffee meditatively.

I propose:

"Why don't you report it to the police?"

He ruminates. Smugly:

"The police...? Maybe. Later, when we get to the station."

"Use the phone, that's what it's there for. If you wait, the thief will get away."

"There's not one here."

"What, there's no thief here?"

"There's no phone."

"Of course there is! It's in the bar, I saw it myself."

"There's no point, it doesn't work."

"You're making things up! Someone was using it just a moment ago."

He gets flustered and grumbles:

"The police don't know about these things. No one will find anything."

Hearing his unease, I risk offending him:

"Come on, Turì... You really don't think the police are up to it, or is that bike maybe stolen?"

He casts a sly glance at me, but his words are ingenuous:

"How, Sir, could I know if it was stolen? The bicycle doesn't belong to me. They loaned it to me, you saw that."

I resign myself to not leave off prying: he lies so truthfully...

Then he recovers, as though leaping up:

"In the end, what does the bicycle matter? A walk in the sun is enough! It's so nice..."

I admire his mechanisms, his flair for living.

In the end – I tell myself, repeating his words – he's right. He is reviving the vagabond he carries inside, or that perhaps he once was, while I have come to look for life in the open air. I'm a tourist, no? Better – even just once, with a guy like him – to be a vagabond, too.

I exaggerate. I can't call myself a vagabond after taking a straight path for three miles into safety. If I thought this, it was due to the influence of Turì, who arranges reality to suit him.

Infected by his mood, I haven't noticed I'm walking barefoot. The hot street's pavement makes it clear to me. I confess: "I can't do it." Turì thinks I can; it's just a question, he says, of getting off the asphalt, since the soil is sandy and won't hurt my feet. Easy for him to say: he's shod in what look like open-toed espadrilles, held on by laces that wind up to the top of his ankle.

I don't want to look bad, so I make an effort. The sand is there, and though it's hot, it doesn't burn like the tar on the road; but it's stippled with patches of wild herbs, some stiff and even sharp, they're hard to dodge, and they wound me.

I'm one step away from giving up, but I hold onto the tatters of my stoicism and refuse to hitchhike. My resolve falters:

"This is the way to the sea, there must be buses that pass by here."

He says: "They pass by," nothing more, keeps walking, and I lag behind him, to keep from flaunting my deplorable gait.

I say:

"We could catch one."

He assures me:

"We can't."

He ponders, like a hermit, and I won't put up with it any further.

He continues dragging out the explanation, and finally he says without my urging:

"We can't because I'm out of money. I spent it in the bar, and you don't have any."

He knew it, he's known it the whole time, the cur. Or he's known at least – I correct myself, in his favor – since I couldn't give the hundred lire to the boys in the village.

I venture:

"We can get on the bus, tell the driver what's happened, and pay when we get there. I'll pay for us both."

"They'll take you, even without money. But not me. And it could be the driver will recognize me when he sees us along his route and he'll keep driving, pretending he doesn't see us. You go alone. I'll stay on foot."

While I wait, undecided, he takes off his shoes. He stretches out his hands, presenting his espadrilles, their laces dangling loose.

I accept.

He carries on, walking over his bare soles. He clowns around now and then, perhaps to amuse me: he jumps on the pavement, pretends it's scalding him, pretends he's hopping on hot coals, that he's a human torch, returns to his natural gait, strolls with ballroom elegance, cracks up laughing, and dances with an unseen partner.

Almost there, beneath the shade of the first trees, I proclaim:

"Shade before sun, the promenade before the beach. I deserve it," I say.

He agrees:

"Good idea."

And he uses the opportunity to recite his part:

"The sea is rough. I think the swimmers might need me. I shouldn't take too long, otherwise I'll lose my job…"

(Strange that he remembers.)

"… besides, people don't pay for their tents if there's no attendant…"

(There's the real reason.)

"… so you can stay here until you're feeling better. I'm going. Bye."

"Hey, just a moment!" I shout. "What about my clothes, my pants with the money?"

"That's not exactly how you told it to me, Sir. You don't trust me. Didn't we agree that your money disappeared while you were in the sea…?"

"We didn't agree on anything. I've said one thing since the beginning, and it hasn't changed: when I went to the beach, I left my money in the tent. While I was swimming, someone stole it."

"And now you're saying you've got money in your pants inside the tent…!"

He feigns astonishment, gives me a reproachful look, as though he's caught me in a false testimony, and pretends to censure me benevolently:

"Are you trying to drag me into some predicament, Sir…? What's the point of these antics, anyhow? Why did you make me waste my time, my bicycle, my tips, and maybe even a friend…? No, Sir, no: you don't play around with a Sicilian…"

I have let him prattle, fleshing out his nonsense (he has to know they didn't take all my money, that some of it remained in my clothes); but this hint of a threat I won't tolerate:

"This is it! I've put it off all day. But now…"

I cut off our conversation and take off walking resolutely, my mind on the police station, until I realize I don't know where it is. It won't be difficult to find. I ask a passerby, and since it's obvious I'm not from there, he thinks I don't understand his language, and he directs me with gestures. They are so extravagant that if Turì is spying on us, he will realize without effort what I'm doing, though he can't hear us and I wasn't open or clear with him about my intentions.

It doesn't matter whether he knows. He can likely imagine what's awaiting him. The best thing would be for him to repent and come to me, cash in hand.

Done! There he is, calling to me from behind my back. I pretend not to pay him any mind.

"Hey, Sir. Don't go, listen to me. Wait a minute."

I continue, almost running.

We are attracting the attention of the passersby.

Agile as he is, I'm unsure why he doesn't run and catch me, and though I don't see him, I conclude he's got a plan working in his favor. I'm not wrong. He shouts at the top of his lungs:

"You're taking my espadrilles! Hey, stop! Those are mine!"

Now the people do look at me and gather round to witness the drama that will surely take place.

He's done it, the bastard. I have to stop, and beyond that, I've now been embarrassed in public. If they know him, that's even worse: a village pickpocket is accusing me of being a shoe thief...! And secondhand shoes, at that...!

Indignant, clumsy, violent, I try to untangle the complex knots, break a lace, and throw one espadrille to the ground, before arming myself with the other to smack him across the face.

I see him coming, with Giuglielmino at his side, cold-blooded. The people open a path for him. They have the second bicycle with them, the green one...

Calm, keeping a distance – wary of the espadrille I'm wielding – he warns me loudly:

"Keep them, I can go on without them. Anyway, I loaned them to you."

He observes the effect of his words and steps forward, just a little, saying as he does so:

"Giuglielmino saw Fungo, and I know I can catch him this time. Have faith in me. I'll come back with your money."

Before I can reach him, he backs away, hops on the bicycle, and departs.

I let a bench bear the weight of my weariness.

Then I see the boy. He has stayed there, as though left to watch over me. If that is true, he's carrying out his duties in an unnerving way. He's quiet and alone, and he looks straight at me, cold, unwavering.

"What are you waiting for?"

He doesn't answer.

"Where did he go?"

He doesn't answer."

"Will he be back?"

He nods up and down expressively, and I feel we're starting to communicate.

"Will he bring the money?"

He doesn't answer.

This boy, is he mute? No. This morning, in my presence, he whispered in Turi's ear. Does he have a voice defect? No. He spoke normally on the hill leading to the village.

I want to pretend he's relaxed among his people and timid in the presence of strangers. I want to trust that he's on my side, or at least that he's defending Turì and helping him to trap the real criminal, who is supposedly this Fungo.

With these hopes, I keep interrogating him, deliberately, patiently.

"Giuglielmino, tell me, what's your part in all this? It's not about the money, right...? Turì is your friend, that much is clear, maybe even your brother..."

My words are muffled, to our surprise, by a deafening helicopter that rushes forth and hovers recklessly just over our heads. I can see it belongs to the navy.

I sense a current of turbulence in all those around.

Giuglielmino has disappeared.

An alarm appears to have mobilized the residents, who pour out from every place in sight, along with tourists better informed than I and eye-catching women who close their boutiques to come look.

I join them without knowing why, something about them draws me, and the call of the sea throbs inside me; I can't tell what's happening, because the trees on the avenue have covered my visual field.

Again the helicopter swoops over, buzzing, and its hoarse whirl takes me back to the beach in Valencia where the three Nordic girls lay in death.

Moments later, I emerge on the shore. Between myself and the sea stands the wall of the multitude, but I step in, as though consciously proceeding toward some determined place, while the row of heads blocks my view of it and whatever is occuring there.

At the risk of stirring things up, perhaps even starting a fight, I struggle forward, impelled by growing preoccupation: I need to see if what I've foreseen has really come to pass. If the aircraft's flight, with its somber sound, has brought about on this beach a repetition of what happened in Valencia. If already, on the sand, the waters now flirt with those bodies that inspired, this morning, when they were alive, such fascination in the four Sicilian boys.

From tenderness toward them, those lovely girls from elsewhere; from romantic attachment to the magic scene proffered by the sun, which I sought out; perhaps from the day's commotion, which has shattered my presence of mind, so that, though I struggle onward, with shoves and pushes, my sentiments are troubled. If it is visible, I am not ashamed.

Then those who held me back, those who rejected me, withdraw and allow me to cross through, and I do so idly, attended by a vast silence that seems almost pious.

At the end of the path they've opened for me lies the coast: on the edge, the clear outline of a woman's body, very white.

My stride is unsteady and rattled: from confusion and from the feeling of the burning sand on my scalded feet. Around me, people give voice to their pity:

"He can't even walk…"

"Poor soul…!"

"A star-crossed lover…!"

Someone corrects them:

"He's not the lover, he's the father."

And I proceed, my determination immovable.

Some women are sobbing. One of them wraps her arms around my neck and tries to hold me back:

"Don't look at her, don't torment yourself any more, it will only hurt you. Remember her as she was in life, the luckless creature."

I pull her off me and cry, "Miss, please…!"

How does she know that when I found her, her immobility was different, that it quivered under the sun, stiff and wistful, held an interminable instant by the veneration of the boys…?

Over the last stretch, some swimmers – women as well as men – give me their hand and utter words of condolence in various languages. I look at them with impatience.

I arrive.

For a long time, I ponder her where she lies.

I hold back the impulse to bend my knees.

She reminds me of a movie star, I don't know which; but she's not one of the girls I saw this morning.

My grief evaporates, because I'd let my foreboding convince me. Naturally, I'm sad that such a pretty girl has drowned, but…

I've fallen still, thinking about all this… Another hand comes forward, interrupting me, presumably to offer condolences, but I will reject it, now that I've emerged from my daze. It is the hand of a man in uniform, with epaulettes, an official from the police.

Amiably, but without letting me go, he spouts a litany of phrases that he may think opportune or comforting:

"Now, Sir, that the first shock is over, I hope you've managed to reconcile yourself at least slightly with the Lord's unfathomable plan, and I ask you, if you feel capable of aiding in our grim but necessary mission, to proceed to the identification of the body. Would you care to tell us the first and last name of your unfortunate girlfriend?"

I've borne his discourse, unwilling to interrupt him, but now that he's finished and I find myself so tired, I simply shake my head and tell him, in a voice that sounds hoarse to me, though not at all sentimental:

"Officer, I don't know her."

I can see his disappointment, and also that he doesn't believe me.

Nor do the people close by who have heard me, for one woman, highly aggrieved, remarks:

"The pain has broken him. He's gone mad."

Another knows better:

"It's not madness, he's had an attack of amnesia."

Another empathizes:

"To not even be able to recognize your own daughter…"

"Wife, I'd say."

"It's not his wife, jeez. It's his fiancée. Don't you see how he's babbling…? Nobody loses it like that when they've lost their wife."

I let them talk. It seems that the policeman, like me, has loosened up, though he may be waiting for a reaction that will reveal my true relationship with the girl. Since I should set him straight, I repeat:

"We're not related, she's not my girlfriend. In fact, I don't know her at all. I'm sorry for the upset…"

("See…?" someone says triumphantly, "he just said he's upset.")

"… but I can assure you that I've never seen her before. I confused her with Valencia."

I understand that I've now encouraged misunderstandings and suspicions. I want to backtrack, but I can't, because the helicopter blades are whipping above us and the air they displace practically sweeps us off our feet. I nearly stumble over the dead girl. I look at her with apprehension.

The machine makes a wide arc and comes back around, now no longer surprising anyone. I analyze the reason for its extreme, even dangerous approach: undoubtedly there's no radio communication between the police on the ground, in the thick of things, and the pilot, and so he's trying to send them a message via signs that all of us attempt to decipher. He seems to be saying they're bringing in another cadaver, but it doesn't interest me, I'm exhausted.

While the officer, who may have drawn the same conclusion after observing the pilot, hurries to give technical commands, I try to pull away without giving rise to more misapprehensions.

But the crowd doesn't open for me as it did when I arrived. Now I have to walk among the faces and eyes, and I sense that they have formed two groups.

One rebukes me: "joker," "jackass," "you don't play with a dead woman's feelings like that." This last consideration may have inspired whoever then stuns me with the following phrase: "Mental degenerate."

From the other side, more timidly, comes a measure of mercy, an admission that the loss of my beloved has plainly deprived me of my wits as well.

And so, amid the expectation provoked by the imminent arrival of the sea's next victim, a certain uproar rises up about me.

Worse yet: one group closes in. Someone rescues me: "Let him go! He's not on trial. He'll come to his senses once the shock of it is past, and if not, he'll go through the world without knowing what has happened to him."

I return to the coolness of the tree-lined promenade.

For a while, no one bothers about me, the center seems to have emptied out, everyone is clustered on the beach.

The sea air comforts me, whistling its way through the leaves, leaving them trembling and stealing their scent, which it brings me.

I lie down on the bench, facing heaven, which pleases me as though I were up there.

I call myself a vagabond, and doing so tickles me because I know I have a hotel and in the hotel, a suitcase, and in the suitcase a billfold, and in the billfold a sum… which is missing something! Yes, the francs and the lire. It occurs to me I should at least recover what was left in my pants on the beach. But now, the masses are out on the beach, drawn there by the tragedy. I imagine the many children. I imagine them marauding through the rows of tents. I imagine the thieves delighting in their thievery.

Forget it! I decide, and do the numbers to figure out how much is left in my billfold. Lazy or fatigued, I pass the time memorizing numbers, recollecting expenses, and computing the exchange rates before returning to the hotel. I even put off showering, and the snack I've been hankering for since my early breakfast. Face up, I contemplate, from a wooden bench on a public promenade, the harmonious motion of the sky, invaded by absurdity, above my head.

⌐

A bicycle brakes. Easy to know, without even looking, which one it is and which person is riding it, looking, perhaps, to entrap me once more.

I don't move, I'm still on my back, and my eyes are closed, so Turì grabs my foot and shakes it cautiously. I stop myself from exploding, in indignation or laughter, I don't know which will emerge.

He whispers to me, as if ordered to wake me in bed without disturbing me:

"Sir, Sir…"

I let him, without reacting.

He tries again. I pretend to snore.

I don't see him, but I imagine that he's surprised and has taken a step back. Then, without touching me, perhaps believing he won't be heard, he grumbles:

"Get up, sleepyhead."

I sit up and examine him: his clothing is tangled and tattered, his hair unkempt with blades of grass poking through.

Seeing me awake, he smiles meekly. He reaches in his back pocket and hands me several banknotes without uttering a word. I recognize the design and color of the French francs.

We both pause serenely, each comfortable with the other, reconciled. I ask:

"How'd you do it?"

He explains discreetly:

"He hid out in the forest. Guglielmino showed me where and told me he saw him hide the bundle of lire under a rock."

"So you went there, lifted up the stone, calmly took the money, and now you're back here to give it to me."

"Exactly as you've said."

"You sneak! You lying dog! Don't be modest, Turì. Your shirt's torn, you're battered and bruised, how are you going to stand here and tell me it was that easy. You've been in a fight. For me, right?"

"No, Sir, not for you. For my honor and the honor of my family."

"Yes," I say.

I appreciate Turì's gesture, and I feel I need to acknowledge it. A noble action, I tell myself, deserves more than just a tip. What would he do for me in this situation? I try to imagine, and see myself sitting around the table with the family, invited to share a savory meal cooked by his mother.

I will share my table with him, though the time for lunch is past, and I will do it my way:

"You want to have a drink?" I propose, without saying where. "This time, I'll pay," I declare, contented, with the sense that I've won his trust.

"I appreciate it. But not wine, not at this hour..."

"...and especially not on an empty stomach," I add, showing that I've understood. "A whiskey or a beer, maybe? A couple of toasted sandwiches, or some thick-cut ham with white bread, what do you say?"

"Beer sounds good, and ham, too. Really, I can't wait," he says, clearly satisfied.

We set off through the streets, which remain unpeopled, and he comments:

"There's something strange here, it's like everyone's gone to sleep. This place isn't normally like this. Did something happen while I was in the forest?"

It's evident he knows nothing of the tragedy in the sea and the grotesquery I took part in on the beach. I say: "Nothing, just the misfortunes of a delirious man."

Guileless, he inquires: "Delirious, in the middle of the day?"

I don't know how to explain it to him, so I distract him:

"Let's go for that beer."

And on we go, the three of us: me, him, and his vehicle.

I ask him what he'll do with the bicycle when we go inside to have our drink. He tells me: "We won't go in anywhere. I don't trust people. We can drink something out on the street." I make a recommendation: "Let's leave it in a garage."

"This bicycle, in a garage...? What garage?"

"The one at the hotel."

"You're taking me to your hotel?"

"Why not?"

I've hit the bullseye. It's certainly not every day he gets treated to this kind of courtesy. He doesn't hide his gratitude, which grows when he finds out which hotel it is – the best in the area.

I notice, without taking it to heart, the porter's confusion as he hears me order him to put my companion's bicycle in the parking deck. Turì acts as though it's natural, but I have no doubt that for him, it's a kind of game, one not inconsonant with his brazen and haphazard way of life.

In the swimmers' elevator, I go up to my bedroom to put on a pair of shorts and a polo, and in minutes, I'm back with Turì.

A man from reception calls me gingerly aside. I can imagine his misgivings, but I won't succumb.

He ought to warn me, he argues, since I apparently know nothing of this guest I've brought along with me. "He's a grafter," he whispers, "with a bad reputation and a nasty background, a swindler, a fighter, you name it."

I reply, simply and categorically, that he is here in my charge. And to Turì, I point out the bar.

Turì responds sanely: "No, Sir… like this…?" and submits himself to a head-to-toe examination. He makes plain what I, in my affection and hospitality, had overlooked: he truly is shabby, a lowlife.

I take him to my room. I invite him to cleanse himself at his leisure and he takes me at my word, singing as he showers. I offer him a brand-new shirt, with broad, colorful stripes. He resists accepting. Then he accepts.

We go down to the bar.

We enjoy two rounds of ice-cold beer, the second with succulent country ham. Turì refuses a third. He implies that he knows his limits.

I study him and think: *He's a guttersnipe, but he was loyal with me, and I didn't know how to appreciate it.* I'm ignoring his contradictions and outbursts, trying to home in on what's essential.

I even believe he may be pondering the pleasures of honesty, in that instant, when a person – like me – has come along and finally recognized something noble in him. *I'm no longer afraid that you'll lie to me again, Turì,* I think, without sharing my profession of faith with him.

Suddenly, I have a vision: Giannina's body against the white walls of the village on the hill. In my daydream, it is the signs, the rewards, of honesty that surround her.

Then I reconsider, and see her cornered, like a martyr.

I don't ask Turì to confide in me. I assure him, manfully:

"You were cruel with Giannina, a bit of a dog, wouldn't you say?"

I've surprised him, and he wavers. His face shows he's bothered, defensive, but he admits:

"I offended her, it's true. But it was just words."

"Hurtful words, that much is clear."

He moves to leave, and I stop him:

"… but the fact is, you love her, and you can't run away from that feeling, can you, Turì?"

He looks at me from the depths of his torment.

I want to reproof him: *What will you do with her?* or else *What will you do for her?* but I decide not to intervene and propose: "Now it's time for whiskey, no?"

He says "Yes." He understands I won't meddle more in his personal affairs.

"So a whiskey, then?"

He clarifies jovially:

"I'm not much for whiskey. Maybe another beer?" and soon, he's back to his old self.

We drink. He does so as zealously as before.

I call over the waiter and ask for the bill, and mechanically reach into my pocket. I take out the bills; they're the French ones, they may not accept them here, and it's silly for me to pay in cash if all I need is to sign the check.

I joke with Turì about the ruffled state this singular day has left me in.

Then I remember how, when he described his caper, he said: *Giuglielmino saw him hide the bundle of lire under a rock.* I repeat the phrase to Turì in order to ask him: "Why did you say lire? These are the bills you handed me back. They're French francs."

Fearless, he enlightens me:

"You were robbed."

"You admit that's what happened?"

"Of course I admit it now. You lost your money…"

"The French francs."

"Yes. Fungo took them, and to be able to spend them freely, he converted them to Italian lire. The bartender at the restaurant did it for him. My thought was, if it was francs that you lost, then it was francs you needed to get back. I made Fungo confess where he had exchanged the francs for lire; I made him take me to the restaurant and get the francs back. But the bartender had already gotten rid of them. I was so mad I hit him again. I said to him, 'You son of a bitch, you've already tried my patience too much, now I'm going to pound on you until you get together every last bit of French currency we need to settle things with that foreigner.' Fungo tried to argue, he said there was no need, that giving you lire would be enough, but I said to him: 'This is a question of manners, the gentleman deserves our consideration.'"

"Thank you."

"It's nothing. But the truth is, he didn't understand, the poor guy, so I had to smack him around to get it into his head, and so he goes off looking for francs in every bar we come across, always with me watching him, you know. And this way, we get a couple of bills here, a couple of bills there, and finally we've got the total, 200 francs. Is that correct, Sir? Have you counted them? Is anything missing? I wouldn't be surprised, knowing that bum had his hands on them…"

I don't need to tell him: I don't need to look again, I already counted them while he was in the shower, there are twenty ten-franc bills, each one new. Not only that, they are the exact same ones I had before.

I recognized them when he gave them to me, then I looked them over and made sure. They were clean and crisp before, now they're a little grubby and worn after the day's hijinks. They have a peculiar, arbitrary fold: not only are they creased in the middle, the usual way you fold banknotes, but there's another pleat, parallel to that one but a centimeter to the side, which passes over Voltaire's nose. I didn't put it there, it was that way when I got my change in Orly.

All of which means that these bills are mine and the twenty of them have been together from the time they were filched; it's not true that Fungo, threatened by Turì, had to ambush place after place, searching near and far, to gather them…

So the both of them are thieves, or they cover for each other and share they spoils afterward. If Fungo is a bandit, so is this weasel whose thirst I've just deigned to quench.

⌒

I don't let the deception rankle me. I'd rather say goodbye to Turì in a pleasant, dignified tone.

I imagine the scene. I ask him, *Friends?*, he shakes my hand, and he replies, assuredly, *Friends*. Perhaps he adds: *Forever*. Each takes his separate path and we never see one another again.

I scold myself for these thoughts, for if I am with a thief, he's not just any thief, and he has repented.

A very wide street passes in front of the hotel; in the middle is a canal, rather narrow, rather tranquil.

When we exit the garage, him in the front, holding his bicycle by the handlebars, Fungo is wandering around on the other side of the canal. He waves and greets us cheerfully: *Ciao*, as though nothing had happened.

Turì seems to be emerging from a tender dream, and raises his hand and shakes it to acknowledge him:

"Ciao, Fungo. Wait. We'll go together. Where are you headed?"

"Dunno," Fungo calls out from the distance.

"Doesn't matter," Turì responds.

Feeling rushed by the uncanny encounter, he pulls away from me, saying, "See you, Sir. Thanks, thanks so much for everything." Not a word about *Friends*!

He gets on the bike, and before he treads on the pedal, his back turned so I can see the nape of his neck, I look at his lone ear and ask myself if this lucky madman isn't racing away foolishly to give up the other to be eaten, in this way completing his vow. (Today, Fungo could allege a new set of motives.)

Turí crosses the nearby bridge to reach the second section of the canal, where Fungo is waiting for him. Turì stops, Fungo climbs onto the bike frame, and they go. They ride in figures of eight, mouth off, make merry.

The sun-soaked day still presents me with infinite possibilities. But I need to sleep, and I enter the hotel.

It's five in the afternoon.

from *Stories from Exile* (1983)

Tropics

I don't know what you did to find me, I thought I was in the furthest corner of the Universe.

I made you a guest in my house (my cabin, my shack), where all this time I've lived alone, with a dog and a lizard as tame as the dog. The lizard doesn't care for rocks in the sun or caves or nooks and crannies, he likes water, and since the river here is so calm... The dog is well-mannered, too, maybe a little passive, being so fat... In times of hunger, I've thought of eating him.

I have neighbors out on the coast, three hundred yards or so from here. A French couple you've gotten along with perfectly in English.

It was hot – we're in the tropics – and the woman provoked her husband nonstop. She refuses to let me be witness to their lascivious goings-on.

When you got here, I put on some music, nothing that would remind us of our country.

The French woman stretched out like a mulatta on a hammock spanning two trees.

You wanted to make a paella to get on their good side, but I refused: "It's too heavy, no offense. We're right on the equator."

You wanted us to reminisce about the names of people from there, those of friends, of people from school. I said to you:

"Get off it, brother. I'm dead to them."

Graciously, you lent me your sandals, so I wouldn't ruin my feet walking over the sand and splintered shells.

I saw you were still just a colt, a young stallion, and I advised you:

"Don't take the Frenchman's woman, she's the only thing he's got. Don't get sly and tell me you're just going to borrow her and you'll give her back once you're done.

I went on telling him:

"I know you well, Andrés. You can't fool me. The Frenchman either, hell he played a pimp in a Jean Renoir movie. Let's go get a bite. I'm hungry. On the way, you can tell me how you wound up here. Crossing the river, I get it, but how could you know…"

Quetzaltenango, Guatemala

The Impossibility of Sleep

The impossibility of sleep is horrific. If you don't sleep, you can't dream. You can think and remember, but poor you if wakefulness turns loose memories and labyrinthine thoughts. You will suffer, from them and from the yearning to sleep, because if you can't manage it, when tomorrow comes, you'll fall asleep standing up, and you won't understand your orders, and they'll beat you.

During the day, the prohibition against lying down in bed: the prohibition against sleeping or dozing.

The prohibition against sleeping sitting down in your seat, which has no backrest anyway and offers no support. If you fall asleep despite the prohibition, you'll freeze. You are surrounded by cement walls and windows without panes, with nothing but bars across them.

At night, the guard wakes him, time and time again.

One evening, the guard doesn't show, not even to glide down the corridors and pound the bars with his baton. Suddenly the light comes on, controlled from outside. It goes out, and with it the fear of a nighttime inspection, when you would have to jump up naked and chaos and destruction would ensue.

The light turns off and when the tension goes slack, I return to my sleep and my fancies. Then the light erupts again, over and over, cutting off and on, with interims of brightness, as though to let flower, all at once, fear, disgust, and hope. It comes on, it goes off, all through the night. It goes off.

The man dreams he is dreaming that the guard won't let him rest.

The guard wakes him with a violent shove and rebuffs him: "You're asleep…? Get up, it's daytime!"

Lazarillo of Hermosilla

On my usual route, from the office to my room and vice versa, I pass through the subway tunnel that opens in Goya, dips under Calle Doctor Esquerdo, and emerges in front of the honey store. Around the corner from there, on a street lined with what once were gaslights, is where I live.

Where the tunnel flattens out under the sidewalk and buses, where the sound goes dead, was the dog. I saw him in wintertime, wrapped in a blanket.

His owner lay dozing, most often on the tile floor. He didn't make a show of the dog, and he had no gift for music, playing the violin or the accordion for tips, as so many do; nor did he have a cardboard sign set out, appealing to the charity of the public: *I'm out of work, my wife died, I have six children, and my hovel burned down.* His hat did all the work, upside down on the ground.

I found his very somber approach interesting, and admired the patience of the dog, who must have received some nourishment from his owner at certain hours, bought with whatever the daily haul of pesetas could afford.

But I didn't care enough about them to let down my guard.

One day, when things had gone well – they weren't going to fire me at work, not yet – I wanted to show my gratitude, but I didn't know how or to whom. I let a coin fall into the upside-down hat.

Then I was angry I had done so, because from then on, when the man saw me come down the tunnel with my respectable beard, he would stare at me, albeit discreetly. Despite that test to my compassion, my action wasn't to be repeated.

My resistance was bolstered by what he said to me when I indulged my weakness and paid him mind.

I asked:

"What did you do before, what were you?"

He replied:

"Not what was I, what *am* I."

"What then, what is it you do?"

"I'm an inventor."

"Of what?"

"What kind of things does an inventor invent?"

"I can't imagine."

"I'm an inventor of what doesn't exist."

"Ah… so what's your most recent invention?"

"The dog."

I let it go. All that arrogance, and the suspicion he was having a laugh at my expense, relieved me of any inclination to help.

Dog and man disappeared. They'd changed spots, I supposed with relief, and I wished them a more prosperous destination.

Then the dog came back, but alone. No man, no blanket. I couldn't ask after his master.

Later on, it was the same thing: the solitary dog, not laid out, as usual, but rather sitting on his hindquarters, expectant, with an anxious demeanor. The man is ill, I thought, or he's busy with something and has left the dog to mind his post, so some other beggar doesn't come along and take it.

Supposing his owner would be back anytime and knowing the dog had to eat, I laid a few pesetas at his feet, or rather paws.

A woman watching me followed suit, without excessive conviction, perhaps, since, it looked a little stupid at first glance, giving money to a dog.

Wednesday was no different. Save that the money from before had vanished. I imagined something magic had occurred, either to the money or to the dog. Then I tried to clear the conjecture from my mind. My life has no room for the marvelous: not a single fancy has ever embellished it. Nothing extraordinary has ever happened to me, nor have I ever encountered anything I might even consider strange.

Thursday: dog and coins intact; there were even a few *duros*. I concluded he had passed the night there, that his owner hadn't returned, that he was used to people leaving him alms, but if someone tried to take them away, a little growling and baring of fangs had sufficed to run them off.

I was convinced the man had died, and I went to the offal shop to get some tripe and oxtails for the poor thing, something hearty to help him through the wait, which was possibly pointless now, but from which there was no dissuading him. I suppose he was thankful for what I'd given him. Either way, he bit into it. Not with voracity: he still had his good manners.

I don't work on Sundays, and this past Sunday I stayed in my room. At one point, a voice rose up from the lots around the square where the children play... a dog's voice. It was barking energetically, peremptorily.

I stepped out onto the balcony and there he was down below. I think he saw or smelled me, and since I hurried like a coward to shut myself up inside, he started moaning, with woeful tones, at my absence.

A boarder has lost his patience and shouted at him, a neighbor lady pitied him, other dogs showed their support with dull, fatalistic howls.

The lapdogs seemed to be sobbing. When night fell, a lonely ululation rose up, and there, between my four walls, I heard the hoarse, accusatory murmurs of the families.

At daybreak on Monday, I pricked up my ears to check whether the plaintive howling had abated. Not a single note hovered in the air. Feeling safer, I went over to look. I peeked over the potted geraniums: nothing.

It occurred to me that he must be wandering along the sidewalks in search of leftovers or castoff food in the doorways, and that soon he would return to his post in the subway. So I walked to the metro via the overground route, since at that hour, the cars aren't yet hurtling en masse down Calle Goya.

The shadows lurking in the office pummeled me with their claws, and a few remained stuck in my flesh. They fired me, I mean to say.

I've spent weeks without work, more than a month now, taking care of the dog, which I usually see in the square – the park, as they call it – in front of the Church of the Holy Family. Properly speaking, the park is called Fuente del Berro, and that's where the dog cheers up and feels better. He's young, and he makes it clear he'd like to romp around, but I can't follow him on his diversions.

Since we get along well, I still don't have a job, and his owner hasn't come back, I've taken over his old post in the pedestrian tunnel that runs under Calle Doctor Esquerdo.

With the dog at my side, without pleading, without a cardboard sign – we keep up appearances – I stand there, as though I'm waiting. My face does the begging for me, it seems: it's pale, wounded, weakened.

If its argument isn't persuasive enough, I stretch out my arm before the good people who pass. To fool myself into thinking I'm not reaching my hand out for charity – aware of my hypocrisy – I hold a plastic bowl instead.

I envy a skilled competitor who drops in every two or three days, presumably when his funds have run dry, and holds a guitar in one arm, fingers with the other hand, and blows accompaniment into a harmonica held on by a chinstrap, attracting more attention than I.

I envy the young couple in the Goya metro, the man with his flute like Manuel de Falla and the woman with her long gauze skirts and black braids that make her look like a real live gypsy.

All I have is my hunger, my bowl, and my face. A lady who stopped, her attitude hesitant, as if not sure that I'm an authentic beggar, opens her mouth to tell me something, with a defiant air, never looking away: Am I not ashamed to use a poor dog to rouse people's compassion?

The stern reprimand, uttered wrathfully to my face, does not manage to unnerve me; but I check myself, and don't respond as I should.

"He's my seeing-eye dog, Miss, don't you understand? What do you want from me, should I tear out my eyes so you'll have a perfect portrait of blind man and guide dog to stir your heart? Is your money worth all that, Miss?"

I turn to walk away. The dog is slow to react, but he may have a sense that the woman has pushed me to the peak of humiliation, for he follows me, his head down, on wobbling legs.

Halfway to who knows where – my confusion has actually blinded me – my thoughts grow clear and I began to conceive of something that makes me whistle. I see if the dog's paying attention and yes, he's picked up on my lifted spirits.

I stop suddenly, struck with an idea. Now I know what I have to do.

I retrace my footsteps, back down to the tunnel. The harpy is no longer there. No matter, I'll put the show on for myself.

When the dog reaches his customary spot, he looks at me inquisitively, and when I say nothing, he lies down, as usual. In a tyrannical voice, I order him up. He stands. Then I move into his place. I throw myself to the ground and start barking.

Calle Hermosilla, Madrid

Orthopterans

I'll tell it the way they told it to me. This clarification is necessary as the language, meant to be as plain as that of the original story, is a bit casual. The speaker, in this case, is not a resident of any of the settings evoked, but rather a man of the city, a journalist. For whom the story began, or was lived, though later he may turn his eyes into the depths of a timeless past, sometime around the 1930s.

Or maybe earlier, because the phenomenon frayed the nerves of Don Jacinto Benavente, and given the circumstances, this could only have happened when they awarded him the Nobel Prize for Literature, that is to say, in 1922.

Don Jactino was traveling by train, with a theater company, maybe Lola Membrives's... No, it can't be, he repeated that journey, but without its perilous exploits, with Membrives, thirty years later.

The itinerary the travelers were meant to cover took them from Buenos Aires to Santiago de Chile, with an obligatory stopover in Mendoza. The arrival in this city in the Andes, anticipated at around midnight, did not take place till the following morning, with muted alarm among those who had some sense of who Benavente was and were already informed, by means of the telegraph, that as they passed through the San Luis station, a messenger came onboard with something important in his leather satchel. This man, an employee of the post office, went from car to car, asking which among the passengers was a Mr. Benavente, and when he found him, he passed him a telegram. The four lines contained the message from the Swedish Academy.

Back then, that train was known pretentiously as the Buenos Aires-Pacific Line and was run by the English, who were both punctual and proud of their punctuality, so that its late arrival meant a black stain on the service record of those responsible for every subsequent stop on the line. When it pulled in, and the swiftest bystanders, the stationmaster among them, leapt at the diminutive and now venerable figure of the *Nobelized* Spaniard, the latter, still bewildered by his impressions, received them with a cry of terror in his throat: "Locusts! Locusts!"

What did he mean? That the delay was the fault of the locust invasion. Thanks to the diligence of the telegraph services, the stationmaster knew this, but neither he nor the other enthusiasts there to receive him could have imagined the news would make such an enormous impression on the face and the eyes of the newly crowned Nobel Prize winner.

For he was frightened, and his fright was tenacious, as if the creatures were still crawling over his face. They say he asked, as soon as possible, to be taken to the zoo, to confirm the existence of the animal kingdom, but in a place where he was certain to find it behind bars and inoffensive. He wouldn't enjoy such vengeance this trip, because in 1922, the zoological park in Mendoza had yet to be founded.

But that is not the main story, and the occasional interruption was foreseeable, for when it comes to confabulation, not even Borges can be expected to cleave to a strict chronological order. The other story, the one mentioned in the opening lines of this report, is of such uncertain origins that it may have come down to us from the earliest Indians. Such a hypothesis rings plausible so long as one keeps in mind that what it describes, or attempts to revive in the imagination, is the fantastical origin of the plagues, or at least of one of them, and related treacheries.

The most recent chapter of these events, which defy common sense, takes us to the 1930s, a period marked by what occurred then to the person now writing. A young journalist, I was assigned, because of the economic harm this disorder had done to the rail services, to a kind of inquiry or journalistic documentation. I was to ascertain whether the official excuse was valid, that the trains could only arrive slowly because, with the enormous weight they were carrying, the steel wheels slipped and couldn't cross the zone between the pampa of Buenos Aires and the pampa of San Luis, where limitless rows of famished, ravaging locusts were perched. When the vermin came to rest on the rails and a train passed, the first car would crush them, and as the body of the locust has an oily consistency, that car and those behind it, now skidding and unable to maintain their normal forward motion, would be turned to a giant iron caterpillar. A laggard one, moreover, hence the chaos on the B.A.P., the Buenos Aires-Pacific Line.

The journalist's entry into the infested region was not greeted by herds of insects, nor even a solitary specimen posed on the windowpane as a foretaste of what was to come. The only symptom was the convoy's slowness, a precaution, as though it were yielding to placid lethargy. The journalist and the photographer yielded to that abandon without question until a locust appeared, swooping down from the air and trying to brace itself against the windowpane. In accordance with the proudest tradition of those lands, the creature began to buck and primp like a horseman on the glass, determined to send us a warning. Then it let go and departed, windborne.

The train didn't derail. The conductor had a knack for dealing with the plague. He maneuvered with consummate care, arriving at the station in a large village, the present one, where the plot unfolded.

Climbing down onto the platform was like stepping into a crab marsh. The people who didn't get off at the station watched the journalist and his photographer with commiseration, recognizing that, if they were going to be devoured, it was by their own choice, they had tamely turned themselves over to that holocaust.

They managed to move forward, though doing so meant treading on cadavers that they themselves were the cause of. The journalist made a rapid conjecture: *if those tiny beasts had a soul and their souls were inclined to vengeance, they will feed on me as soon as I fall still.* Even more, it dismayed him to consider that subtle movements wouldn't save him: the wheat ears, though shaken by the gales, still bore up the locusts which never ceased, even in these unstable conditions, to devastate their grains and stalks.

He relaxed when the photographer led him to the steps of a corner bar in front of the station.

They ordered a wine in the shade and protection of the roof and walls, where the multitude of insects that tormented human life found their only emissaries in the flies, which were intolerable as well, but more familiar, at least.

The journalist's glass of white wine, flung by the owner, whipped swiftly across the tin bar top and disrupted the journalist's musing, though not so fast as to free it from the suicidal stratagems of a green gleam that plunged diagonally into the beverage. The green gleam was a locust, which lay across the glass like a mint sprig in a cocktail, with the same color and vegetal appearance. Insufferable, given the visitor's growing irritation.

He proposed to his fellow adventurer the calm of the small, tree-lined plaza next door, and wondered if the leaves had a repellent scent, since they'd remained immune to that devouring fury that had rained down from the heavens.

Once in the shelter of those verdant shadows, so predictably close to vanishing from the urban landscape, the journalist's myopia revealed to him a kind of surface or bark on the trees, less furrowed than mobile and mimetic, being green and seeming composed of the bodies of locusts. Not content to merely seem so, it was so. This provided the occasion for the man with the camera to exercise his profession; to act, but without fanfare, as the subject wasn't still, it roiled, and begged for the aptitudes of an instant camera, an impossibility at the time.

Nonetheless, inspired by the challenge, the photographer threw himself into the task, trying to shoot a masterpiece, moving from tree to tree in the little distance the plaza had to offer. Those shifts left the journalist alone at the behest of his absurd curiosity. He noted that the corner of the building belonged to an agricultural bank, that it was Saturday afternoon, or siesta, which is even drearier, and was surprised to find a business of this kind open.

He stood up and went to look closer. The rolling blind on the window was lowered halfway, so the journalist had to find a better position to get a glimpse of the interior. He stood on a low barrier and, his objective achieved, came back down, after witnessing the vulgarity of that workplace.

Whence he felt drawn to another gentle scene: a young woman, seated on a bench, caring for two children. She didn't look old enough to be their mother. He approached her to ask her flat out. Just then, one of the children intruded, bursting into vigorous tears at the stranger's appearance and causing the other child to burst into tears in turn. To round off the spectacle, the second child began throwing a tantrum that robbed the reporter of his good judgment, so that he stepped forward with a menacing mien, utterly out of sorts, with an amiable request on his lips, but his probable intention of (he later thought) seeking a sentimental alliance with the babysitter already frustrated. He stopped before the group and demanded that the children quit crying. The effect, as was foreseeable, was the opposite. The journalist, now intractable, tried to save the situation by censuring the young lady emphatically: "Make them quiet down! If they don't, I'll take one of them with me."

Which threat must have astonished him, when he recollected his words at the police station, where he was dragged by an officer moved by therapeutic instincts who, once called upon to proceed, found that the journalist's outburst required jail time, not as a punishment, but rather as an indispensible reprieve.

Which intuition he explained when explanation was demanded by the station chief.

For, when the journalist told off the children and the babysitter, the photographer set aside his photographic undertaking to remedy the incident and witnessed the young woman, spilling buckets of tears, make her escape, soon returning with a uniformed policeman who didn't mince words before charging the aggressor.

The photographer, mortified at the sight of a colleague brought low, but lacking the will to intervene, thought it urgent that someone with some sort of authority intervene, and knowing no other person of comparable influence, called on the stationmaster where they'd disembarked an hour before. He showed his credentials, trotted out his photographic equipment, and brandished those verbal defenses he had swallowed only just before.

The railway man, likewise a uniformed servant of the state (with the word *gefe* or *chief* embroidered in hold thread on the breast pocket of his jacket, beginning a *g* rather than an *j*, in conformity with the peculiar orthography of the British rail lines in South America), was indignant and, though not so expeditious as to make his feelings evident by the expression on his face, he did not fail when it was time to act. At the station, he made much of the journalistic calling of the accused, which at that time and place had no significance whatsoever. The same cannot be said for the weighty assertion that this same party had been hired by the Buenos Aires-Pacific Line to document the scandal, in which the railway authorities were naturally blameless, of the train delays occurring precisely in those parts as a result of the swarms of locusts, the consequences of which were evident, not so much there as on the other end of the line.

The spirit of law and order, as embodied in the officer in question, might have been compelled to let the matter drop, had he not found himself with a certain advantage over the ordinarily superior powers of the railway company: the stranger was already locked up in the clink.

So that instead of fretting, as a preliminary step to the refusal of immediate release, the policeman, his bearing triumphal, let slip a suspicion. He asked the stationmaster if he really knew who the offender was:

"Offender against what?"

"The law."

"What law?"

"What law, I can't say. Later, when things have calmed down, I'll find out. But there must be one that forbids kidnapping."

The stationmaster didn't show his cards for all to see, but he did adduce a defense, affirming the impossibility of a visiting delegate perpetuating a crime of such magnitude:

"Kidnapping? Who? The girl? He tried to run off with the girl to commit some dishonest act?"

"No. I'm not saying that. But he did warn her he would steal the little boy."

"But he didn't, did he? There was no kidnapping."

"Kidnapping, no, but threats… And you know how things are nowadays…"

And thus, the defense was plunged once more into confusion, and barely managed to ask:

"How are things? Did something happen?"

With the authoritative bearing of one who knows better than his neighbor, the officer explained:

"What, you don't know?" (He addressed the stationmaster alone, preferring to ignore the photographer.) "You haven't heard…?"

"What?"

"The kidnapping of the Lindbergh baby, the aviator's child."

All this, that is to say, the incarceration of the journalist investigating the delay of the trains that led to the sea, to the edge of the Pacific Ocean in other words, took place, as has already been made clear, in the decade of the 30s, at the same time as the famed kidnapping of the child of Charles Lindbergh, the "Lone Eagle," who had, in 1927, crossed the Atlantic Ocean in a single flight, from New York to Paris, and whose little boy was stolen and murdered years later.

The stationmaster accepted the policeman's excessive zeal when the latter advised him of the need to respect formalities, declaring that it was a mere matter of hours, and that the journalist would be in safe hands with him, drinking yerba mate. "Just in case the boy's father, who's a bank manager, comes around hooting and hollering: the police… don't you do anything, with all the bandits showing up here from one day to the next?"

In fact it was precisely two hours, though the detainee himself was unaware of the designated period until his traveling companion informed him of such.

Two hours of chitchat and mate with the officer who, dispirited and cordial, illuminated the journalist with regard to his theories concerning the plague of locusts.

He spoke to him amicably of a man and a suitcase, or maybe a trunk. The man was like him, like the journalist: a stranger who took up residence in the village, from love, it was said. But he was a loner, and he went by the name of Professor. A loner who, by all rights, was determined to deepen his solitude. At first he'd go to the post office to send off letters, and he received letters as well. Then people noticed he no longer took that road to the post office, not to send mail and not to receive it. From which the policeman concluded that he received no responses because he no longer wrote to anyone.

In the meanwhile, the professor restricted his nourishment, he made do with a few packets of noodles from the store, a daily loaf of bread, some potatoes... and more rarely, a single hen's egg.

As his purchases dwindled, his flesh began to wither, and since he customarily dressed in black, and deep purple rings had formed beneath his eyes, he made a funereal impression when he showed up in the street.

"You told me," the journalist ventured to ask him, "that he arrived in the village for love. Love for what, the place or a person: was there a companion involved?"

"It could be she existed. It could be she died before he came. Anyway, no one knows where she's buried, if the professor's lady friend ever did live here."

"Did he visit the cemetery? Did he take flowers to any grave in particular?" The journalist fears he's overstepped and tries to emend his words with the following inanity:

"I'm sorry, but do you all have a cemetery here?"

With a tinge of pride, the officer informs him:

"Of course we do, my friend! A big one, well tended, though it must be said, not all of the dead are from around here. The cemetery's shared between two municipalities."

He picks up the thread:

"Was he ever seen paying respects to anyone in particular? My feeling is no. Why deny it, I... given the nature of my profession, I distrusted him, even more when the thing happened, I mean when he got started with his plans. Because he did want to teach us things, I'll admit that much, but they always came out twisted. He didn't talk much, he wasn't confident or the sort to give long speeches. But he made himself heard when he got started with his flower craze. He said lots of them reproduce thanks to pollen from elsewhere and that in order to be fertilized, the plant has to receive pollen. It's the air that brings the pollen, he said, but it's best if there are insects to help. And he had chosen a flower the bees like, and when the bees have fed on those flowers, they make honey. He saw beehives as the future of this village.

"He offered to bring these pollinating insects, hopped on the train, and came back after a while with a suitcase or a trunk, I never saw it, I wasn't yet assigned to this detachment. I heard about it, and that's why I'm not certain."

"Well, suitcase or trunk, what did it have inside?"

"Locusts. He opened the trunk and the pests started flying out. Whatever they landed on, they stripped it raw, whether it was grain, flowers, vegetation, or wild shrubs."

"That's the origin of the plague you're suffering?"

"I wouldn't go that far, because the professor's stunt was ages ago."

"How many years?"

"I wouldn't rightly know. Who can say? Could be what I'm telling you happened back when the Indians camped out in these parts, or even before…"

"Why, then, did you say he was a professor who wrote letters and traveled by train?"

"You don't think it's possible he was was the chief of a tribe or a witch doctor and maybe with the passage of time, as the story went from person to person, he turned into a man of knowledge, a professor?"

"So what you're telling me has come down from an age-old tradition, maybe from before the Spanish arrived?"

That's the only objection the journalist dares to proffer, taking care not to accuse the chief of pulling his leg, so as to avoid raising hackles at a moment so decisive for his upcoming release.

But the officer seemed oblivious to his incredulity, and merely responded by musing, without a trace of bitterness or annoyance:

"From before the Spanish…? Could be. There's so many of these stories, but just a few have to do with the village, this village. I'll go ahead and tell them to you."

The journalist, alarmed by this declaration, glanced uneasily at his wristwatch.

The officer noticed and chided him courteously:

"Don't worry, you'll be out soon enough. There's time for everything. Death is the only impediment. And speaking of death…"

The journalist didn't meekly endure this intimation that the officer would now move on to another tale. Unwillingly, he made an impatient face, which the other registered before returning to his theme:

"You were asking whether the professor visited any grave in particular, and we left aside the matter of the professor's love. Love for whom? We found out later. There was a strange death. I worked the case. The schoolteacher disappeared. We tracked her until we found her sleeping in the countryside. What am I saying, sleeping? Dead. The clue was a column of locusts shaped like a whirlwind rising up over the sunflowers."

"What relationship did that death have with the professor?"

"What relation? You tell me: 1. The whirlwind or spiral of locusts rose up from the teacher's body. 2. The body was empty; inside there was nothing but locusts. 3. The professor brought the locusts to the village."

"Still, I don't understand the relation between the professor and her death."

"Well, I did, and I wasn't alone."

"You weren't alone, you say? Who else thought so?"

"The coroner."

"How do you know?"

"Sometimes the coroners take over the functions of investigators or detectives. That was the case back then."

"And the judge, did he not pay attention to you or your suspicions?"

"No."

"How did the professor take the death? What did he do that you could see?"

"He made his desperation obvious, in a surprising way, too. He made a public confession, in the schoolroom where we held the viewing."

"What did he confess to, the murder?"

"Not so fast, my friend, just wait. Who said murder? The professor declared he had brought the locusts so the seamstresses could copy their wings. He wanted a fabric, not a white one like every bride wears, but a light green, diaphanous one, like the wings of those insects he called… what was the word? Orthopterans."

"Very good. So what was your conclusion then, officer?"

"My conclusion? My conclusions!"

The journalist again consulted his Longines, no longer hiding it, faced with the prospect of another song and dance, as indeed occurred:

"One. The professor was involved in her death, though it was never proven, nor was much effort put into doing so, because what can a miserable little police department in the countryside do without the help of criminalistics, who never show their faces around these parts? Two. It was never discovered how the teacher died, nor will it ever be. The coroner didn't wash his hands, I mean to say he didn't abandon his obligation to put forward a hypothesis, but the one he came up with was useless. He said the locusts had eaten her from the inside out, entering through her nasal cavities or her mouth, which was open when she died. I've heard talk of killer wasps, but never of killer locusts. Anyway, it's one thing for an insect to kill someone and another thing to eat them, especially if you recall that, as the coroner admitted, the locust is not a carnivorous beast. Three, putting the teacher's death aside, I can assure you I have another conclusion, of even greater importance. Shall I tell you?"

Before continuing, the officer asked the arrestee what time his watch showed, if he'd already passed the time limit he himself had set. The journalist responded with an *almost, almost...* so feebly that the narrator felt free to proceed.

"I understand you've taken my account to be a fantasy and the death of the teacher to be magic, and it should be said, that part doesn't correspond to the Indians' recollections. But whether you admit it or not, you are listening to me with malice, and knowing that, I'll go ahead and tell you the conclusion that has worried me the most, and I'll save another one, in case you feel like killing an afternoon with me some other time before you return to where you're from. I'd say you've been listening to me, and if you believe me, you'll add things up and realize that this is, at the very least, the second invasion of locusts this village has had to endure. It must be two, right?"

"True."

"Not counting the one in Egypt."

"What's that have to do with anything?"

"Listen, I don't remember too well what I had to learn in school or in catechism. I'd have to ask the priest, but we don't speak to each other. Regardless, I seem to recall that locusts were one of the seven plagues of Egypt, right? You must know. So from what I can tell, with or without Egypt – though Egypt would be good to include, just to make the accounting more serious – we have to face the fact that locusts, like every other plague, return. And as I see it, everything returns, except for us. When we die, just like the teacher, the jig is up."

"Conclusion?"

"You've got to enjoy life, as long as you hold out. Without hurting anyone, understand?"

It was almost night – not completely, because in the summertime, in the sky presiding over all those fields, the light, before emptying its heavy shadows over the land, wavers at the prospect of a total retreat, and lingers there, concentrated, in the moon and stars, which spread out as though inflamed with vibrant glimmers.

It wasn't night, and yet something inside his organism was ordering him to eat. At the door to the station was the photographer, who had drawn once more on the fund of saintly patience he exercised in the course of their association. For which reason the journalist, who took care of the money their company provided for travel expenses, proposed not the best restaurant, because the village didn't have one, but simply finding nourishment suited to what they both were: a pair of hungry men.

But after making short work of the cold cuts and beef empanadas, the photographer reasoned against ordering further dishes:

"Tomorrow, we have to work."

Which the journalist took to mean, *Tomorrow, we have to start working*, and he saw it as fair counsel:

"Truth is, instead of working, I've passed my day in leisure, as a prisoner."

As they had agreed to rise early, they set forth with the first gleams of daylight in search of their feature, hoping the locusts had not yet taken flight. They had calculated correctly.

The insects still covered the trunks of the trees, and those laid out on the ground had remained there, heedless or practicing some morning gymnastics with the aim of getting into shape, the journalist thought, attributing human intentions to the frolicking little beasts which leapt nimbly on their elongated extremities.

Then, while the photographer, absorbed in his work, amused himself urging them on – Pose, my pretties! What are you doing! Don't look around, look at the camera! – the journalist brought his eyes close to those locusts still in the clutches of their nocturnal lethargy, hoping to confirm the similarity between the wings of the orthopteran insects and the lace the professor chose for the wedding gown in which he hoped the rural schoolteacher would marry him.

The position of the newly born sun, piercing the cloudscape that sheathed its ascent, dispatched rays that brought the mass of locusts into view: their angular bodies, long, with four folded wings.

Later, when the sun's disc rose a bit higher, its beacon cast shadows from behind, and he could imagine that lace over the young flesh of that woman; and just as he could never know what struck her down, he would never delight in the sight of her face.

He lost track of time, submerged in these divagations, while the creatures crawled closer together, and when they were a single mass, they took flight in perfect formation, temporarily blocking the view of the sky.

Everything happened soundlessly, and the journalist asked himself if those airborne creatures' silence masked a voice that humans couldn't hear. How wonderful! he said, not quite knowing the source of his wonderment, perhaps still imagining those thousands of locusts had taken flight to form, before the blue canvas of the everyday sky, a Nile-green sky destined for a single day, like the green of that wedding dress.

They photographed locusts sitting still, locusts busy eating, and locusts posted on stationary trains that couldn't move forward without sliding off perilously and risking derailment. They photographed locusts up close and from afar, but from too far away was impossible, the camera couldn't capture them. The photographer knowingly squandered his plates, aware of the loss of material incurred but wishing to catch sight of a locust's mandibles as it chewed, while not certain whether locusts had mandibles.

They photographed the stationmaster, the stalled trains' engineers, the neighbors from the village, who offered opinions...

They lunched on leaner rations than the evening before, rested a while in the beds in the pension, and when they left, the journalist told his colleague he was taking the road to the police station.

"Again?" said the photographer, astonished.

"My conversation with the officer was cut short. And he owes me some mate..."

"Best if we be sincere: you got used to prison life."

The officer said he'd been waiting for him and showed him the kettle on the coals and the strong yerba mate he was brewing.

He said if the journalist was looking to find out the professor's fate after the death of his secret love, he would share with him the last part of the story.

He doubted he would be believed, even supposing the journalist lent credence to what he'd heard before, because, he clarified, the professor's conduct became even more perverse thereafter, not because he caused problems per se, but because he proposed something that struck the neighbors as extraordinarily strange.

The professor knew he'd disappointed them before, promising pollinating insects and instead bringing locusts that loosed rack and ruin and the countryside, laying it waste before stopping one day and setting off in a dark cloud, doubtless to pillage crops and threaten men's bread elsewhere, and so, he proclaimed he would procure them the blessing of water.

They didn't lack for water in the village or the fields, but it wasn't enough to satisfy their longings to increase the arable land, and securing them more, and others of nature's bounties, was the meat of his new proposition.

He didn't come back with a suitcase or trunk, but with a bearded character with a black head of hair trimmed to resemble a fakir at a fair. At first he kept him from the public eye, and even when he lowered his guard, he merely introduced the man as Garrick, neither mentioning details concerning him or praising whatever virtues he might possess. Nor did he speak again of his promise of water, and yet the population couldn't help but see Garrick as a magician who would make it rain more than before, filling the ponds and lakes from which the canals snaked out to the thirsty fields.

One day, when the time seemed right, the professor and Garrick set to work. They set up vertical wooden pillars, unfurled a canvas cloth, and raised a spacious tent.

He summoned the population and tried to dispel doubts, telling all that Garrick was neither magician nor acrobat nor trapeze artist. He was an actor.

Someone asked from the stands:

"A comedian?"

And the professor smiled by way of a response, but there was something ambiguous in his smile.

The people took the professor at his word, keeping in mind how gruesomely he'd lost his beloved.

The professor explained then that Garrick was a dramatic actor, although – a curious intuition from the man in the audience, he said – in England, he was renowned as one of the great artists of history for his ability to make others laugh.

Perhaps, he clarified, the English had their reasons for cataloguing him as they had, but on coming to America, he had pursued his true vocation, that of the art of drama. And so, after passing through the big city theaters, in Buenos Aires, for example, he found he preferred the circus tent. Beneath it, he said, in the circle of sand, he had acted out gaucho sagas of love and courage, from Martín Fierro to Santos Vega and Hormiga Negra, the protagonists of which he'd known in real life and with some of whom, the last two, for example, he had even shared the stage.

This announcement didn't please the audience.

There were murmurs, and some said to others that Santos Vega and the other gauchos were noble and capable of greater feats, facing off against an armed band or mouthing off to the devil while playing guitar. But that wasn't what they wanted, what they wanted was water, and if not, if this was how things had to be, then the foreigner, the actor, could be an actor, but he'd best be a comic one.

"Comic and otherwise," said Garrick, with the visible approval of the professor, who had heard the murmurs and shared them with the artist.

Garrick stepped away, then returned weighed down with masks and disguises, a whole array of clothing suited to clowns, jesters, mummers, acrobats, mimics, buffoons, and gagsters.

But he left aside, ostentatiously, the contraptions for the masquerade, and devoted himself naturally and effortlessly to making them laugh, with stories, gags, wit, impersonations, much brilliance, and occasional grimaces, but tactful ones, without any sort of exaggeration.

And the people reveled and laughed unrestrained, laughed until they cried.

Their tears flowed together like a rivulet, which grew as it coursed through the town and emptied its current in the outskirts.

And in that way, through the magic virtue of joyous tears, lakes, lagoons, and other deposits which, if they are large enough, are given the name *mar chiquita*, spread across the vastness of Spanish America.

Madrid, winter of 1982

Uncollected Stories

Hands in the Night

The man has come back to the big, mysterious city. It was his homeland, but after a period of absence, he feels like a stranger. By day he plunges into the maze of streets and the multiplicity of means of transport, confused and stymied in any attempt to arrive at any place in particular. By night, he wrangles with his insomnia in a borrowed room, lacking means to buy his own or rent one.

Tonight, he's overcome his fear of falling, of tripping on the sidewalks with their pavers upturned, as if they'd suffered a bombardment; he's overcome the fear of bumping into the hooligans who wantonly rob passersby. An obsession compels him: held in a hand that waits to pass it to him somewhere in the undeciphered city. Aided by this improbable illusion, he has walked past the streets constantly rumbling with the clamor of cars in motion, arriving at the outskirts where an unseen dog howls, baneful and haunting.

He can't see why the beast isn't in the open fields instead of behind the wall he's just come upon, and all alone, he follows the linear structure, finding neither a single person on his path nor a single opening that might permit anyone to emerge or approach him.

The man stays there, in the midst of the dreadful silence, startled by the bellows or cries of the big dog which he cannot describe as such, for he hasn't seen it.

The man walks and walks, endeavoring to reach the end of the wall, never getting past that band of stone or brick that hovers beside him, blocking his access to the plane he suspects lies beyond it. He imagines he's arrived at the Great Wall of China and consoles himself with the thought of coming across some sentry box where a man will say a word and give him shelter. This guardian or watchman could be a soldier, he reflects, and armed, and instead of giving him his hand he may stab him with the bayonet on the tip of his rifle. The image makes him cringe, but doesn't deter him from his mission of walking to the place where he knows a hand is waiting for him.

The journey along the wall lasts so long that the man starts to think there is nothing behind it, nothing promising at least, though his conjecture is belied by the barking, for if there is a dog, then presumably, a human being, master or executioner, is with him.

Without rescinding its shadow, without permitting the least infiltration of light, whether from the sky or along the surface of the ground, the night follows its course, stretching on longer than what might be thought normal.

The man feels an irritation, like an itch on his chin and cheek. He brings a hand to those parts of his face and finds his beard has grown. How long, how many nights has he spent walking, besieged by that hound, bloodthirsty, or so it seems, which would have pounced to destroy him, had it not been for the wall?

He questions the tension making his chest tremble, and he grasps at another theory: there is nothing to fear, there is nothing behind the wall, no living beings nor beings of any other sort, the world ends beyond that barrier; but that is no comfort, either: if the barrier fell, abstractly or materially, with an intolerable bang, the man – he thinks – would run up against the shell of the universe or if not, a surface empty and barren, like the crust of the moon.

The perspective of a solitude so vast torments him and smothers him with fear.

But over and over, he returns, as to a kindly hope, to his intention when he began his walk: to find the hand outstretched to him, the lost loner in the night.

He advances obstinately, ignoring his fears, weighed down by the likely danger, the nature of which he still doesn't know.

He has faith, a dark and indecipherable faith, that regardless of the risk, it may be benevolent. But he has to find the hand, the fraternal hand that welcomes him, only then will he have passed the test.

Now the hungry void is behind him, the one that called him as though to devour him, the immense black emptiness behind or alongside the surrounding wall, which has, in the meantime, ceased to be a barrier, and is now like an orange peel, a twisted strip of rind. Inside, it protects or cushions what resemble monuments, more than one of them, more than ten.

He goes over to look more closely, and finds they have doors. On this door, and indeed, on the one further off, hangs a heavy knocker which, looking closely, betrays the form of a hand. He is tempted to lift it from the bottom and let it drop to test its weight. Then the hand vanishes: it is now a dangling serpent with an upraised head.

Then the hand manages to capture it in its grasp. The hand is a ruse, a deadly instrument. And to overcome terror and misfortune, he must ignore it. Just when he's due to pound the door with the knocker, he suspects it to represent vengeance against him, but he knows he is innocent, and must maintain his composure.

He takes the knocker, which is heavy, and his hand hurries down, with a muffled but powerful sound of bronze banging against the door. He knocks, and the dull sound is like a magic invocation: the lights open up, and the wall that obstructed his vision vanishes. The man recognizes the Calle Junín, close to Las Heras, where the cars and buses are passing at this late hour.

Joyous – somewhat – he sees he's been saved, admits that his fear made him panic and led him astray, that there neither was nor is a Great Wall of China, that the serpent hasn't bitten him, and all he has to do is take a few steps to reach the corner of Las Heras and take the number sixty.

Premature Wait

I'm the master of my time, and that's saying quite a bit, and would indeed be worth something if my continual waits were not the masters of my time.

Yesterday I waited for the mailman, and if that has ensnared me in complex and absorbing proceedings, I am happy because, if in a muddled way, I have clarified something that allows me to define myself to myself.

I waited for the mailman from very early, with an anxiety my chest showed through my shirt, as was evident to the entire family. I need to permit myself a minimum of aloofness, even with those close to me, as concerns my most secret hopes. It's not selfishness or dim pertinacity, it's simply the terror of being deceived by expectation and thus of deceiving those who expect things of me. And so my heart's treachery made me uncomfortable at home, and I had to wait in the door leading to the street; then, soon after, I moved to the corner, to avoid my indiscreet neighbors; and lastly, I wound up at the post office, where the mailman was due to emerge on his route toward my house. He left through that very door, surprising me, as I had no idea what time he went out. But, whether from unkindness or because he doesn't know me, he had nothing for me but an indifferent glance.

I had to follow him through street after street while he labored meticulously, passing out letters until his leather bag was empty, and we understood that he'd passed by my house some time back and he'd brought nothing along for me. Then I walked with him like a friendly neighbor, trying to salvage my dignity with my attitude and conversation, still paying great attention to anything that might prove advantageous to me when the time came, assuring a letter would arrive in my hands, in mine, and mine alone. We reached his house, and he insisted on presenting me to his wife, against my wishes, but that was all, he neither invited me to the drink my lips were craving nor allowed me access to the bedrooms, which would have led, I'd like to believe, to a greater closeness and, in the long term, incalculable advantages.

At least, I found out his address and thus, quite soon, that very same day, I could take another stab at friendship, sending a bouquet of flowers to the lady. I spent the night calculating the results of my daring, without casting aside the possibility that the sneaking character I had noted in the mailman, conjoined to a hot-blooded, jealous temperament, might lead him to receive my gift with ill humor. What I invested in these calculations I lost in sleep, and in the morning, my body sought recompense, so that my plan to repeat my wait from the day before came to nothing.

It was this same mailman who later came to my door, demanding my presence in a way that my sister, ever timid, took as a threat, which she could neither deflect nor prevent me from reading on her face. As I was ready for anything, I immediately left my bed, fearless, or else pretending flawlessly to be so, and presented myself in pajamas before that imperative, impatient, and irascible mailman, who was not, however, spurred by jealousy, to all appearances and to my good fortune.

He demanded categorically that I explain what it was I wanted from him. I stammered: "Well, I'm waiting…" and then I understood what he was after. I told him frankly and clearly, confessing, man to man: "Well now, I'd like you to sell me one of your paintings. My spirit compels me to have one, but my economic situation, with the current problems which impede me from making use of my talents as I should, puts me in the unpleasant position of having to ask you for a discount, the biggest discount you can possibly concede. And I will tell you even more. It is not in the least true that I propose to acquire one of your paintings, though I really do have the ambition of possessing one, and would buy one from you at any price, no matter how extravagant. If I turn to you as a likely buyer, it has been from mere vacillation, though my firm tone of voice makes this difficult to believe. I was vacillating because I may be neglecting my duty by telling you early what I must absolutely inform you of if I wish to strictly comply with regulations (though I should have done so by letter): we have voted for you, and you will receive the Grand Prize, and with the Grand Prize a recognition that, admittedly, is of no use to you, because you already enjoy it. Now, you know, and you may do what you wish with me, though I trust in your discretion."

Each of my phrases brought a shadow of a smile to my listener's face, no less malicious for its faintness; though it could have been the smile of a person informing another that his problems are already solved, or on their way to being so. He smiled, and tried neither to interrupt me nor to answer. He listened to me courteously until I'd finished. Then, employing such a tone as would make me understand him, he said: "Neither what you ask of me nor what you're announcing is possible, yet; but don't fret, and don't torment yourself. You should not be troubled in the least, because the painter, the artist, is you and not I."

I understood, and after squeezing with all my heart the hands he'd placed in my own, I went back to my brushes.

Paternal Epistle to Fabia

To Fabia:

Today I've been conversing with Don Vicente and his wife; you will see what I told them.

They live on the third floor of this same building. I ran into them on my way from church, in the little park next to Calle Peñascales; today is almost like a Sunday, it's the Feast of the Virgin of the Pillar, no one works and everything is calm.

My neighbors invited me to their apartment, for a glass of beer; they are older, and it's the only vaguely alcoholic beverage they allow themselves. They were waiting for their son to come for lunch along with their daughter-in-law and the grandchildren.

It didn't seem improper for them to ask if I have family in America, they always see me all alone… I confessed to them I'd split from my wife, it was my fault I said, and I had the urge to tell them a bit about you. An incident you may have forgotten some time back, because I don't believe it left a mark on you, it can't have affected you the way it did me, it left me addled with an enduring shame that I still feel and that goes on gnawing at me.

You must remember, though, that first encounter – which was a farewell – the day they conceded to restore my freedom, in the same manner in which they had dispossessed me of it earlier: without explanations, without telling me why. Naturally, confinement was worse: without an indictment, without taking me to trial, without the least opportunity of defense…

After that year and a half of immobility in La Plata, no longer accustomed to walking the city streets, I thought it might not be utterly senseless to risk staying a few days in Buenos Aires before departing for Europe, from whence, I already inferred, I would not be returning in life.

With this forlorn conviction – as I told the couple – I asked my daughter to travel to the capital from our home in the foothills of the Andes, to say goodbye, as I could not return to my region, even briefly, without facing the most ominous risks.

We arranged to meet when her plane landed at Ezeiza, on such a day at such an hour, as you well know. I went to the airport, overcome with anticipation, and rested my body, which had grown so fragile, in the sanctuary of the waiting area.

Assorted machines landed in brief succession, and soon, many travelers filed into the room. From among them, I paid particular attention to a contingent of young girls looking energetic and cheerful. I supposed they were companions of yours from some end-of-the-term excursion; the exam period had just ended. I didn't see you with them, but I did notice some of them looking at me and whispering. I slunk down into the chair, trying to pass unobserved. Who knew whether they might be saying they'd identified me as the father who'd been the subject of that story?

Faced with this circumstance, I kept my head low, I recall, bowed, that is to say, without wishing to face forward. Until I realized that someone, one of those girls, had stopped before me. I looked up, and the situation became clear to me. Wavering, almost timid, I asked: "Are you one of Fabia's classmates?" Very considerately, as though taking care not to deprive me of my serenity, she answered, with a respectful rebuke: "Papa, I'm Fabia. You don't recognize your own daughter…?"

In that year and a half – I tried to convey to the couple – you had changed, at that age teenagers change so fast, and you ceased being what you had been as preserved in my recollection of my last day at home – do you remember?

Your mother had moved to Córdoba for treatment of her singular and agonizing illness and you and I were left alone. As I couldn't care for you properly, you ate and slept in the home of that classmate of yours with the remarkably hospitable family. For my part, I remained at our home, but only to sleep or at midday, for a bite to eat; dinner I always had at the Press Club.

That day, I bought tomatoes, bread, and cheese in the morning and carried them back home. I was in the kitchen cutting a tomato, which I was about to bathe in oil, when you rushed in to look for school supplies or notebooks you needed for class. I offered to share my food with you, you were flustered with your tardiness or worries. I gave you what I believe was a gentle and comprehending look. Once more, like always: our fleeting encounters, the fault of my existence, sapped by journalistic duties, with no time for family, and when I did show up at home, you were asleep.

"Did a letter from your mother come?" was all I could find to say, a single, otiose question, do you remember? Those were the last words you would hear from your father for a very long time.

Later, when I was in that place in La Plata – which, despite its rigors, I prefer to imagine as a hotel, or a monastery – the pain of leaving you so poor weighed on me. Just as it plagues me now, because – as you know, suffering the consequences – I have been incapable of remaking myself in exile.

My poor, defenseless child, without even a sister. I think with torment of those nights she had to spend, afraid, in her lonely, quiet room. Walled in, so needful of affection and company to sleep and play.

My poor, fatherless daughter. Her father crucified on responsibilities unfulfilled while she grew and learned: to be the child's mentor and support.

I sigh as I recall this episode I confided to Don Vicente and his wife, though without disclosing to them the enormity or nature of my distress at my failure to be near and help you.

You see, dear, if I've searched for solace by entrusting my secrets to strangers, still, I have not been sufficiently sincere, and I continue to feel ill at ease. Knowing it's impossible, still I look for you, not so much in airports as in the people around me.

With this misgiving, which sticks in my throat: if I found you, how would I recognize you? The last time, I forgot your features after a year and a half without seeing you... now, seven more years have gone by!

This morning, prudently Don Vicente's wife gave voice to her curiosity, which did not strike me as untoward:

"Your daughter... does she write?"

"Yes, yes. She sent me a portrait, a postcard-size photo. You can see it. I'll bring it another day."

I made a show of flaunting a certain still-intact dignity, without stooping to convince them that the feeling is still there between us, that you haven't abandoned me.

While I kept to myself the bitter taste of disappointment at my failure to help you, my waiver of a father's duties: to educate, direct, to listen to his little girl, to converse with her... No one who's aware will feel these things like the person incapable of doing them.

I say this, Fabia, because of the letter where you tell me about your life. Only a little, not too much. I don't reproach you, I suppose you do so to save me the heartache. In that letter, there is a paragraph, a line that cuts to the bone:

When I come home at the end of the day, and there's nothing to eat...

Without reading it again, I will go on hearing it.

With affection,

Papa.

Very Early Morning in the Cemetery

So much cold.

"Did it have to be so early? Why?" she says, not in protest, but toneless, as though declaring acquiescence to her torment.

"You know. I already told you... It's to preserve the scene from onlookers. It has to be before the visitors come in with their flowers. The spectacle's not for them."

"The scene, the spectacle...?"

He doesn't answer.

From the frozen darkness of the garden at the entrance, a man comes forward. He speaks to them through the grating in the doorway:

"Are you all...?"

"We are. Good morning."

He leads them through the first rows of tombs to a squat administrative building, a contrast to the grandiosity of the structures for the dead.

Inside, behind a desk of medium height, so wide it blocks their path, a man busies himself with his coffee and milk and rushes them:

"It's getting late...! If we're not careful, they'll see everything."

A flicker of alarm is visible in the sister's eyes.

The functionary opens bound volumes, registries, and loose papers. He reads quickly and badly, his words unintelligible. He asks expeditiously if everything is clear. Both the new arrivals say yes. The sister doesn't intervene, she lets him continue.

She pays. The sum makes her raise an eyebrow. She understands what she must do: pay. The service he's performing for them is not the sort one niggles over.

He swallows the rest of his coffee with milk and looks nostalgically into the bottom of the cup. It's the only respite from the restive brusqueness of the procedure.

"Over there, over there."

"It's dark. Where are we going? No one's going to take us?"

"There's no need, you'll figure it out."

The sister in her fur coat cringes, while the man, in a dark, slender suit, with no other protection from the elements, regrets thinking only of the ceremonial aspects.

They walk forward blindly, among blocks scattered at random, and are forced onto faint, weed-infested trails.

They manage to emerge, irritable and confused, from the muddle of concrete blocks, stone, and marble, and neither utters a word.

Further off opens up, on all four sides, a field of crosses, of graves dug in the earth. Stone angels bow down over them in compassion. Bolstering this vision is the sight of the masses, not yet clearly discernible, despite the return of the dawn with its purpose of bringing clarity to all things on the face of the earth.

The air, as though agitated, redoubles its frozen rigors. The light seeps slowly into the atmosphere.

They go back. Disoriented, defeated, to the bureaucrat's office, to appeal for help.

They will receive it: the same character who opened the door for them will guide them.

With him, they will not cross, as they had in their ignorance, the terrain of the dead, who hoist their Nazarene emblems just above the surface of the earth.

He leads them through one of the galleries to the side, where the niches sit as though posed on balconies over ledges of reinforced concrete. It's a relief, this transit over the tile floor, beneath the relative shelter of the vaults.

Among these hoards of dead, he thinks of how many have died. He cannot calculate the number. They appear before him, a bare few, but those are not there. The man asks himself: where are those dead? And he is not asking about their bodies. Who is he speaking with, who does he want to answer? Not his sister, who is turned inward, walking beside him, in mourning and relinquishment.

The man hears music, and asks himself if she does as well. Why ask her? She will tell him: What do you mean? Music?

And yet…

It's a song, maudlin and soothing, without lyrics, set to strings. Soon it stretches forth, like an arm, as though wailing, but not in a spirit of reproach. Chords like the sonorous steps of a ballerina who has choreographed her heedfulness and whose every footfall treads a feeling beautiful but sinister.

The music comes and goes – a dance for two – spins vertiginously – a soloist's turn on his axis.

A voice turns majestic and harmonious, a voice of universal nostalgia, like a score performed by a symphony orchestra.

It diminishes, and takes on the air of a song and the rhythm of a rocking raft on a tranquil lake.

But then, more dynamic sounds, intensely warm sounds rise up, like love thriving in the twin hearts of a man and woman embracing.

The classical tone and manner of the score that sounds – perhaps – for a single listener permit the intrusion, real or vulgar, of chirping birds, which is not impossible, as the dawn has announced its arrival and that chirping may come from the birds greeting the day.

Without time to consider whether it comes from the border of trees, the nascent trilling turns to ayes, to the piping of despair. Another, crueler vision passes before his eyes: two fledglings fly or fall in concert, as if feuding, or fighting tooth and nail, never managing to gain a foothold in the air, unable to resist the force that unifies and binds them. With their frantic warbling, they plummet into the void, and their flimsy heads and bones shatter against the mosaic floor. There they remain, with a final shudder.

The guard explains, without waiting to be asked:

"The sparrows nest in the upper niches. The children hawking flowers or water for the vases climb up there and tie their feet together, one bird to the other. After a few days, when the birds grow up and they try to fly for the first time, what you just saw happens."

The man pushes aside this cruel impression by returning to his earlier question: how many have died. He is not concerned with multitudes, but with individuals. Friends, acquaintances, the odd person he admires but never met.

Manuel de Falla, Lorenzo Domínguez, the Chilean sculptor who came for Easter, Sergio Sergi, who made engravings in Trieste, rubbing elbows with Joyce, Neruda, his uncle Ángel, who pierced his chest with those five sharp prongs he had used to eviscerate the soil, Ramponi, who died of poetic rapture; Cúneo, a poet, not for nothing, nor was it for nothing that he bore the name Víctor Hugo, who set himself on fire in the Plaza Independencia, at the foot of the rose bushes, and the flames scorched them one morning, around breakfast time.

Before advancing toward a patch of dead grass where there stands something like a shack or barn, the maudlin music grabs him, as though tugging him back to the trees: it's returning, majestic, rife with harmony, the voice of universal nostalgia performed by a symphony orchestra.

The hovel is like a workshop, for a carpenter or marble mason, with an abundance of tombstones and coffins, half-complete or half-dismantled.

Among the officiants, gruff, thankfully silent, one gestures with his chin, to indicate he's here.

Before entering, he pulls away prudently from his sister. He goes in alone. The wooden lid has been unscrewed and the metal lining of the interior is exposed, with its small oval of glass. Beneath the glass, slightly misty but still clear, is the face of the eternal sleeper.

The music has receded, or else remains outside.

Without waiting for instructions, the workers run the torch around the edges of the metal box, which cede tranquilly, arcing apart.

The mourner leans over to look as deep inside as he can, to take in whatever detail or expression can still reach him.

But his curiosity is overrun by the irresistible impulse to bow his forehead over his progenitor.

Does he bow before a beloved being or before the immutability of death? Or before the beyond that in a certain way has come so close?

It's me, he tells himself. *I am there. My father is my copy.*

He reacts: *I was my father's copy. He is more distinct than I because he is preserved at thirty-three years old.*

He tells himself to wait before drawing conclusions, because, for now, they are muddled: *He is what I will be. Just as I will be. How is it he keeps his hair so black, that death doesn't whiten it, his natural color doesn't recede, even as life has receded from him?* And then: *So well combed, with that natural wave caught by the painter in the portrait we had hanging at home.*

And yet it seems there is something missing from that intact head. The eyes? No, the stare! He has lost his stare. It's not that his fallen eyelids cover it. It's that death has pulled from the upper left corner and dislodged the force of that absent gaze.

But this pulling is someone tugging at his jacket, with care and respect, to wake him or bring him to order.

He holds himself firm with a question, like a person returned from elsewhere:

"Yes…?"

"We need to get to it."

"Just another moment."

He still doesn't have the proof, the secret ulterior motive of this undertaking.

Nose pressed again to the pane of glass, he scrutinizes the forehead. Terse and serene, without signs of decay. The mouth, neither cracked nor deformed into a rictus. *It must have been in his chest then*, he thinks, *level with the heart, perhaps.*

The workers finish opening the metal cover, just as with a can of preserves. The solder bows and flakes, they strip it from the edges in their dogskin gloves, and for the first time in thirty years, it has contact with the air: this body, which his son recollects as lively, dynamic, handsome; this body, which managed to achieve immobility. Managed…? Achieved…? Was it something he did himself? Today, as the operation goes forward, as they disrobe him, his son may find out. Because it's nothing more than an execution, starting with cutting off the head. With a handsaw that sinks in at the Adam's apple, or where it was, because his neck is now smooth, and no blood will spurt from it, no moan will emerge, save perhaps from the bereaved himself.

The head removed, so dry it didn't tear, they carefully place it aside, and the eyes led astray by the violence of death contemplate what remains of his former body.

Knives and saws enter the corpse, with destructive exuberance and a striving for neatness. But where the bones, in their shell of hard skin turned to leather, oppose the exemplary sacrifice, the axe goes in bluntly, and now, fruit of rage, as the profession's ruthlessness bares its claws, they let loose, giving rise to what the witness hadn't yet known: the sound, the roar of battle, of hatchet blows against bone, the stiff metal blade as it grazes the marble, raising sparks and other sounds of a different timbre, a dreadful symphony performed by the very composers, still unaccompanied by theater music.

There must be something irresistible here, because even with his back turned to this place which ought to have a door, but doesn't, he can sense someone's ingress, and afraid it is her, he turns and sees his sister, her fists over her mouth to suppress something: is it nausea or screams?

He steps in front of her and leads her away.

He stays with her outside, blaming himself for relaxing his vigilance... She responds with a simple litany:

"That noise... that noise..."

Her brother understands: the noise of the saw cutting through the bones.

"Was it Papa?"

"You didn't see him?"

"I tried, but your back hid him."

"Better."

"Why better? He was my father, too, wasn't he?" She sobs. "And I never saw him, or if I did, I was so little I don't remember. Even now, I don't recall the last time... Can I, now?"

To keep from telling her nothing's left but pieces, he responds despotically:

"No."

They have stayed outside. He embraces the orphan, as if she were still a girl, with a late or retrospective intimation of their childhood and their need for sanctuary. Amid this rapport or communion of souls comes a slackening, or a pause for distraction. His gaze wanders. Far off, he notices a swarm of mourners for the unknown dead, with offerings of flowers, advancing along the alleys between the crosses and angels, and closer, he sees, amid the monuments to the deceased, crowning a pedestal some two meters in height, the bust of an older woman, her hair in a bun: she is the mother of the sculptor Domínguez, her image preserved for the ages by her artist son. He draws a comparison between this sculpted work of lasting material on its marble pedestal and the head of his father, severed by a saw and set on a wooden stool, which may fall and roll around like a ball or simply shatter its cranial bones, which must be as fragile as those of the tiny birds.

Looking over his sister's shoulder, he suspects these observations, and the digressions following them, have only been possible because the noise of the sawing has ceased. Maybe he only notices this because the workmen emerge, with the refuse in hand, toward where?

Boards, rags; their boots transported in hand. A short trip, toward some pits he hadn't noticed, over there, a kind of common grave. Where, moments later, another of the workers will carry what's left of the desiccated flesh and the shapeless bits of bone. They are scattered there, and he looks to watch them vanish, until a gravedigger, maybe an underling, starts to shovel the dirt for their second interment. The definitive one, perhaps, because there, in that hole, the bones will intermingle and identity will come to an end. Goodbye, Papa. They didn't give him time to see if there was a wound in his chest, they pulled off the elegant suit and stylish shirt while he was away, consoling the man's daughter.

They invite him to pay homage:

"Do you want to come?"

The larger bones and head remain, with a certain order, in the hut from which the diaspora of all that had composed a unified human being proceeded.

He asks himself whether the same will now occur with the body of his mother, who is still a living memory, because she died only moths ago, while his father was fossilized, a bundle of parchment, nothing more.

No, it will not occur.

They explain to him what he knew well enough, though it had slipped his mind:

That he cannot buy or even rent a niche for his mother in the gallery of reinforced concrete, where the coffins and their contents are less prone to rot and crumble away, because spaces are scarce, and at present, there is not a single one available. (A lack of final dwellings, or overpopulation among the deceased.) That, as he is the rightful owner, in perpetuity, of his father's niche, it is possible to pair the two bodies, even if they are sealed, and since two coffins won't fit, they will employ what is known as reduction. They will reduce, in other words, the volume of one of the bodies, so that both will fit in a single coffin. Hence the dismemberment and fragmenting of the bones.

Consequently, the mother's body will be preserved intact.

Not the coffin, which they will have to open, why?

"To put in his bones and head?"

"That won't be necessary, we've prepared another one for him."

He notices it, though it has been in his sight the whole time: an oblong casket, like the ones for deceased children.

An assistant knocks on it with his knuckles, to show him it is solid, quality wood.

They carefully deposit the femurs and a few ribs, and a strip of black cloth from the suit, as a symbol, perhaps. Everything fits without difficulty until they lay the head inside, and they try the lid, which won't close. They press down, as you do with a suitcase overstuffed with clothes.

He fears – and then perceives – a crackling, like the grinding of bones.

"Don't, please! I'll buy a bigger coffin."

"It can't be done, we have to finish now. Regulations... Anyhow, a bigger one won't fit in the niche."

He agrees, but dissuades them from pressing down on the cranium, because he can't bear, whether on his way out or in the days and nights to follow, that macabre music, which seems to rise up from the soul.

They find a solution: they will avoid sealing the box completely. The lid will remain in place, but they won't screw it down, it will stay loose, balanced and tottering over the peak of the cranium.

They ready an old wagon, with wooden rails a palm in height, barely big enough for anything, but sufficient for the two coffins: the larger one, which is now the mother's, and the tiny one that serves to hold the father's bones. The whole scene seems a parody of a family in mourning for a mother boxed up with her child.

The shafts are lying on the ground. Presumably they'll fit them to one of the donkeys he saw in the corral behind the shack. But no. With great strength and determination, a worker lifts them up and sets off walking forward, not pulling, with the load behind him. Since this, apparently, is the ordinary course of things, the man simply asks:

"Where to now?"

"To the niche."

"To the niche...?" and he stretches out his arm, pointing to the eight or ten rows, one above the other, of inset tombs, overflowing with a haunting succession of bouquets of flowers and green branches. His gesture must be an eloquent testament to his stupefaction, for the worker reacts, albeit with scorn:

"Don't you get it? We have to take them over. Isn't that what you wanted? If not, why'd we bother doing the work?"

Those who carried out the reduction stand around, their silence and their faces showing their agreement with their spokesman. The man understands what he has to do: hand out tips and follow the wagon.

He doubts it is sturdy enough for the journey, but it's already on its way, guided forward vigorously by the worker, and he takes the arm of his sister, who is half-lost, half-horrified. He won't let her think, he drags her onward.

They pass through a narrow sort of alley, flanked by trees that lose their leaves at that time of year. The cold – not the sun, because the first light of day, which was golden, has decayed into a gray insinuation of rain – hangs down like invisible icicles from the bluish branches, while a fire strikes up inside the man and makes him sweat. Pity for his sister and himself: humiliation, shame.

The group has begun to attract the stares of the people decorating the many graves on each side of the path that runs through the very center of the cemetery.

He is ashamed to let the worker make the effort alone, he waves him away from one of the shafts and takes it in his hands.

He asks if it wouldn't be easier to change the cart's direction and pull on the shafts. It seems more reasonable, but the worker doesn't agree, and tells him, maybe disdainfully, he'd do better to make sure the lid of the small coffin doesn't slide off.

And as the cobblestone pavement is highly uneven, the load begins to shift, and a few meters on, the lid does fall down and the head is left uncovered. A child shouts, with wonderment and fright:

"Mama, a dead man's coming out of the box!"

He rushes to cover it.

The turmoil passes, and afraid the same could occur again, he walks beside the cart with one hand covering the unstable lid.

Once he's calmer, he becomes aware of other details: of himself, in his dark suit, with one hand over the coffin, as if a terrible, captive animal might leap out. The porter in his nurse's smock, inexplicable for those ignorant of the preliminaries. His sister, with her elegant layer of furs, which conceal her agony and dread, shattered and austere in her commitment to take part in that shabby cortege… The cart that creaks and creaks again, its groaning sound growing in their ears, which is not an illusion, because it draws the attention of those formerly lost in their respects for the dead, who look with a curiosity that he takes as insolence and disrespect.

He looks away from the rest, decides their gazes will no longer pierce him, there's a long stretch ahead, and he devotes his attention to not letting the lid slide away to reveal the badly hidden horror, though it shouldn't matter one bit.

In this way, he is left alone, shrunken or gathered in himself, wounded in the flesh that has suddenly become no less sensitive than his soul, and in his ears, which dread and attend every squeak from the decrepit, dilapidated cart.

Everything is sad, and the music returns, and the music is sad, too.

Borne up or led by a line of melody formed of tribulation or nostalgia and a pounding rhythm like that of waves, coming together, rising up in a breaker, and then receding. Or one that reaches out to you, not managing to touch, and withdraws, coming forward and falling back, over and over, over and over.

There is no love for the wounded, no tenderness in reach of the humiliated; it seems to come, but it doesn't touch you, grief mounts upon grief. God, what merciless music! And with that insidiously dissonant creaking, obstinately ruining any harmony, black as it may be in this music which, so far as he can see, neither disturbs his sister in her subdued anguish nor exasperates the weary worker.

"Done."

He has to repeat it: done. They have arrived.

He moves toward a part of the galleries that he recognizes easily from his constant visits to his father's tomb, and now, because empty, it is easier to locate, like a deep hollow, a pure, dark, uncovered chasm.

The cart and the carter fall quiet, the latter gasping. The music has left the man's ears and mind. He fears the discordant squealing has only withdrawn, and will later return, even when he's no longer there.

A pair of workers charged with cleaning the galleries and a long suffering gravedigger come to help. The four of them unload the caskets, and for a moment, to catch their breath, they lay them on the pavement with the rectangular mosaics, alternating black and white.

Now they will enter the hollow that will afford them perpetual rest. Another slab of marble will seal it, with both of their names, and the immobile stone will remain between him and his parents. The end. A chord sounded and broke off. *Did you hear it, sister?* She doesn't even hear the question, he didn't utter it, he was talking to himself, my God!

Perhaps the exclamation, perhaps the solemnity of the coffins that have stopped their rattling as they lie there on the mosaic, perhaps the expectation of what will take place just afterward, visible on the faces of the assistants and the occasional kindly lady who is leaving a few chrysanthemums for her mother, make him turn, illicitly, to his recollections of the seminary. Shielded by his dark monastic clothing – though given away, without noticing, by his ordinary necktie – he utters, like a murmur, in Latin, the viaticum. Transported, and heartened by the solemnity he has produced in those around him, he says, out loud, in a language they all understand, the Salve Regina, and, without pausing, begins an Our Father, and all present accompany him. It is presumed, as he is the son, that no one will hurry ahead of him, and he will finish with devotion and strength: *Amen.* In the meanwhile, a thought has crept into his mind, intertwined with tortured sentiments, which prevent his uttering this formula: *I am a parricide. Today, I have laid the weapon in the hand of the man who has cut off my father's head.*

His sister, wretched, has quivered through the ceremony and her wretched body falls to the ground. Soundlessly and without ostentation.

archipelago books

is a not-for-profit literary press devoted to
promoting cross-cultural exchange through innovative
classic and contemporary international literature
www.archipelagobooks.org